Also published in Large Print
from G.K. Hall by Johanna Lindsey:

Brave the Wild Wind
Captive Bride
Defy Not the Heart
Fires of Winter
A Gentle Feuding
Gentle Rogue
A Heart So Wild
Hearts Aflame
Love Only Once
Man of My Dreams
Once a Princess
Paradise Wild
Silver Angel

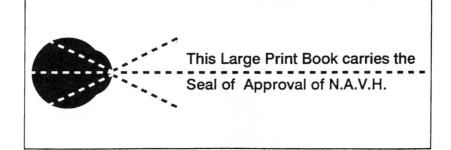

This Large Print Book carries the
Seal of Approval of N.A.V.H.

ANGEL

ANGEL

Johanna Lindsey

G.K.Hall & Co.
Thorndike, Maine

Published in Large Print by arrangement with Avon Books, a division of The Hearst Corporation.

G.K. Hall Large Print Book Series.

Set in 16 pt. News Plantin by Juanita Macdonald.

Printed in the United States on acid-free, high-opacity paper. ∞

Library of Congress Cataloging in Publication Data

Lindsey, Johanna.
    Angel / Johanna Lindsey.
        p.   cm.
    ISBN 0-8161-5760-X (hc : alk. paper : lg. print).
    ISBN 0-8161-5761-8 (sc : alk. paper : lg. print).
    1. Large type books. I. Title.
[PS3562.I5123A83 1993]
813'.54—dc20   93-31159

In memory of Misti Jewel, my own toe-biter.
She was a talker, a sweet pest, my deskmate.
Lord, please don't mind that she likes to clean
her teeth on bare feet.

Chapter 1

Texas, 1881

High noon . . . an hour synonymous with death in a great many Western towns. This town was no different. The hour alone told folks who hadn't heard what was going to happen when they saw other folks running to clear the street. Only one thing could cause such an exodus at that particular time of day.

High noon . . . an hour without advantages, no shadows to distract, no lowering sun to blind and tip the odds. It'd be a fair fight according to the standards of the day. No one would stop to wonder if the man being challenged might not want to participate, or see anything unfair in the fact that he was forced to. A man who made his living by the gun had little choice in the matter.

The street was nearly deserted now, the windows along it crowded with folks waiting to see someone die. Even the November wind paused for the moment, letting the dust settle under the bright rays of the late autumn sun.

From the north end of the street came Tom Prynne, the challenger, though he was calling himself Pecos Tom now. He'd been waiting an hour since he'd issued the challenge, time enough for him to wonder if he might not have been a bit hasty this once. No, just silly nerves that bothered him before every fight. He wondered how many gunfights it would take before he felt as calm as the other fellow looked.

Tom didn't mind the killing. He loved the power and the triumph he felt afterward, the feeling that he was invincible. And the fear. God, he loved it when folks feared him. So what if he had to deal with a little fear himself before each fight? It was worth it afterward.

He'd been hoping for an opportunity just like this, a chance at a known name. His own name, or the one he'd taken for himself, wasn't traveling fast enough to suit him. No one had heard of Pecos Tom this far south. Hell, they forgot him even where he'd been because until now his gunfights had been with "nobodys" like himself.

But his opponent today, Angel — *his* name had no trouble preceding him. Some called him the Angel of Death, and with reason. No one could say how many men he'd killed. Some said even Angel couldn't name a number. He was reputed to be not only fast but accurate.

Tom wasn't that accurate, but he was faster, he knew he was. And he knew exactly how many men he'd killed — one card cheat, two sodbusters, and a deputy who'd tracked him last year, thinking he ought to be hanged for shooting an unarmed man. No one knew about the deputy, and just as well. He wanted a name, but he didn't want it plastered on Wanted posters.

There'd been other gunfights in his short career, and he'd been fortunate in that half of them he'd won simply by the draw, the other fellow so shocked at his speed that he'd drop his gun and concede. Tom was counting on that happening today, not that he figured Angel would drop his gun, but he hoped to surprise him enough so that he'd have time to steady his aim and be the only one standing when the smoke cleared.

He'd been in this town only two days himself. He would have been riding out today if he hadn't heard that Angel had drifted in last night. It was sure as hell that no one had passed the word around when *he'd* ridden in. After today, they would.

But Angel wasn't exactly what Tom had expected when he'd stopped him from leaving his hotel this morning. Somehow he'd thought the gunfighter would be taller, and older, and not so emotionless in the face of his challenge. His reaction had been as if he didn't care one way or the other. But Tom hadn't let that worry him.

He'd blocked the other man's way, demanding in a loud voice so everyone present could hear, "Angel? I heard you was fast, but I'm here to tell you I'm faster."

"Suit yourself, mister. I won't argue the point."

"But I aim to prove it. High noon. Don't disappoint me."

It was only after Tom had walked away that he'd realized how cold and emotionless Angel's eyes were, eyes as black as sin, the eyes of a ruthless killer.

With outward calm, Angel waited to meet his challenger. He'd walked out into the center of

9

the street, but that was as far as he would extend himself. He patiently let the young gloryseeker come to him.

To look at him, you couldn't see his anger. What he was going to do was so senseless. It wasn't like killing someone he knew deserved it. He didn't know this kid, didn't know what sins were to his credit, how many men he'd killed seeking a name for himself, or if he'd even killed any. He hated it when he didn't know.

Knowing wouldn't change what he was going to do, however; it would just eliminate the regret of a senseless killing. But most of these young gloryseekers wouldn't have the nerve to start with him. They'd have quite a few gunfights behind them before they attempted a name, and that meant they'd done some killing — and the odds were, some innocent men had died — to establish their gunfighting careers. Angel had no regrets killing men like that. He saw himself as an executioner in that respect, getting rid of the scum a bit sooner than the law would, and maybe saving the lives of some decent folk in the process.

Having a known name was a curse and a blessing. It brought out the gloryseekers. That couldn't be helped. But it also made his work easier sometimes because some men would back down, thereby saving lives, since he absolutely hated having to kill a man whose only crime was working for the wrong boss.

He was a gun for hire. It was what he knew, and he was good enough to make his living at it. He could be hired for just about any job if the price was right, though folks had learned not

10

to ask him to do outright murder because they were likely to end up dead themselves if they did. He simply saw no difference between the man who pulled the trigger on the unsuspecting victim and the one who hired him to do it. Both were murderers in his book, and if Angel couldn't find an excuse to kill them himself, he'd turn them over to the law's judgment.

He made no excuses for his life. He could wish it might have been different, but circumstances made it otherwise. And though his instincts might lean toward mercy, he followed the creed of the man who'd taught him how to defend and protect himself with a gun.

"Conscience has its place well and good, but not in a gunfight. If you're gonna shoot, you shoot to kill, or they come back to haunt you . . . some dark night, out of an alley — a bullet in the back, 'cause they've tried you once and know for a fact that you're too fast for them to take the chance of trying you again. That's what comes of just wounding a man, that, or they might figure you're fast, but your aim's lousy. Those ones you'll be facing a second time in the street, and that's purely a waste of time and what luck you're allotted. It'd be a damn shame if that bullet with your name on it came from a man you had the chance to kill but didn't."

Three times he'd come close to dying at the hands of lawless men before he'd learned that creed. Three times he'd been saved, not by his own efforts, but with help from strangers. Three debts he'd owed for that, and he was not a man who felt comfortable being beholden. Two had

11

been paid, the second only recently.

He'd come to this town hoping to pay back the third debt. He didn't know why he'd been sent for. He'd been on his way to locate Lewis Pickens to find out when the young gun had stepped in his way.

He only knew his name, Pecos Tom. Someone had had to check the hotel register to find that out. He was a stranger to the town, just as Angel was, so no one could tell Angel if he was facing a killer or just a foolish young man. Damn, he hated this, hated not knowing. He hadn't asked for the fight, had tried to avoid it, but no one expected him to ignore it once the challenge had been issued. Pecos Tom had every intention of killing him. Angel had to settle for that simple truth to assuage his regret.

Pecos was taking his sweet time coming down the street. Twenty feet away, fifteen. He stopped finally at ten. Angel would have preferred more distance than that, but this wasn't his show. He'd heard that back east a man got to choose the weapon when he was challenged, even no weapon, just fists if he wanted. It would give Angel plea-sure to beat some sense into this kid, instead of killing him. But the West didn't offer a man choices. When you carried a gun on your hip, you were expected to use it.

Pecos's sheepskin jacket was already tucked out of the way, his hands out at his sides, ready. Slowly, Angel moved his yellow mackintosh out of the way. He didn't watch the hands, not even to note if they trembled. He watched the eyes.

And he tried one last time. "We don't have

12

to do this. These people don't know you. You can just ride out."

"Forget it," the boy replied, relaxing now, figuring Angel was afraid to fight him, that he was the one who wanted out of the fight. "I'm ready."

No one was close enough to hear Angel's sigh. "Then make your peace, mister. I don't shoot to wound."

Twenty-year-old Tom Prynne didn't shoot to wound either, and his draw was faster, about two seconds faster, all the time he would have needed if he had had the patience to perfect his aim before he'd gone gloryseeking. His bullet flew past Angel's shoulder to lose itself in the dirt at the end of the street. Angel's momentum was too quick to stop even if he'd wanted to, and his aim was deadly accurate.

Tom Prynne had made a name for himself after all, though it wouldn't travel far. But he'd be talked about here for a good while to come, and his epitaph would read: *Here lies Pecos Tom. He challenged the Angel of Death and lost.* The undertaker in this town had a morbid sense of humor.

Chapter 2

Cassandra Stuart absently dropped a piece of wood into the fireplace as she passed it. Across the room a feline lifted its head and hissed in complaint. The slim girl glanced at the cat and shrugged.

"Sorry, Marabelle," Cassie said as she resumed her agitated pacing. "Habit."

Both Cassie and her pet were used to much colder weather in Wyoming, where she'd grown up. Here in the south of Texas, where her father's ranch was located, it probably wasn't more than fifty degrees outside, and they were a few days into December. One piece of firewood would have sufficed to take the chill out of her bedroom. With two . . . It wasn't long before she stripped down to her camisole and drawers.

The small desk that she had been avoiding for the past half hour was still sitting in the corner, her stationery in a neat stack on top of it, the inkwell opened, the quill pen sharpened, the lamp turned up high. Her father had given her the old-fashioned writing set right after she'd arrived in the fall. And she'd been faithful in her letter writing, sending off one or two letters a week to her mother — at least she had been up until six weeks ago.

But she couldn't avoid writing any longer. The

telegram had arrived late this afternoon. IF I DON'T HEAR FROM YOU IMMEDIATELY I'M COMING DOWN THERE WITH AN ARMY.

That last part was an exaggeration — Cassie certainly hoped it was. But she didn't doubt her mother would come, and that wasn't going to help anything. Her father most definitely wouldn't appreciate it when he returned. But then her father wasn't going to appreciate that his neighbors were now his enemies, thanks to his interfering daughter.

Cassie had sent back a reply that she'd have a letter off by tomorrow to explain everything. There was no help for it now. But she had been so hoping that the Peacemaker would have arrived first, so that when she told her mother what she'd done, she could at least also tell her that she'd fixed it and there was nothing else to worry about.

She made a sound resembling a groan that had the sleek black feline following her to the writing desk to investigate the problem. Marabelle was very sensitive to Cassie's moods. The cat wouldn't settle down until Cassie gave it a reassuring scratch behind the ears.

At last she took pen in hand.

Dearest Mama,

I don't suppose it will surprise you to hear that I've meddled again. I don't know why I thought I could put an end to a feud that's been going on for twenty-five years, but there you have it, my infernal optimism letting me down once again. By now you must realize

I'm talking about Papa's neighbors, the Catlins and the MacKauleys, whom I told you about after my first visit here.

This was Cassie's second visit to her father's ranch in Texas. She had been amazed the first time she'd seen the house he had built here ten years ago. It was an exact replica of the one he had left behind in Wyoming. Even the furnishings were the same. It was like being at home — until she walked outside.

Her father had wanted her to visit for a long time, but her mother had refused to let her travel without her until she'd reached the age of eighteen two years ago. And Catherine Stuart wouldn't step foot on Charles Stuart's ranch unless there was a dire emergency — involving their only child. She hadn't seen her ex-husband in the ten years since he'd left Wyoming, hadn't spoken to him in twenty, even though they'd lived in the same house for the first ten years of Cassie's life. Their relationship, or their lack of one, was the one thing Cassie had never tried to meddle in. As much as she wished it were otherwise, her parents despised each other.

But Cassie had told her mother all about the Catlins and the MacKauleys when she'd returned home in the spring of last year, and about her new friend, Jenny Catlin, who was two years younger than Cassie. Cassie had found Jenny nothing but melancholy this visit because she was at an age when she wanted to get married, and lamented that the only good-looking young men in the area happened to be R. J. MacKauley's

16

four sons, who were, unfortunately, her sworn enemies.

Cassie really wished that Jenny hadn't mentioned the MacKauley men in the same breath with marriage. It had got her to thinking that maybe Jenny didn't see them in the same light that her mother and older brother did. It had got her to noticing how Clayton MacKauley, R. J.'s youngest son, stared at Jenny in church, and how the young girl blushed each time she caught him at it.

This probably won't surprise you, either, Mama, but I've managed to include the Stuarts in the feud — at least the one with me. Papa doesn't even know about it yet, but I'm sure he won't be happy about it when he finds out. I'll get to leave, after all, but he'll still have to live with these people after I'm gone.

And before you start cussing him for letting me meddle, I have to tell you he wasn't here to stop me. Actually, it started before he left, not long after I arrived, but it was all done in secret like a conspiracy, and then Papa got a letter from this man in North Texas whom he'd been bargaining with for two years for the purchase of a prize bull, and the man finally decided he'd sell. And don't cuss Papa for leaving me alone, either, to go get his new bull, because he was only supposed to be gone for less than two weeks, and I *am* twenty now and fully capable of running his ranch — when I'm not meddling. Besides, he wanted me to go with him, but I begged

17

off, since I had already begun my . . . well, there's no easy way to put this. What I did was try my hand at matchmaking again, and unfortunately, this time I succeeded.

I managed to convince Jenny Catlin and Clayton MacKauley that each was in love with the other. And it really did seem as if they were, Mama. They were so surprised and pleased by my fabrications. It was so easy to get them together and, after only three weeks, to help them leave for Austin to marry secretly. Unfortunately, on the wedding night they discovered that neither one loved the other, that the romance was only in my own wishful imagination.

Apparently I mistook the situation entirely, but that is nothing new. I seem to do that quite frequently, as you well know. Of course, I have tried to set things right. I went to the Catlin ranch to try to explain that my intentions had been good, if misguided. Dorothy Catlin wouldn't talk to me. Her son, Buck, advised me to leave Texas and not come back.

Buck hadn't put it as nicely as that, but her mother didn't need to know how nasty he'd been in his anger, or about the threats she had received from the MacKauleys, who had actually set a date for her to vacate, or else they'd burn her father's ranch down. There was no need to mention that Richard MacKauley had been picking up her mail and then telling her he'd lost it, which was why she hadn't had a letter from her mother these past six weeks, or that she'd come out of the bank in Caully to find molasses dumped all over the seat and floor of her carriage, or that three of her father's hands had been intimidated into quitting, including his foreman. Nor did she intend to mention the note slipped under the front door that said if her cat was found out on the range again, she'd be invited to the barbecue.

And it was best that her mother not know that Sam Hadley and Rafferty Slater, two Catlin hired hands, had cornered her in the livery in town and frightened her badly with their manhandling before someone happened by to put a stop to it, or that she had been wearing her modified Colt gun to town ever since that incident, rather than just out on the range, and would continue to do so despite the amusement it was causing the good folks of Caully.

And she most especially wasn't going to tell her mother that her father had been gone seven weeks now and wasn't expected back for another three because his new prize bull had kicked him and he'd broken two ribs and one foot in the fall. It sufficed for her to say:

> They are such nice families, but when they don't like someone, they are pains in the asses, and right now neither family likes me very much.

She thought about scratching out the "pains in the asses," but decided her mother could use a laugh about now. Cassie certainly could, but then she had only three more weeks to set things right, because she knew exactly what her father would do when he returned. He'd simply abandon what he'd built here over the past ten years and relocate. After all, he ranched because he enjoyed it, not because he needed to earn a living from it, not when he came from one of the richest families in Connecticut. But Cassie would never forgive herself if the situation came to that.

Since they won't even listen to my apologies, I did the only other thing I could think of. I sent for Grandpa Kimbal's good friend, the man they call the Peacemaker. I have no doubt whatsoever that he will be able to end the hostilities here the very day he arrives, and I expect him any day now.

Actually, she had expected him several weeks ago and was definitely starting to worry over his delay, after he'd assured her that he would come. He really was her only hope. Perhaps she ought to send him another telegram when she went to town tomorrow to post her mother's letter.

So now you know why I haven't written. I really hated having to admit that I'd put my foot in it once again, at least before I'd mended what I'd wrought. And I will write again just as soon as it's all over and Papa's neighbors are back to just hating each other.

Cassie bit her lip, frowning at the letter. She'd saved the worst for last — how to convince her mother not to rush down here to save her "baby"

20

from another catastrophe of her own making. Deviously. She'd invite her.

I know you were just exaggerating when you said you'd come down here with an army, but you are welcome to come if you don't mind traveling in the middle of winter. I'm sure Papa won't mind if you pay us a visit. Of course, the trouble here will be over before you could manage to get here, so he might wonder at your reason for coming. You don't suppose he might think you were interested in a reconciliation, do you?

Cassie decided to end the letter right there. She knew her mother well, and after reading that last question, Catherine Stuart would most likely rip the letter up and toss it into the nearest fire. She could also imagine her mother's verbal response to the question. "Reconcile with that faithless whoremonger? When I'm dead and buried, and you can tell him I said so!"

Cassie had been telling *him* or telling *her* what the other had to say for as long as she could remember. If there was no one around to relay their conversations through, would they break down and speak to each other? No. One or the other of them — depending on which one was the most determined to say something — would search until he or she found someone who would speak for them.

Cassie pushed herself away from the desk, stretching, and then looked down at Marabelle. "At least that's one worry out of the way —

for the moment," she told the cat. "Now if the Peacemaker would just show up to solve the other, we might be able to stay until spring as planned."

She was putting all her hopes in her grandpa's friend, but she had good reason to do so. Once she'd seen him say a few words to a man who was in a murderous rage, and he had him laughing within five minutes. His talent for soothing folks was incredible, and he'd need all of that talent for the animosity she'd stirred up.

Chapter 3

The Double C Ranch wasn't hard to locate. If you rode due north out of town as directed, you sort of ran into it. But it wasn't what Angel had been expecting. This far south, most ranchers took a cue from their Mexican neighbors and built the Spanish-style adobe houses that helped to ward off the worst of the summer heat.

What Angel rode up to was a two-story wooden house of mansion size in a design more common in the Northwest. A half-dozen steps led up to a porch that surrounded the lower floor and was wide enough to accommodate chairs, rockers, and even a two-seater wooden swing in each corner. A balcony with double doors that opened onto it from what he assumed were bedrooms circled the second floor of the house and shaded the porch below.

The house seemed vaguely familiar to him, as if he'd seen it before, though he'd never come this far south before. The outbuildings, or what he'd seen of them before he got this close, were spread out behind the main house, so that twenty feet from the front of the house, you couldn't tell that this was a working ranch. Even the carriage drawn up in front was more like the fancy rigs you'd see in a large city than the smaller buckboards favored in the country.

23

Angel got no farther than that twenty feet when the front door opened and a black cat the size of a mountain lion was suddenly loping in his direction. He had no time to wonder where the hell it had come from — it was inconceivable that it had come from inside the house — before he was fighting to control his terrified mount and reach for his gun at the same time.

He hadn't quite reached his gun before his hat flew off his head to the accompaniment of a shot, and he heard, "Don't even think about it, mister."

Angel had only seconds to make up his mind as his eyes went to the speaker to find a woman with a gun trained on him, then back to the cat, which had been somewhat arrested by the shot and wasn't coming at him quite so quickly now. But it was still coming, and his horse was getting desperate, sidestepping, wildly tossing its head, and finally rearing up on its hind legs.

While he was fighting to keep his seat — he was damned if he was going to face that enormous animal on the ground — the woman spoke again, one word. When his horse had all four hooves back on the ground, he saw that the cat had stopped and was just sitting there now, not five feet away, looking up at him with large yellow eyes.

Marabelle, she'd said, in a tone meant to be obeyed. He hadn't heard her wrong. Marabelle . . . and he did something he never did, something he couldn't afford to do in his line of work. He got mad and showed it.

"Lady, if you don't get that animal out of my sight immediately," he gritted out in what was by force of habit a very moderate tone, "I won't be responsible for what happens."

She seemed to take exception to that, probably because she was the one holding the gun — still trained on him. "You aren't in a position to —"

What happened took only seconds, Angel palming his gun and sending off one shot that knocked the weapon from her hand, her cry of "Son of a bitch!" as she shook her stinging fingers, the cat snarling, *loudly,* in response to her cry, and Angel's horse starting to buck wildly in response to the cat's snarl. Angel ended up in the dirt this time, the horse lit out for the next county, and the now hissing cat was no more than a foot away from him before she said it again, that one word that stopped the feline immediately. *Marabelle.*

He had a mind to shoot it anyway. He had a mind to shoot her, too. He couldn't remember when he'd been so out of control of his emotions. An idiot could surmise that the cat, whatever it was, belonged to her. A pet. It had to be a pet to obey her like that. And she'd let it out to terrify his horse, terrify him, too, he didn't doubt.

Even as angry as he was, and realizing that the cat had to be tame, or somewhat tame, he still had considerable courage to take his eyes off an animal that size that was sitting no more than a foot away, especially with him down on the ground with it, the two of them eyeball-to-eyeball. But he did it, found her again, still up on the porch, and narrowed his eyes on her.

She'd managed to retrieve her gun and was holding it in her other hand, the hand with the sore fingers squeezed between her arm and her side. It was doubtful the gun would shoot now without a visit to a gunsmith first, but she didn't seem to think of that and was pointing the damn thing at him again.

"I'll tell you right now that my aim's as good as yours, mister, but I won't have to shoot you. You move that weapon you're holding even a quarter inch in my direction, and Marabelle will tear you to pieces."

Whether she could hit what she aimed at was debatable. Shooting his hat off could have been deliberate, just to get his attention, or she could have been trying to kill him and missed. The second threat he didn't doubt, however. But she had to be afraid of him to issue a double threat like that. Well, she'd seen what he was capable of. He'd disarmed her when she'd had her gun pointed right at him and his had still been holstered. And she had good reason to fear him right now, as angry as he was.

"You're crazy if you think I'm putting my gun away with this thing breathing down my neck." They could have had a standoff at that point, neither willing to budge an inch. In fact, several long moments of silence passed before Angel decided he'd rather get rid of the cat, so he added grudgingly, "Call it off, lady, and *maybe* we'll talk."

Her chin rose a notch. "There won't be any talking, since you'll be leaving. And you can tell them they had no reason to bring in a fast gun."

"They?"

"Whichever of them hired you."

"No one hired me, lady. Lewis Pickens sent me to —"

"Well, for God's sake," she cut in, and lowered her weapon. "Why didn't you say so to begin with?" And then: "Marabelle, come here, baby. He's harmless."

This had to be the first time Angel had ever been called harmless since he'd reached manhood. He didn't take exception to it. He waited to see if the animal would obey, and damned if the large head didn't swing around to look at the woman, then the long, sleek body slowly followed as the cat ambled across the yard and went up the steps. Angel let out a sigh, but he didn't put his gun away until the feline was inside the house.

"You can go back to the kitchen, Maria," the woman said to someone just inside the door, adding before she closed it, "Do you actually know how to shoot that rifle?"

Angel cringed. He'd had another gun trained on him and hadn't even sensed it. He was getting careless. No, his senses had all been attuned to that monstrous black animal and that idiot woman on the porch — please, God, don't let her be Cassandra Stuart.

She was coming down the steps toward him now. For the first time he noticed her fancy attire, a long black coat with fur trimming over ice-blue lace at her throat, and five layers of blue pleated ruffles in the skirt, which was seen only from her knees to her toes. A small beaver hat was perched at a jaunty angle on dark brown hair. Citified clothes, to be sure, but the incongruity of the outfit was that she wore a gun holster on the outside of the coat.

She slipped the gun into that holster just before she held out her hand to him. "I'm Cassandra Stuart. Will Mr. Pickens be arriving soon?"

Angel ignored the hand, unsure what she expected him to do with it. There was even a smile that came with it, as if she hadn't shot at him, sent that man-eating cat after him, and run off his horse. He ignored the smile, too. That she was apparently the woman he had to deal with made him curse silently as he got to his feet and dusted off his slicker. At the moment, the last thing he wanted to do was help the woman. But that's what he was here for. A debt was a debt.

He went after his hat before he answered her. Seeing the bullet hole that had passed dead-center through the crown had him swearing again, this time aloud. Hell, she could have killed him!

He swung around and gave her a dark look. "When you get that six-shooter fixed, I want to see proof that you know how to use it."

All she did was frown, take out her gun again and examine it, then exclaim, "Damn, you've ruined it!"

"And you've ruined my hat."

She gave him a narrow look. "This happens to be a special-made weapon, mister — who are you, anyway?"

"Angel — and this happens to be a twenty-dollar hat, *ma'am*."

"I'll replace your damn hat —" She paused to take a step back. "What do you mean *Angel?* You aren't *the* Angel, are you? The one they call the Angel of Death?"

28

His lips twisted sourly. Most folks never said it within his hearing. "I don't care for that name."

"I don't blame you," she replied.

But there was a wary look in her silver-gray eyes now that gave Angel a wealth of satisfaction to see. It should have been there sooner. Even folks who didn't know who he was usually gave him a wide berth. He simply had a look about him that said "Beware."

"Well," she said with a nervous laugh when he just stared at her. "It's lucky for you that I have more than one of these modified Colts, or I would probably be quite angry now."

"You better hope it don't take me long to find my, horse, lady, or you'll find out what angry —"

"If you lay a hand on me —"

"I was thinking more along the lines of shooting you."

He didn't mean it, but she didn't know that. And he wondered what the hell he was doing, letting his anger build back up again when he'd had it under control. He *never* made idle threats. But there was something about her that just irritated the hell out of him, even when she wasn't pointing a gun in his direction.

"Forget I said that," he said curtly.

"Gladly," she replied, but she still took another step back from him.

He almost smiled. Her nervousness was soothing his temper as nothing else could.

"Do you make a habit of taking potshots at folks paying you a visit?"

She blinked, pursed her lips — lushly shaped

29

lips, he now noticed — and straightened her spine. Damn. He could see it coming. She'd just got her courage back.

"You were about to shoot Marabelle. I couldn't let you do that just because she'd sneaked out the door before I could stop her."

That gave him pause. "Then you didn't set her on me?"

"Certainly not," she said in an indignant-sounding tone that implied he was stupid for asking.

"I saw no 'certainly' about it, lady."

"Common sense —"

"I think you better drop it," he warned before her insults got any worse.

She stiffened, taking his meaning. "And I think you better state your business and then go."

If only he could — go, that is. "Pickens isn't coming," he said tersely.

She stared at him blankly for a moment, then gasped, "But he *has* to! I was counting on him — why isn't he coming? He said he would."

Her genuine distress made Angel uncomfortable with his other feelings. He didn't like the young woman, and with good reason after what she'd done to him, but he had trouble maintaining his animosity in the face of her upset.

Angel unbent enough to assure her, "He was coming. In fact, he was at his bank taking out enough money to get him here when this bunch of comancheros rode in from the Staked Plain with the idea of making a withdrawal of their own at gunpoint. 'Course, Pickens couldn't just mind his own business and let them go about theirs. He felt obliged to stop them and got shot

30

up pretty bad in the effort."

She'd gone from pale halfway through his little speech to sickly-looking at the end, her distress switching causes. "Oh, God, he — he didn't die, did he? It'd be my fault. Grandpa will never forgive me —"

"Now, how do you figure you're to blame when you weren't there?"

"I asked him to come. He wouldn't have been in that bank if —" She paused, seeing him shake his head at her, and her tone as well as her expression turned stubbornly belligerent. "I'll accept blame if I choose to. I'm quite good at it."

At that point he shrugged, not about to try to convince a fool woman she was being foolish when he didn't care one way or the other. "Suit yourself."

The fight went out of her instantly. She bit her lower lip. She suddenly looked like she was about to cry, which had Angel's stomach clenching. Shit. He'd never tried to deal with a crying woman before, and he wasn't going to start now. One damn tear and he was walking.

"Is he . . . ?" She couldn't manage to say "dead."

"No!" Angel couldn't get the word out fast enough. "The doc says Pickens will live, but he won't be traveling for a while, which is why he had his lady friend send for me."

That got rid of Cassie's teary-eyed look. She was frowning now. "I don't understand. This was nearly six weeks ago. Why didn't he send me word sooner to let me know he couldn't come? Now I'm almost out of time."

Angel could accept blame as easily as she could. "That'd be my fault. Pickens tracked me down easy enough, but I got delayed up in New Mexico for a few weeks. But then, his message didn't mention a time limit."

"I see." She didn't. She looked confused as all hell. "Bearers of bad news are rarely appreciated, but thank you all the same for coming out of your way when a telegram would certainly have sufficed. And I'm sorry about your horse. You can borrow one of ours to find it. Just return ours when you're through." She reached into one of the wide pockets on her coat and came out with a twenty-dollar gold piece. "And this should get you a new hat."

All Angel did was stare at the hand she held out to him, forcing her to say, "Take it." He still didn't, so she shrugged and closed her fist on the coin. "Suit yourself. But if you'll excuse me now, I was leaving for town when you arrived."

She actually turned and walked away from him. Angel rocked back on his heels, letting her get halfway to her carriage before he drawled, "I guess I should have spelled it out, ma'am. Lewis Pickens sent for me to take his place. I'm here to settle your problem, whatever it is, so maybe you ought to tell me what it is before you head for town."

She'd whipped back around at the words "take his place," her eyes incredulous, but she had her belligerent expression back on by the time he finished. "I beg your pardon."

"You heard me plain enough."

"I know I heard you," she gritted out, giving

every indication of a woman about to lose her temper. "I just don't believe it. What could Mr. Pickens have been thinking of to send you, *you* of all people? I need a peacemaker, not a gunfighter. You'd only make the situation worse."

"Just what is the situation?"

She waved a hand impatiently. "There's no point in my discussing that with you when you can't help. If a gun was the answer, I'd use my own."

He couldn't help it. He grinned at the image her words brought to mind, of hats flying through the air. But he turned aside before she noticed. There were very few people he allowed close enough to glimpse his sense of humor. *She* wasn't going to be one of them.

"You got a bunkhouse?"

"Yes, but — wait a minute!" she cried when he started toward the back of the house. "You can't stay here. Weren't you listening?"

He stopped long enough to say, "Yeah, but you weren't. I'm here to see to your problem as a favor to Pickens. I owe him, so I won't be leaving until my debt's paid."

She hurried to catch up with him as he rounded the side of the house. "Whatever debt you owe has nothing to do with me, mister."

"It does now."

"That's unacceptable. I'm only going to say this once more. You can't —"

The roar coming from inside the house stopped them both. Angel turned to see the large cat sitting in front of a window looking out at them. Fortunately, the window wasn't open, but that fact

33

didn't settle his nerves as fast as it should have. Knowing the cat was a pet didn't make it look any less dangerous.

"What *is* that thing?" he finally asked.

"A black panther."

"Didn't know they had such things in Texas."

"They don't. Marabelle came over from Africa."

He wasn't going to ask how. "Just keep it away from me as long as I'm here."

She visibly bristled at that. "*If* you were staying, which you're *not,* I would insist you get along with Marabelle. And you'd have to introduce your horse to her for obvious reasons — but you're not staying. The stable is there." She pointed to a long building next to a barn. "Go find your horse and go back where you came from."

She must have thought that settled the matter. In a way, it did. His slow drawl told her so as she started to turn away from him for the second time. "Then I guess I'll have to take care of your problem in my own way."

Her eyes flared wide in understanding. "You wouldn't." He was silent. "All right!" she snapped. "You can stay, but you can't kill anyone. No shooting. No dead bodies. Is that clear?"

She didn't wait for an answer. She stomped away this time, leaving no doubt that she had conceded under protest. Irritating woman. If he didn't figure he'd need her input to fix her trouble, this would be the last he'd see of her. He'd still handle it his own way. But as he heard her carriage leaving for town, it occurred to him that he still didn't know what the trouble was. *Damned* irritating woman.

Chapter 4

It wasn't going to work. Cassie had had enough time to consider all the repercussions on the way to town, including the worst, that the Catlins and the MacKauleys would think she intended to fight back. What could a gunman do anyway, except issue threats? And if the threats were ignored, then the shooting would begin. Just what her father needed to come home to — a war.

She should have been firmer with that man. She should have called his bluff and stuck to the "no-thank-you." She didn't have the kind of problem that a hired gun was needed for. Well, maybe she did, but that wasn't the answer — at least, it wasn't an acceptable answer for her, and she'd have to tell him so as soon as she returned to the ranch.

She wasn't looking forward to that. She had known he was a gunfighter before she'd heard his name to prove it. But then she'd also known him, or of him. For half her life she'd heard his name, because he came from the same part of the country she did, and he'd been in and around Cheyenne for the past eleven years. But she'd never seen him, even from afar, never met him until today. Because he stayed in Cheyenne between jobs folks around there were quick to brag that Cheyenne was his home. If he had a real home somewhere, no one knew about it.

He wasn't what she might have imagined *the* Angel to look like, if she had bothered to try to put a face to the many tales she'd heard of him. He wasn't that tall, not like the MacKauley men were, at a little over six feet, but you didn't notice that about Angel unless you were standing right next to him. Of course, Cassie was on the short side herself, so he was still a half foot taller than she was. But height wasn't what you noticed about Angel.

From a distance you saw a man dressed all in black, except for the yellow mackintosh slicker that framed his sleekly muscled body. You saw the exposed gun on his hip, the silver spurs that flashed in the sunlight, the wide brimmed hat pulled down low, and the easy way he sat his horse that belied his keen alertness, the quickness he was capable of, the blurring speed Cassie had witnessed firsthand.

But up close, the first thing you noticed was his eyes. You sensed the ruthlessness there, the violence he was capable of. What he was was all in those eyes, black as pitch, soulless, conscienceless, fearless. They were so mesmerizing, it was a while before you saw that he had a starkly masculine face to go with them, a square, clean-shaven jaw, a sharply chiseled nose, and prominent cheekbones. It took even longer to realize his face was ruggedly handsome. Cassie hadn't realized that fact until she was halfway to town.

But it was a moot point; all that mattered was the kind of man he was, and he wasn't the kind she wanted anything to do with, for help or any

36

other reason. The plain truth was, he frightened her. There was simply no getting around the fact that he killed people in his line of work, and he was quite good at it.

She could only hope her neighbors wouldn't find out that the man known as the Angel of Death had paid her a visit. There was the possibility that his notoriety hadn't reached this far south, but that wouldn't matter because just the look of him told what he was, if not who, and that was just as bad. So she had to hope no one would learn he'd even been out to the Double C, and to hope he'd be gone before the end of the day.

To that end, she was going to send off another telegram to Lewis Pickens before she left town. She would thank him for his concern — and lie. She'd tell him she no longer had a problem, so his Angel of *Mercy* wasn't needed here. Then she'd tell Angel exactly what she'd done and that he no longer had a reason to stick around. He'd go — and she'd be back where she was six weeks ago, only with hardly any time left to figure out what to do about it.

Cassie left the gunsmith's, where she'd dropped off her gun, her last stop before heading for the stage depot to send her telegram. Today she was forced to carry the rifle that was kept in the boot of the carriage for emergencies. She knew how to use it as well as her Colt, but it was unwieldy, not to mention heavy, to carry around. She should have retrieved her matching six-shooter before leaving the ranch, but she'd left angry and hadn't even been thinking about it.

Carrying no weapon at all was out of the question, however. Though she hadn't seen any MacKauleys or Catlins about, nor any of their loyal hired hands, she hadn't left town yet, and it was rare that she came to town and didn't run into one or more of them. But it was Rafferty Slater and Sam Hadley who really worried her, the reason she wasn't going to be found unarmed again.

Those two hadn't worked for the Catlins all that long, and they'd already gotten into some trouble in town because of their rowdiness. They weren't the type that Dorothy Catlin usually hired, drifters who never stayed in one place for long, and worked just to have enough money to raise hell on a Saturday night in town. They'd no doubt get themselves fired eventually, but in the meantime they'd taken sides, and Cassie happened to be on the wrong side.

She got nervous just thinking about that day in the livery when they'd cornered her between them, blocking her from escaping, Sam shoving her, Rafferty holding her and touching her in places he had no right to. And there'd been a look in his eyes that said she'd be getting more of the same if he found her alone again. Sam had just been trying to frighten her. Rafferty had enjoyed it.

Nothing like that had ever happened to her before, and it wasn't going to happen again. If she saw Rafferty Slater in town and he even looked like he was going to approach her, she'd shoot first and ask what he wanted later. That man was *not* going to get a chance to put his hands on her body again.

The incident even had her leery of using either of the two livery stables anymore. Today she'd left her carriage in front of Caully's mercantile store, where she'd posted the letter to her mother. She had walked to accomplish the rest of her errands, but as she headed back that way to get to the stage depot, which doubled as the telegraph office, she saw that her carriage was still where she'd left it but now had two horses tied to the back of it.

Upon seeing the horses, Cassie stopped instantly and started searching the area for the gunfighter. She didn't doubt for a minute that it was Angel's horse and the one he'd borrowed, even though she was still too far away to get a good look at them. She located him easily enough. It wasn't hard to spot that yellow slicker.

He was leaning against the wall of the Second Chance Saloon, across the street. With his hat tipped down so low, she couldn't tell whom he was watching, but she had a feeling he was watching her.

It made her uneasy, that feeling. She didn't know why he'd followed her to town. And he didn't come forward now to say why, didn't move at all from his relaxed position. But just about everyone on the street knew he was there. Caully was a small town, after all, and Angel was a stranger. It would be natural for folks to wonder about him even if he didn't look like a gunfighter.

Cassie ground her teeth in frustration. So much for keeping his business with her a secret. There was no way she could leave town without speaking to him, not with his horse attached to her carriage. Even if the direction in which he had headed this morning could have gone unnoticed, this wouldn't. By the end of the day everyone in town would have asked the question: what was the Stuart girl doing with a gunfighter? But her currently hostile neighbors wouldn't merely wonder about it, they'd be out to the ranch by tonight to demand an explanation, and unless Angel was gone by then, all hell could break loose.

It was her own fault. She shouldn't have let that man rattle her like she did. She should have called his bluff. But no, she had to go and give him permission to stay, which in turn gave him permission to stick his nose in her affairs. And his following her to town and keeping a close eye on her, as if he had elected himself her personal guardian, said he was going to do things his own way after all, no matter what she had to say about it.

She didn't look his way again as she continued down the street. But she hurried now, afraid that she would be stopped before she could send off that telegram. And she was stopped. Only it wasn't by Angel.

Morgan MacKauley stepped out of Wilson's Saddle Shop right into Cassie's path. She almost ran into him. And seeing who it was, she tried slipping past him before she was noticed. No such luck.

Morgan considered himself something of a ladies' man. Whether that was true or not, his eye was drawn to anything in skirts, and it didn't take him but a second to catch sight of Cassie's and turn toward her — and step back to block her path. She tried going around him the other way, but he made it clear she wasn't passing at all by moving into her path again. She finally stepped back to give him a baleful glare, which had no effect whatsoever coming from her.

It galled her that no one down here in Texas took her seriously. They laughed when she wore a gun. They ignored her when she got mad. She was like a ladybug, easily flicked out of the way — unless she had her black panther sitting right next to her. Even the fearless MacKauleys were wary of Marabelle.

But Cassie never brought her cat to town, and the frown Morgan cast down on her right now was much more effective than hers had been. It was downright intimidating.

Of R. J.'s four sons, Morgan was the second youngest at twenty-one, but they were all big men, all over six feet tall and hefty for their size. All took after their father with their reddish-brown hair and dark green eyes. Cassie didn't think for a moment that any of them would actually do her physical harm, but that didn't stop the fear their animosity engendered. They were hot-tempered, and a hot-tempered man in a fury was capable of doing stupid things he wouldn't ordinarily do.

"Didn't think to see you in town this week, Miss Stuart," Morgan said nonchalantly.

Just two months ago, he had called her Cassie, as most of her friends and family did, rather than Miss Stuart. He'd also invited her to Will Bates's barn dance on a Saturday night, and a Sunday

41

picnic up on Willow Ridge a week later. His intentions had been clear. He'd actually been courting her. And she'd been terribly flattered — and interested. After all, the MacKauley brothers were exceptionally handsome men, every one of them, and as she'd been discovering in recent years, it was hard to find a man willing to marry her *and* Marabelle.

Morgan hadn't exactly liked Marabelle, but that hadn't kept him from courting Cassie — up until she'd meddled in his brother's life in a way none of them were going to forgive, or forget. And after she'd become the focus of all their anger, he'd let her know that it was only her father's ranch he'd been interested in.

Whether that was true, or if he'd only said it in anger, it had still hurt Cassie more than she cared to remember. She didn't have much confidence to begin with when it came to men. Morgan MacKauley had made her confidence drop even lower. And the sorry fact was, she'd really liked him. She'd had such hopes there for a few weeks. Now . . . there was nothing left, not even the slightest stir of pleasure to be this close to him. Regret was what she felt — and a good deal of annoyance.

She wondered about his casual remark, which from recent experience she thought probably wasn't casual at all. Warily she asked, "Why's that?"

"Figured you'd be too busy packing."

She should have known she couldn't pass a MacKauley, or a Catlin for that matter, without some unpleasant reminder of her current pre-

42

dicament. It was the MacKauleys who'd set an actual date for her to vacate the area — and threatened, if she refused, to resort to mass destruction of the ranch with lit torches.

"So you figured wrong," she said in a tight little voice, and attempted once more to step around him. Once more he moved so she couldn't, prompting her to add, "You're being obnoxious, Morgan. Let me pass."

"First you tell me 'bout that stranger directed out to your place this morning."

Cassie groaned inwardly. She hadn't had time to come up with an acceptable reason for Angel's visit, and she needed time, because when it came to lying and avoiding issues, Cassie was hopelessly inadequate. Unless she devoted a lot of thought and rehearsal to getting it out right, anyone who knew her could spot a lie immediately.

She still had to try with Morgan. "That was nothing. He — he was just a drifter looking for work."

"You should have sent him over to our place, then," he replied easily. "You ain't gonna have work for no one come the end of the week."

Cassie stiffened at that second allusion to the deadline that had been set for her to depart the area. Somehow she had hoped that the threat to burn down her father's ranch had been just anger talking, with no substance behind it. These were people she had socialized with, been friends with; she'd even been courted by one of them. But all that was before she had meddled.

She skipped the subject of Angel, since Morgan had given her another to address. "I need to talk to your pa, Morgan. Tell him I'll ride over to-morrow —"

"He won't see you. Fact is, Clayton's got him madder than ever, and you want to know why, Miss Stuart?"

She started shaking her head as his tone got sharper. She really didn't want to know, because whatever the reason, she knew the blame would be set at her door whether she was actually to blame or not.

But Morgan was determined to say it, and he did, scathingly. "That fool brother of mine hasn't been right in the head since he come back from Austin. Can't get a lick of work out of him these days. And now he's talking 'bout 'rights' and how he's got some where his 'wife' is concerned. He even mentioned that he might go over and collect the Catlin girl, seeing as how they ain't divorced yet. 'Course, Pa whipped that notion out of him."

Cassie was incredulous and didn't even think to contain her reaction. "Are you saying he *wants* to stay married to Jenny?"

Morgan flushed bright red at that question, denying it, or the very idea of it. "The hell he does," he practically growled. "He's just had a taste of her, thanks to you, and now he wants another. It ain't no more'n that."

Cassie was flushing now because of the subject matter, which was outrageously inappropriate for her innocent ears. Morgan knew he'd just stepped over propriety's line, but he didn't care. He was furious with her for what she'd done, since it had put an end to his hopes of marrying

44

her, and furious with himself for not having the courage to defy his pa and stick up for her as he'd been inclined to do. The fact was, he still wanted her.

Morgan hadn't noticed her very much the first time she'd come to visit her father. She had been eighteen then and nothing much to look at, could just barely be called pretty, and Caully had its fair share of pretty women, beautiful women even. And she was much too tiny and childlike for Morgan's tastes. There was simply nothing passion-inspiring about her, or so he'd first thought.

But there was something damn strange about Miss Cassandra Stuart, something that made her more interesting and attractive each time you saw her. She sort of grew on you — at least her looks did. You began to see that although she might be small in stature, there was nothing child-like in the way she was put together. And the more you saw her, the prettier she actually seemed to become.

Morgan had found himself thinking about her a lot before her visit ended last year, and he'd been in a fighting mood all that summer because he hadn't realized before she left that he wanted her. Then she hadn't come last winter and his interests had turned elsewhere, nothing serious, but he'd buried his feelings for Cassie, forgot about them — until she'd showed up again.

Strangely, upon his seeing her again, it was like the first time, nothing much to make a man sit up and take notice. He thought he must have been a bit lazy the previous year to have let her into his thoughts and even his sexual fantasies. But it had taken less than six months for his feelings to turn around this time. He was back to wanting her within the first month of her arrival, and he was serious enough about it to ask his pa's permission to marry her.

It was telling of R. J. MacKauley's hold over his sons that his approval was the only one they considered needful for whatever they wanted. Charles Stuart's blessing on the courtship of his daughter was secondary, Cassie's not even considered. MacKauley men were unbelievably arrogant when it came to taking some things for granted.

That was one of the things R. J. held against Cassie, that she'd managed somehow to convince his youngest son to break from tradition and do as he damn well pleased, without R. J.'s permission. That what Clayton "pleased doing" was with an enemy just threw salt on the open wound. But Morgan's wound was open and festering, too, because he still wanted Cassie and knew he'd never have her now.

He didn't blame his father, who was too rigid and set in his ways to change. He didn't blame a feud that he didn't even know the cause of, but that had been going on for as long as he could remember. He blamed Cassie for butting her nose in where it didn't belong. If he had married her, he would have broken her of that interfering habit she had. Now he'd never have the chance.

But she'd never know how he still felt about her. Not by look or deed would he let her know.

And come the end of the week, she'd be gone, and he could get on with the business of forgetting her again. Looking at her now, he decided it couldn't happen soon enough to suit him.

Cassie wasn't paying attention to the fact that Morgan's green eyes were drifting over her diminutive form as they stood there. Despite the embarrassing way he'd put it, she pounced on the possibility that Clayton MacKauley might be regretting returning his bride to her family. The idea was so unexpected, so guilt-relieving, she grasped it and hugged it to her breast. It meant her instincts hadn't been so far off the mark after all. It meant her plan to join the two families in marriage to end their feud still might work — eventually. Of course, she wouldn't be around to see it happen.

"What are you doing with that, Cassie?"

She focused her eyes back on Morgan to see him frowning at the rifle in her hand. He was surprised enough at seeing it that he'd forgotten to call her Miss Stuart. But then, this was the first time she had run into him since she'd started arming herself.

"I had some trouble with . . . actually . . . never mind what I'm doing with it," she ended on a stubborn note.

But she was chagrined with herself for still trying to keep the peace between the two families, as she'd been in the habit of doing before the trouble started, when it was just as likely that Morgan wouldn't get upset over what the Catlin hired hands had done to her if she mentioned it now. He would probably applaud them instead for the fright they'd given her. So she wouldn't mention it.

But Morgan's frown just got deeper as his eyes fixed on hers. "What kind of trouble?"

She didn't answer him. She tried one more time to walk past him. And he didn't move to block her this time. He grabbed her arm instead, which was much more effective in stopping her.

"Answer me," he demanded.

If she didn't know better, she might think he was displaying some unexpected concern over her welfare. But when his own family intended to come and set fire to the Double C at the end of the week, that just couldn't be. Perhaps it simply annoyed him that the Catlins had her more worried than the MacKauleys.

At any rate, she didn't owe him any answers, truthful or otherwise. "You have no right to question me, Morgan MacKauley," she said stubbornly, and twisted around to free her arm. "Now let me —"

Her demand for release lodged in her throat, her movement having turned her enough so that she nearly faced the street, and was able to catch a flash of bright yellow out of the corner of her eye. She turned her head the rest of the way to see that Angel had come up behind her at some point and was casually leaning a shoulder against one of the posts that supported the saddle shop's overhanging roof.

He didn't give the impression that he was with her. In fact, he seemed no more than a casual observer of the interesting scene she and Morgan were enacting. But his casual pose was deceiving

48

if you bothered to look closely. The thumb of his left hand was hooked through a belt loop, his mackintosh was open and tucked back, his right hand rested loosely on his hip — directly over his Colt .45.

He was about seven feet away, close enough to hear — close enough to aid. And Cassie was absolutely horrified, imagining what could happen in the next few seconds.

She jerked her eyes away from him, pretending she didn't know him, hoping Morgan hadn't even noticed his presence. No such luck. Morgan was looking directly at Angel now, having followed Cassie's wide-eyed stare, and his frown hadn't lightened up any.

"You want something, mister?"

Cassie winced upon hearing the aggression in Morgan's tone. The trouble with MacKauleys was that their huge size gave them a feeling of superiority as well as invincibility. But a bullet had a way of cutting a man down to size, evening up the odds real quick. Angel would know that from experience, which was probably why he didn't move a muscle, didn't seem the least bit impressed by the bigger man, didn't even seem like he would answer. And no response would be even worse. No man liked to be flat out ignored, and a MacKauley would take exception to that, since no one *ever* ignored them.

Cassie jumped into the prolonged silence to distract Morgan, saying the first thing that came to mind. "Tell your pa I'm not leaving until he agrees to speak to me."

That got his eyes back on her instantly. "I

told you he won't —"

"I know what you said," she cut in anxiously, "but you give him my message anyway, or it's going to come down to the day of reckoning, Morgan. Will *you* set the torch to the house with me still in it?"

"Don't be . . . now listen here . . . dammit, woman!" he ended, so flustered he couldn't get any more words out.

Cassie was pretty flustered herself, not to mention appalled at her own daring. She hadn't intended to call the MacKauleys' bluff, if bluff it was. She wouldn't have had the nerve to do it if she had given it any thought. But she hadn't thought. She'd just wanted to get Morgan's hostile attention off Angel — which wouldn't have been necessary if Angel had kept his distance.

And unfortunately, her ploy gained only temporary results. If Angel had simply left during the time she had distracted Morgan, it would have been worth it. But he was still there, still watching them with those black-as-sin eyes, still provoking with his mere presence. And Morgan, embarrassed over stammering and at a loss as to how to deal with female stubbornness, figured he had a convenient outlet for his current frustration in the form of a nosy stranger. He hadn't yet made the connection that this was the stranger he'd asked Cassie about.

"Either state your business, mister, or get lost. This here's a private conversation."

Angel still hadn't moved from his relaxed position against the post, but this time he answered. "This here's a public boardwalk — and I want

50

to hear the lady say she's not being bothered."

Morgan puffed up indignantly over the very notion. "I ain't bothering her."

"Seems otherwise to me," Angel replied in his slow drawl. "So I'll hear her say it."

"I'm not bothered!" Cassie snapped out with a warning look for Angel to mind his own business, then hissed quietly at Morgan, "Now let go of me and prove it. You've detained me long enough."

Morgan had to drag his eyes away from Angel to look down at Cassie. He showed some surprise at finding his hand still wrapped around her arm and let go instantly. "Sorry," he mumbled.

Cassie just nodded stiffly and walked away. As upset as she was at the moment, considering she'd just taken a stand she hadn't intended to take that could backfire on her by the end of the week, she didn't care that she was leaving the two men alone, one arbitrary, one unpredictable. They were welcome to shoot each other, as far as she was concerned.

Chapter 5

Angel kept half of his attention on the woman as she hurried away, half on the man she'd called Morgan. She was walking so briskly she was almost running. Morgan also was staring after her — and swearing under his breath. Angel wasn't sure about what he'd just witnessed, but he knew he didn't like it. And it was past time he found out what was going on.

The tall Texan turned to him, finally recalling his presence, and was about to say something, but Angel didn't have time to oblige him. "You'll have to excuse me, but she's about to take off with my horse."

And damned if she wasn't doing just that. He did some swearing himself as he realized he'd have to run to catch up to her carriage, which she'd already set in motion.

By the time he reached her, she was nearly out of town, he was out of breath and composure, and the first words out of his mouth weren't meant to alleviate her alarm at finding him suddenly in the seat next to her. "Lady, that's called horse-stealing!"

Her mouth dropped open and her eyes grew saucer-round as she whipped about to see the horses trailing behind the carriage. "Oh, God, I forgot . . . didn't even notice . . . certainly didn't mean to —"

She ended her disjointed explanation abruptly, her mouth snapping shut. And she was so slow in turning back around, she was wearing a completely different expression by the time she faced him, one he recognized too well from their previous encounter.

"Don't start —" He tried to warn off the anticipated diatribe, but she was already cutting into his attempt.

"What the *hell* were you trying to do back there? Don't you know how to deal with men without getting their pride all bent out of shape?"

"I reckon not."

Cassie wasn't expecting that answer, or to see him sit back and cross his arms over his chest, as if daring her to continue upbraiding him. It took some of the heat out of her and she turned to face the road.

"Then you must leave bodies behind wherever you go," she said with quiet contempt.

"That's been known to happen."

She had no rejoinder for that. They could have been speaking of the weather instead of his killing people for all the emotion he gave the subject. She quite honestly didn't know how to deal with someone like him, and didn't care to try anymore.

He *had* to go, today — this very minute. And with that thought settled firmly, she stopped the carriage to tell him so. But he sat forward when she pulled up on the reins, and when she turned toward him it was to find him no more than inches away, so close she had to tilt her head back to see his face, and she got ensnared by those coal-black eyes, not so frightening now, merely curious, but still mesmerizing.

"What'd you stop for?"

Why had she stopped? She had no idea . . . and then she did. She gasped, and moved as far back into her corner of the seat as she could get. She wasn't sure what had just happened, why every thought she'd had had gone right out of her head. Or why she'd felt strange and breathless, as if she were scared witless. But she hadn't been scared, not then. And Angel wasn't exactly frightening her now with his bemused look.

She was forced to glance away just to get her thoughts back to the matter at hand and recall her determination. And it came quickly enough as long as she wasn't looking at him. So she decided to continue facing forward to say what needed saying — to be sure it got said.

"I don't like what happened back there. Morgan I could handle. *You* and Morgan I couldn't. I even took a stand I wouldn't have just to get his attention off you before you drew him into a gunfight."

"I wouldn't have done that," Angel replied with a cold edge to his tone. "I don't pick fights, 'cause there wouldn't be a damn thing fair about it. Outside of a fight, however, I can draw without shooting, and most folks shut their mouths and go away."

"Most folks aren't MacKauleys, which Morgan happens to be just one in a bunch of, and they're all hotheaded men. Their tempers snap, and they've been known to charge right into a man like a riled bull. Morgan might not have noticed you drawing your gun, and you'd have had to shoot him to stop him, or ended up out in the street getting your face rearranged. But that's done and over, with thankfully no one dead."

"Exactly, so —"

"I'm not finished," she cut in tersely, keeping her eyes away from him, uncomfortably aware that he wasn't doing the same. "I was still so upset by what *could* have happened that I left town without completing my errands, the last being to — well, you might as well know. I'm going to send a telegram to Lewis Pickens to inform him that my problem has been solved and I no longer need his help — or yours. I'm going back to town to do that right now."

"Go ahead," was all he said.

Cassie visibly slumped in her relief. She had expected an argument, expected she'd have to lie through her teeth to convince him she had no trouble that he could help with, especially after what he had witnessed of her confrontation with Morgan. Perhaps he was glad to be out of it. After all, he hadn't seemed overjoyed that morning that she and her difficulty happened to be the favor that would clear his debt.

She turned to him now with a tentative smile that died as soon as she saw the frown he had fixed on her. Had she misunderstood his response? Maybe a few lies would be necessary after all.

"I really don't have the same problem I did six weeks ago when I first asked for help. If I wasn't so shaken up by your arrival this morning,

I would have thought to tell you that. With so much time passed, tempers have cooled, and the situation is so minor now it isn't even worth mentioning."

He sat back again in that lazy crossed-arm pose and drawled, "Now I'm plumb curious, so why don't you mention it anyway?"

She wasn't about to go into it for him, since she might inadvertently say something that could suggest his help was still needed. "It's just a matter of a few people being annoyed with me."

"How many?"

She hedged. "There are two separate families."

"How many?"

His persistence made her eyes narrow and she snapped impatiently, "I never bothered to count."

"That many?"

Was that humor in his tone? She wasn't sure, but this was no laughing matter, not to her. Then again, it wouldn't hurt if *he* thought it was.

So she waved a dismissive hand and assured him, "It's nothing serious. The reason I would still have welcomed Mr. Pickens's help was I would have liked to get things back to the way they were before I got everyone — annoyed at me. I was hoping I could still stay here until spring, as I'd intended. But now I'll just stay until my papa returns, and that isn't going to be a problem."

He said nothing to that, just stared at her patiently as if waiting for her to continue — as if he knew there had to be more to it than that. Well, too bad. She'd said all she was going to on that subject.

"It was kind of you to offer to help, but there's nothing to help with now. I'm not in any, well . . . danger — never was, actually, and the telegram I'm sending to Mr. Pickens will release you from any obligation you might feel."

"Is that so?"

"Certainly. Maybe he'll even consider your debt paid, even though you didn't have to do anything. After all, you came. You were able and willing to help — damned persistent about it, actually," she added in a low-voiced grumble. "You did as he asked, so what more is there —"

"He won't see it that way any more'n I do," Angel cut in dryly. "But since there's 'no problem,' you won't mind if I stick around for a few days and ask some questions, will you?"

Cassie stiffened and demanded sharply, "Now why would you do that?"

"Because you don't lie very well, lady."

She stared at him for a long moment, seeing it in his eyes, in his faintly scornful look, that he hadn't believed a single word she'd said. She let out a sigh, saying ruefully, "I know. But most folks don't notice."

"Maybe because you're so sweet-faced wholesome, they can't imagine you telling anything but the truth."

Had she just been insulted or complimented? And how was it that he had known, without a doubt, that she wasn't being honest, when it was only people who knew her really well who usually had that ability?

She tried one last time. "You still can't help.

57

What happened with Morgan just proves it. You get people riled, and I need them pacified."

He slowly shook his head at her. "I'm not about to take your word for it, lady, not after that crock of bullshit you just handed me. I'll decide for myself whether I can help. But until I hear what your problem is, and the truth this time, I'm staying right on your boot heels, and I doubt you'll enjoy that."

She knew she wouldn't. He might not be threatening at the moment, just pigheaded stubborn, but he still made her extremely nervous. She was too aware of him in every way, of his raw masculinity and the violence he was capable of. She simply had no experience in dealing with someone like him, but she'd better learn real quick, because it looked like she wasn't getting rid of him any time soon.

"All right," she said, slightly bitter, slightly resigned. "But first let me assure you that what trouble I'm in is my own fault. I'm a meddler, you see. I'm the first to admit it. It's something I can't seem to help doing. And I should warn you that if you stick around, I'll probably try meddling in your life, too."

"So I've been warned," he replied.

He wasn't impressed, though, she noted. He was probably confident that he was too intimidating for her to try any such thing with him. Come to think of it, that might be so.

"At any rate," she continued, "what I tried to do this time was end a feud that's been going on down here for twenty-five years. It's between two families, the MacKauleys and the Catlins.

58

Actually, it's not just the families. Whoever works for them takes sides, too. Brawls break out every once in a while between the hands when they meet up in town. If their two herds mix — well, that could lead to shooting before they get un-mixed. My papa has become sort of a buffer these past ten years, at least on the range, since he settled right in the middle of their two properties. So the feud is pretty much past the violent stage, but that doesn't mean there isn't a lot of hate built up on both sides."

"I know all about feuds, Miss Stuart. I've been in the middle of several myself."

She knew that, at least she'd heard about one that he'd been hired to participate in, but she wasn't going to comment on that. "These folks, they aren't hardheaded about their feud. They don't insist outsiders take sides. So I was friendly with both families, in particular with Jenny Catlin, who's near my age — and Morgan MacKauley."

"That ornery young cuss you were talking to? You call that friendly?"

She flushed at his sneering tone. "He was friendly enough before I got his whole family set against me."

"And how'd you manage that?"

"I played matchmaker. I figured the simplest way to end the feud was to have the two families joined by marriage. It was a good idea. Don't you think so?"

"If the married couple didn't end up killing each other, I suppose it could've worked. Is that what happened? They killed each other?"

Cassie scowled at his blasé tone. "There was

no killing. But Jenny and Clayton married with my help, each thinking the other was in love with them. I sort of convinced them of that. Only they found out on their wedding night that neither had reached the loving point yet. Clayton dumped his bride back on her family, both families were outraged, and I got blamed for the whole mess, and rightly so, since those two, the youngest of both families, would never have done anything about their mutual attraction if I hadn't noticed it and meddled."

"So you've got half the folks around here hating your guts. Is that all?"

Her mouth dropped open. "All? That's enough for me, thank you," she said indignantly. "I'm not used to being hated. And that's not all. I've been asked — well, *told,* actually, to get out of Texas by both families. But the MacKauleys also gave me a date that I'd better be gone by, or else they'll burn down the Double C. Now, they were generous, really, when you consider this was six weeks ago. They were giving me plenty of time, time enough for my papa to return. Only Papa got delayed with an injury. My time is up this Saturday and the foreman's been chased off by the Catlins, so I can't leave even if I wanted to, and neither Dorothy Catlin nor R. J. Mac-Kauley, the two heads of the families, will speak to me, so I can't even apologize or grovel for forgiveness. So you tell me, mister, how are *you* going to help? I needed Mr. Pickens's talent for talking folks around to being reasonable. From what I hear, you don't talk much at all."

"From what you hear? That's not the first time

you've implied you know me, when we've never met to my recollection. Or have we?"

It wasn't very flattering that he would suppose he would have forgotten her if they *had* met. But Cassie didn't take offense. She was well aware that she was no beauty to turn men's heads. Not that she'd been completely ignored since she'd reached a marriageable age. Of course, the fact that the Lazy S was a very large ranch and the Stuarts had other wealth besides had a lot to do with it. But of the two men who'd shown some slight interest, each had asked outright if she'd be willing to get rid of Marabelle, and their interest had ended when told she wouldn't.

She said to Angel now, "We haven't met, but I do know all about you, what you are, what you do. I grew up on tales of your exploits."

He gave her a doubtful look. "My name's recognized in the North, lady, but only in a few places down here."

"Yes, but I'm only visiting Texas," she explained. "My home is in Wyoming."

He stared at her hard for a moment, then swore. "Son of a — you're one of them eccentric Stuarts from the Lazy S out of Cheyenne, aren't you? The ones that got an el-e-phant grazing out on the range with their cattle. Hell and I should have known."

He said the last with such disgust, she blushed furiously. "You *and* hell don't know a damn thing," she said in defense of her family. "So my grandpa likes to give unusual gifts. He's a world traveler, who goes to many never-heard-of-before places. And he just likes to share a little of his experiences with his family in a tangible way. I don't see any harm in that."

"No harm? I heard that el-e-phant knocked half your barn down once."

Her blush got brighter. "The *elephant* belongs to my mama. He stays out on the range, but every once in a while he comes home — so he's a little clumsy. No *real* harm gets done, and my mama is very fond of him."

"Your mama —"

He bit off what he was going to say, but she could just imagine. Around Cheyenne, it was no secret that Catherine Stuart had lived in the same house with her husband for ten years without saying one word to him — except through third parties. A lot of folks thought that was plain weird. And their collection of unusual animals only added to that opinion.

"So that's how you got that black panther? A gift from your grandfather?"

She could tell he was really having trouble accepting the notion. He probably thought her grandpa was a little bit crazy — or a lot. But then, his was a reaction she was used to. And she was used to explaining.

"Not exactly. Grandpa had intended to keep Marabelle for himself. He found her the day he was leaving Africa. The natives had killed her mother, were going to kill her, too, but Grandpa intervened and brought her on his ship. But he found out after he sailed that he and Marabelle just weren't compatible. She didn't take to sailing at all, was sick the whole trip home, and he wasn't ready to give up sailing himself. And every time he got near her he started sneezing for some reason.

"When he reached the ranch, she was half dead, poor thing, down to skin and bones from having such a hard time keeping food down on the ship. He'd already decided to send her back east to a zoo, but he gave her to me to fatten up first. I'm afraid I got attached to her real quick, as small and adorable as she was then. It took me a while to talk him into letting me keep her, but then, he's a softy where I'm concerned. And I've never regretted keeping her." Even if Marabelle did scare off what few possible beaux Cassie might have had.

"But I believe we have digressed, haven't we?" she continued in a sterner tone. "I asked you what possible help a gunfighter could be in my present situation. Care to answer that now?"

He gave her a narrow look for putting him on the spot. "Didn't you say them MacKauleys were a hotheaded bunch?"

"Yes, but —"

"If you don't want me talking to them for you, which I'd be happy to do —"

"No!"

"Then I'll just be here to protect you if it proves necessary, until they decide to let you live here in peace, or you leave. Guess I'll have to stick pretty close to your boot heels after all."

He didn't seem too happy about that. Cassie was appalled herself.

Chapter 6

He'd be there to protect her. It sounded nice, it sounded safe — if it were anyone but the Angel of Death who'd said it. The trouble was, Cassie didn't trust him just to protect her. He would want to finish his favor for Mr. Pickens as soon as possible. He wouldn't want to merely sit around and let things take their natural course. But she didn't even want to think about what he might do if he got it into his head that he *could* do something to hurry things along.

On the way back to the ranch she'd stressed again that there was to be no killing. She wasn't sure he'd been listening. And even if he had been, she doubted he'd pay her much mind. She hadn't hired him, after all, so he wouldn't feel obliged to obey her orders.

It was a nerve-racking ride. Cassie had hoped Angel would leave the carriage and ride his horse back to the ranch, but he'd made no move to do that when they'd finished their talk. And he was certainly no conversationalist. If she didn't speak first, he said nothing at all, and sometimes even if she did say something, he made no reply.

And his proximity had her fidgeting and paying little attention to the road. His black-clad legs were stretched out next to her and kept drawing her eye. His boots were well made and

64

clearly well cared for, the spurs shining as if they never touched dirt. The boots and his bandana were black like the rest of his attire; everything was black except for his gun, his spurs, and that yellow slicker that let you see him coming from a long way off.

There was nothing normal about his attire. He dressed to draw attention to himself. She wondered why, but she wasn't up to asking him any personal questions. Unfortunately, she'd have ample time to do so later if she got up the nerve, since he was staying — right on her boot heels. God, she hoped he hadn't meant that literally.

Angel found himself glancing at Cassandra Stuart more than once during that ride. His eyes kept coming back to her face, and a profile that was prettier than he'd first thought her to be. It showed off a pert little nose, the soft angle of her cheekbones, a chin that was sweetly rounded, and the fullness of those lush lips. Those lips were downright beautiful, and infinitely kissable. He'd caught himself staring at them when she'd turned to him earlier, and wondering what they'd taste like — which was a thought that confounded him because he wasn't the least bit attracted to the irritating woman.

It wasn't hard to tell that he made her nervous, but that was nothing unusual. Angel made most women nervous, ladies in particular. Her stiff little back, the tenseness in her neck and shoulders, the whites of her knuckles when she gripped the reins too tight, all spoke quite eloquently. She'd even picked up her rifle from the floor and set it between them on the seat. That had so amused him he'd almost laughed outright. He hadn't, though, and he'd had no intention of putting her at ease. It usually was a waste of time to try, but in her case, he simply hadn't felt like it.

Now that he knew who she was, he looked at her differently, though not in any better light after adding lying to him to his list of what he disliked about her. But she was from Cheyenne, and that made a difference, made him see her in a more personal way, though he wished it didn't.

But then, Cheyenne was the closest he came to calling a place home, because he'd spent the most time there since leaving the mountains when he was fifteen — or thereabouts. He wasn't sure how old he was now, somewhere around twenty-six. Didn't know when he was born, or where. Didn't know who his folks were, or how to find them if they were still alive. Old Bear had stolen him out of St. Louis, but he remembered riding a train to get there, so St. Louis wasn't his real home. He'd gone back there once, but no one remembered a little boy disappearing from their town all those years ago. And searching for his past hadn't held much interest for a boy who had spent his childhood the virtual prisoner of a crazy old mountain man. He'd been too busy learning all the things denied him for nine years — and adjusting to living among people again.

He didn't like feeling as if he knew Cassandra Stuart, but the fact remained that she was one of those crazy Stuarts — one of those *rich*, crazy Stuarts — and he'd even met her mother. He'd

66

gone to her ranch once with Jessie Summers when he'd worked for the Rocky Valley spread, during which short time he'd tried ranching — and decided he wasn't cut out for it. But he remembered that day with crystal clarity for a number of reasons.

It was the first and only time he'd met Catherine Stuart, and from what he'd heard about her, she wasn't what he'd expected. She was a handsome woman, a woman of strong character and forthright manner, who looked you right in the eye to take your measure just like a man would. There was nothing soft or shy about her, nothing ladylike, either, at least not that day, since they'd caught her coming in off the range wearing pants and chaps as well as a gun — he could see now where Miss Stuart got the nerve to wear one. Must run in the family.

He'd never met the husband, Charles Stuart. He'd left Wyoming before Angel had ever heard of the crazy Stuarts. But there wasn't a soul who knew the story of their family feud, or thought they did, who blamed him for leaving his wife and daughter.

Some said Catherine had caught him in bed with another woman, but ten years was too long to make a man suffer for one indiscretion. Others said he'd beaten her once and she'd never forgiven him for it. And there was one other version, that she'd had such a hard time giving birth to their only child that she'd never let him back into her bed.

Whatever the reason for ten years of silence, she'd taken over the running of the Lazy S after her husband left, and she ran the large ranch with an iron hand. Men who worked for her jumped when she said jump. Angel could see why after meeting her. There was definitely something intimidating about that woman.

But what made that morning so memorable for Angel were the two flame-red parrots that perched on the railing of the front porch — of a house identical to the one he'd seen this morning, now that he thought of it. The parrots were the most unusual, comical things he'd ever seen. They moved back and forth along the railing in such symmetry, it was like there was only one bird with a mirror following along behind it. And the foul language that they spewed — Jessie had laughed uproariously. Catherine Stuart hadn't batted an eye. Angel had blushed three kinds of red before the two women, mostly at being so surprised, since he hadn't known such birds existed, much less that they could talk.

But that was just the first reason that day was still so clear in his mind. The other was he'd nearly died that afternoon when he'd come across the rustlers who'd been whittling away at the Rocky Valley's herd for several weeks. He'd taken a bullet in his side and been about to get another at point-blank range right between the eyes when Jessie's half brother, Colt, had shown up. It had been damn close, mere seconds to his last breath. He'd even seen the trigger starting to move.

That had been his second debt, owed to Colt Thunder, the one he'd paid back recently that had delayed him getting to Texas. Colt was also

68

about the only man Angel could call a true friend. There were men who called him friend, men who wanted to share in the glory of his reputation. Angel only tolerated them to a point. With Colt it was different. They were both loners, both fast guns, both faced with the strangeness of how folks saw them, though for different reasons. Colt had called them kindred spirits. Angel didn't disagree.

And Cassandra Stuart and her mother were Colt's neighbors. Colt probably even knew them both real well. It was another reason why he was forced to look at the woman differently, now that he knew. She was a friend of a friend. Damn, he would have preferred not knowing.

Chapter 7

Cassie was so eager to depart the gunfighter's company, she didn't bother to take the carriage around to the barn as she usually did when returning from town, but stopped it in front of the house. Emanuel, Maria's son, would come and get it anyway, no matter where she left it, so she didn't spare a thought for the tired carriage horse. She just wanted to get out of *his* sight the quickest way possible.

It had ended up being the longest ride of her life in one of the shortest distances. It had been bad enough that Angel's mere presence disturbed her, but she'd also sensed him staring at her a number of times, and that had been even worse, not knowing what he was thinking, not knowing why he was staring, not knowing what a man like him might do from one minute to the next.

She knew, with what intelligence she possessed, that she was being ridiculous to let him shred her nerves to pieces. He was there to help her, not hurt her. But her emotions weren't interested in being logical or realistic.

She jumped out of her side of the carriage the second it stopped, and was almost running around it to reach the porch. But Angel did the same, and he was there to block her from the steps.

For the second time that day, she just barely

managed to keep from colliding with a man, and this time only because his voice startled her into halting. "What the hell is your hurry, lady?"

Cassie was dismayed to see that her — unwarranted — behavior had annoyed him. And she had no answer for him that wouldn't make it worse. She stepped back hesitantly, enough that she could finally see he was holding her rifle.

As soon as her eyes dropped to it, he thrust it at her. "Forgot this, didn't you?"

That was said in such a sneering tone, she knew that *he* knew she'd felt she needed it to defend herself against him. Her blush came quickly. God, had she ever made such a fool of herself before?

"I'm sorry," she started to apologize, the least she could do after her behavior had insinuated she thought him a depraved monster — or worse.

But he interrupted, saying, "Take it. You might need it — since you got company coming."

His pause was just long enough to make her pale, thinking she'd been right after all, only to have her cheeks flood with color again when she realized he'd done it deliberately. But there was no time for her to lose her own temper over it, which was what she was about to do. She was forced to look in the direction he nodded toward first, and that took care of her temper, for riding hell-bent for leather toward the ranch were three MacKauleys.

"Oh, no," she groaned. "Morgan must have plowed a field racing to get home to tell his pa what I said. That's R. J. MacKauley out in the lead with Morgan, and it looks like R. J.'s oldest son, Frazer, is bringing up the rear. I suppose I should be glad he's along."

"Why?"

"He's the mildest-tempered of all of them — which is not to say he can't explode like the rest, just that he's not as bad as they are. He's the only MacKauley who gave me one furious look when it started, then ignored me after that. But then, Frazer's got a sort of weird sense of humor that no one understands but him. In fact, I wouldn't be surprised if he finds the whole thing hilarious by now."

"Can he calm the others?" Angel asked as he took her arm and led her up the porch steps.

"Occasionally . . . what are you doing?"

"Putting you in a better position. If they dismount, they'll have to look up to you. If they remain on their horses, at least you'll face them eye to eye."

Strategy — while her stomach was churning with dread. "I'd just as soon not face them at all."

She was sure she'd only thought it, not said it, until he replied, "Then go in the house and let me deal with them."

Cassie blanched. "No!"

Angel sighed. "Make up your mind, lady. Thought you wanted a chance to talk to the old man."

"I do."

But she hadn't thought she'd get it, had just a few hours ago taken the stand that almost guaranteed she would. Only she hadn't counted on it being this soon, hadn't had time to think about it at all with Angel on her mind. Yet she needed time to plan confrontations like this, to think out what she needed to say so she could say it right. Without forethought, Cassie tended to mess things up — like she'd done a number of times today already.

But she had no time. The MacKauleys were almost there. And Angel stepped in front of her to face them, causing her more alarm than the MacKauleys did.

She stepped around him to plead, "Please, don't say a word. And don't stand there looking like you hope they'll draw on you. I told you, the MacKauleys have touchy tempers. It doesn't take much to set them off. And this would."

"This" was the rifle he was still holding. Cassie took it from him and set it against the wall. By the time she turned back, dust was floating up on the porch from three horses skidding to a halt.

"Mr. MacKauley," Cassie said respectfully as she moved to the top of the step — putting herself in front of Angel.

R. J. was bigger than his sons; at least he was much broader of frame. Morgan had mentioned once that he was only forty-five. His red hair wasn't touched by gray yet, nor had it started to fade. He'd had his four sons at an early age, and they ranged from twenty to twenty-three — one a year, which was what was said to have killed his wife.

R. J. barely spared Cassie a glance. Morgan and Frazer did likewise. They were all more interested in Angel right now, so Cassie jumped in with

73

what she needed to say while she had the chance.

"I know my still being here is an irritation, Mr. MacKauley, but my papa's been delayed getting back due to an injury. I don't expect him for another three weeks, and the Catlins have scared off his foreman plus two other hands. We have a few men left, but none capable of taking the foreman's job. So you can see why I can't leave yet, at least not until my papa returns."

Cassie drew a deep breath, amazed and pleased that she'd managed to state her major concern without being interrupted — even at the mention of the hated Catlins. But she still had her second concern to address, and the way the three men were continuing to eye Angel, she doubted she'd have much time to finish.

"You never gave me a chance to say how sorry —"

Cassie was right. R. J. interrupted her, still staring at Angel. "Who is he, girlie? And none of that crap you told my boy about him being a drifter."

"Why don't you ask me?" Angel said in a tone so menacing — at least to Cassie's ears — that she panicked.

"He's my fiancé." She blurted out the first thing that came to mind.

That got their attention, including Angel's. But seeing how Morgan was looking so incredulous, then furious, she knew she'd more than blundered by coming up with *that* nonthreatening explanation of Angel's presence. And now she had to further the lie with a logical reason why she'd let Morgan court her if she already had a fiancé.

74

So she added quickly, "I thought he was dead, but he's shown up to prove otherwise."

R. J. didn't buy it. "You're lying, girl," he said without the least doubt. "I don't know where you found him, but he ain't nothing to you."

Cassie was at a complete loss then as to how to support her outlandish claim — until Frazer remarked, "Pa's right. If you two just got reunited, you'd be crawling all over each other. Seems to me —"

Cassie didn't wait for him to continue. She turned toward Angel, wrapped her arms around his neck in a death grip, and smashed her lips against his.

No one was as surprised by her actions as Angel was, but he didn't ruin her attempt at "reuniting" by pushing her away. He did, however, put one arm around her waist to move her to the side, away from his gun, because he wasn't about to leave himself defenseless no matter what point she was trying to make. So he accepted her kiss, even absently returned it, but all the while he kept his eyes on the three men watching their performance, dividing his attention between them and the woman pressed along his side.

As the seconds passed, R. J. turned red in the face, yanked his horse about, and rode off. Morgan gave Angel a killing look before he did the same. Frazer made no move to follow them. He sat there grinning, and finally his amusement became vocal in a burst of laughter.

Hearing it, Cassie let go of Angel's neck and ended the kiss. But his arm tightened around her waist, keeping her pressed to his side. She had to put her hand on his chest to keep her balance as she turned to see who was so amused — as if she hadn't guessed.

"Didn't know you had it in you, Miss Cassie." Frazer's voice came at her with the humor still in it. "This'll have Pa cussing and ranting for a week, which will be a pure pleasure to watch."

Frazer's sense of humor never ceased to amaze her, though she didn't appreciate it at the moment. "But will he still come around at the end of the week?"

"Nah." Frazer grinned at her. "You were supposed to be scared off and run home to your mama. Fact is, Pa was getting plumb worried with the day approaching and you still here. He's probably relieved you've given him an excuse to back off — 'cept for this fellow. Just who are you, mister?"

"My name's —"

"John Brown," Cassie said quickly, cutting Angel off.

But that got only a chuckle from Frazer. "You can do better'n that, Miss Cassie."

She blushed, then paled as Angel tried again. "My name is —"

Her shoe heel stomping on the toe of his boot stopped him this time — and got her released. She heard him swear beneath his breath and lost even more color, though Frazer was having a fit of laughter now.

"Reckon it don't matter all that much," Frazer got out when he wound down, but there was a wicked twinkle in his green eyes as he added, "Maybe we'll be having us another wedding 'fore you head back north. Pa just might get a real kick out of that kind of just deserts."

Cassie ignored his humor-in-full-swing. "But can I count on being left alone now?"

"From Pa? Maybe. Don't know about Morgan, though, since *he* believed you 'bout your friend there. Ain't seen him so mad since Clay came home to tell us what he'd done and your part in it. 'Course, the Catlins are another matter, aren't they?"

With a last irritating chuckle, Frazer tipped his hat and rode off, and Cassie was left with the horrible realization that she was alone again with Angel. After what she'd just done to him — oh, God, the enormity of it, the outrageousness — she wondered if she could just run into the house and slam the door in his face. No, she owed him an apology first — *then* she'd run inside and slam the door shut.

She swung around, only to find him just behind her right shoulder, and too damn close under the circumstances. She started backing up along the length of the porch, away from the door, which couldn't be helped because he didn't stay put, but slowly followed her. He didn't look furious, yet there was a menacing determination in the way he stalked her that set her heart to pounding as hard as it had when she'd thoughtlessly started that kiss.

"I'm sorry," she began in a squeak, then continued in a rush. "I'm *really* sorry about your foot. I didn't mean to — well, I did — no, no, I shouldn't have. But their finding out who you are — I was afraid it'd make things worse. And —"

She gasped as her backside came up against the side railing, ending her retreat. But he kept on coming, until the front of him was pressed to the front of her, at least the bottom half was. She still leaned back, stretching as far as possible over the railing to keep some distance between them, if only a little.

His hands slapped down on the railing on each side of her as he ground out, "I *told* you I'm not known down here."

"You — you don't know that for sure. You'd be amazed how a reputation like yours gets around. There's no point in taking a chance that they might not have heard of you. That wouldn't help matters at all."

"And you think your little lie and demonstration did? Honey, all it accomplished was to show me how sweet-tasting your mouth is. We'll have to try it again sometime without an audience."

The color came, bright flames of it across her cheeks. "You're madder than you look, aren't you?" she guessed miserably.

"My toe's still throbbing, lady. I figure you owe me for that."

Cassie groaned, "Please, I'm a lousy subject to seek revenge on. You saw how unsatisfying the MacKauleys found it. And I never would have stomped on your foot — or done the other — if I'd had time to think about it. But I panicked. I wasn't thinking clearly. I was afraid —"

"You still are, and it's starting to annoy me. You had enough gumption to stand up to three large Texans, two of 'em madder'n hell. I'm just one man."

"But you're a killer."

She really wished she hadn't said that. It rang out like a death knell, hers, and the silence that followed was excruciating. Cassie felt like she'd actually struck him, when all she'd done was state a fact. But the emotion that gathered in his eyes . . .

"You think I'd hurt you?"

Truth time. He wasn't just asking to hear the answer. He was forcing her to hear it, too, and accept it once and for all — and stop acting like a silly goose every time he got close to her. Deep down she'd known the answer. She just hadn't been listening to her own instincts.

"No, you wouldn't hurt me — so back off."

She shoved against him as she said the last, and slipped past him to head for the front door. Her temper was rising by the second as she thought about what he'd just done to her, playing on her fears to get even, then making her *aware* of it. If she had to say one more word to him . . .

"Miss Stuart?"

She whipped around, ready to blast him with her now simmering anger, but she was forestalled by his expression, so intense, with his eyes fixed on her mouth.

"I'll wait a while to collect on that debt."

Her breath caught in her throat. "I — I thought you just did."

He shook his head, a slow, unsettling grin forming on his lips, the first of any kind of humor she'd seen out of him, and this she would have preferred not seeing. He didn't say anything else.

He simply sauntered down the side porch and out of her sight.

Cassie went inside the house and closed the door quietly instead of how she'd intended to. It was her heart that was doing the slamming.

Chapter 8

"I don't start fights, but I don't back down from them, either."

Cassie wished she weren't still nervous around Angel. Yesterday they had established that he wasn't going to hurt her, so this continued unease whenever he got close to her didn't make much sense. She wasn't in fear for her life. She wasn't even in fear for her virtue. That parting threat he'd made yesterday hadn't held much sub-stance, she'd decided after she'd had time to think about it. After all, she knew her attributes, and attracting handsome men wasn't one of them — at least men not interested in ranching. And in-sinuating that he was going to kiss her again to get even, well, the threat of it had obviously been the getting even part. He wouldn't actually do it.

But this morning when Angel had insisted on riding out with her to check on the herd, Cassie had gotten all nervous and flustered again. And this time it came out in chattering that had sud-denly turned serious when she'd asked him how many men he'd challenged. His reply hadn't been the answer she'd been looking for. But now that she'd opened the subject, her curiosity wouldn't let her abandon it.

"They say you've killed more than a hundred

men," she pointed out as nonchalantly as she could manage.

"They say a lot of things about me that aren't true," he replied.

They were riding side by side. She glanced over at him, but his expression didn't warn her off. He looked quite indifferent, actually.

"Have you kept count?" she asked.

He met her eyes for a moment, and she could have sworn there was a spark of humor in them as he replied, "I hate to disillusion you, but the number isn't so high I can't keep track of it."

He obviously wasn't going to share that figure with her. "Were they all fair fights?"

"Depends on how you define fair. I've killed a few who didn't see it coming. But then, I have no qualms about shooting a man who's got a rope waiting for him somewhere. I'll give him the same chance the hangman does — none."

"You don't call that murder?"

"I call it roundabout justice. You think these low-life bastards give their victims a chance when they rape, rob, and kill 'em?"

He was no longer indifferent to the subject. In fact, there was enough heat in that statement to make Cassie wish she'd left well enough alone. So she was appalled to hear herself ask, "How many is a few?"

"Three."

"And the reasons?"

"One tried to hire me to shoot his partner in the back. Figured if he paid to have it done, he wouldn't be accountable. I don't see it that way. His partner wouldn't have, either. But I would have turned that one over to the sheriff if he hadn't made the mistake of telling me the local lawman was on his payroll."

Which was nothing she hadn't heard of before. Caully's own sheriff was more or less in Dorothy Catlin's pocket, since he happened to be her nephew. But then, last term the sheriff had been one of the MacKauleys' cousins.

"So nothing would have happened to that man," Cassie guessed.

"Nothing at all, and the partner, who happened to be a decent, honest man, would have been murdered some night just because he'd gone into business with the wrong man. I didn't feel like letting that happen."

Cassie wondered if she could have made such a decision. Thank God she'd never had to. "And the other two?"

He stopped suddenly. When she noticed, she pulled up and had to twist around to look at him. He was leaning forward against the saddle horn, staring straight at her, his face more shadowed at that distance.

And he stared for a number of tense seconds before he asked, "You sure you want to know?"

Put that way, in that tone of voice, she knew she ought to say no. But she'd latched onto this notion that the more she knew about Angel, the less frightening he'd be. So far it wasn't working, yet her meddling instincts wouldn't let her quit. Still, she couldn't quite get the word out, so she had to nod her answer.

He set his horse to motion until they were riding side by side again. He wouldn't look at her as he spoke. "A couple of years ago I happened upon this man forcing himself on a farm girl. It looked like he might have dragged her out of the field she was working. You could see her farm in the distance with the fields running right up to this river I was following to the next town. He had her on the opposite bank, far enough up behind the trees that I wouldn't have noticed if I hadn't heard her screaming.

"By the time I crossed the river and came up behind them, he was almost finished with her. She'd been beaten, probably for resisting him. Still, for all I knew, they could have been married, though I just can't stomach a man who'd treat his wife that way. So I suggested he leave the girl alone. He suggested I get lost — in some pretty colorful terms. Then I noticed the young boy who looked enough like the girl to be her kin. He'd apparently tried to help her, and he was lying not too far away with a knife stuck in his belly for his trouble. He was already dead."

Cassie swallowed hard before she said, "So you shot him." It was no question.

"I shot him."

"Good," she said so quietly he didn't hear.

"But the girl was beyond caring. She never did stop screaming. And the second I shoved that bastard off her, she up and run into the river. I went in after her, but the water deepened not too far downriver, and she slipped under it. By the time I pulled her out, she was dead — and I felt like going back and shooting that bastard again."

Cassie tried pushing the event from her mind.

It was a tragedy a couple of years old — which she'd just forced him to relive. Some levity was called for to break the somber mood that tale had left, but she wasn't all that adept at lightening moods. Getting folks annoyed with her was her forte.

But she owed it to him to try, so she said, "I hope you didn't save the worst for last."

He actually laughed. "Figured that one would have shut you up."

She cast him a suspicious look. "Was that the truth you just told me?"

"The shortened version — unless you want to hear about her folks' reaction. Those two children were all they had. They blamed me for not saving the girl."

"But you tried!"

"They weren't interested in hearing that."

No, they wouldn't be, but then, grief was a strange emotion, affecting each person differently. And Angel didn't sound bitter about it. He'd probably seen a great deal of grief in his career — possibly some that he'd caused himself.

He suddenly added, "I never told anyone about that girl and her brother."

Cassie was surprised, but his confession also caused a warm feeling akin to pleasure that was more than just feeling privileged that he'd shared the story with her. It flustered her enough that she said, "Then would you like to share the last account with me?"

She'd left herself open to a flat-out no, but instead he remarked, "You really do like to meddle, don't you?" She blushed, but he didn't wait for her response. "It don't make no never mind to me. The third time happened only last month. The rumor was that this fellow by the name of Dryden married rich old widows for their money, then killed them off. He was making a career out of it."

"You actually killed a man based on a *rumor?*"

He ignored the shock in her expression, going on in the same conversational tone. "There were a lot of folks who knew about it, just no way to prove it after the fact. You really think I'd kill someone because of a rumor?"

The blush was back worse than before. Truth time again. "No, you wouldn't."

"No, I wouldn't — though it sure made it easier to pull that trigger, knowing about all those widows who died before their time. But I shot Dryden because he'd just handed over a woman, an English duchess, to a bunch of cut-throats, and he knew full well they were going to murder her. She happened to be a friend of Colt Thunder's, and he asked me to join up with this outlaw bunch who was hunting her, so I'd be there to help her out if she needed it. Turned out she needed it. If I hadn't shot him, Dryden would have lit out of there with his blood money, and I didn't want to take the chance that I might not find him again."

"Did you save the Englishwoman?"

"She was still alive last I saw. Keeping her that way is Colt's problem now."

"I'd forgotten that you know him, and Jessie

and Chase Summers as well. They're my neighbors, you know."

"I know."

His tone was slightly resigned, as if he wished it were otherwise. She looked at him curiously, but he was staring out at the sagebrush-dotted plain, so she decided she'd be better off not pursuing that thought.

"I'm surprised to hear Colt has made friends with a white woman. If I hadn't known him before — well, before the Callan incident, he wouldn't give me the time of day now."

Anyone who knew Colt Thunder knew about that time several years ago when he'd been whipped nearly to death because he'd dared to court a white woman. The girl's father had taken exception to it when he'd found out Colt was half Cheyenne Indian. But Colt had never looked at white women the same after that, at least those he wasn't already acquainted with. The rest he treated like the plague.

"Maybe the term 'friend' was a mite too generous," Angel allowed. "That duchess had somehow corralled Colt into escorting her up to Wyoming, so he's stuck with her for the time being. I didn't say he liked it. Fact is, he don't like it one little bit."

That sounded more in line with what she knew about Colt Thunder, so her thoughts went back to what Angel had confessed about his third "unfair" killing. "You knew you were going to save that Englishwoman, or at least try to, so how do you justify killing Dryden?"

That had him stopping again, and again she

87

had to twist around to look at him. "Lady, *he* didn't know I wasn't part of that bunch that had promised him five thousand to hand her over. As far as he knew, he was bringing her to us to die, and let me tell you something, the plans they had for her didn't include a clean, easy death. Besides, I call it as I see it. If a man's doing something that would earn him a rope, it don't bother me to save the hangman the trouble. So if you think I regret killing that bastard, think again. It was a pure pleasure. But what the hell should I expect? *She* called it cold-blooded murder, too, even though she'd be dead now if I hadn't been there. So you think I give a good damn what the hell you call it?"

Cassie didn't know what to say. He was angry that she was judging him, and rightly so. If she'd been there, she might have called it exactly as he did — though without the courage to take care of Dryden as he deserved.

She faced forward again, and waited until he drew up beside her. The browns and grays of the low plain were starting to give way to the green of the hilly river region where the cattle grazed. The range camp of her father's two remaining hands was just over the next rise, but that seemed miles away when she was presently sitting in a hot seat of discomfort.

"You're right," she said by way of apology. "That man was as guilty as if he'd killed her himself, for intent is equal to the deed."

"Not always."

He was looking at her as he said it, traces of his anger still present, so she had little doubt he'd had some mayhem-type thoughts concerning her. Strangely, instead of causing alarm this time, the idea struck her funny and she grinned at him.

"As long as you only think about it," she said.

"About what?"

"Wringing my neck."

He tipped his hat back, letting the sun touch half of his face, and said in that lazy slow drawl of his, "Is that what I was doing?"

Her eyes widened in feigned surprise. "*Worse* than that?"

He laughed then, playing along. "I reckon neck-wringing's good enough."

"But mine's a scrawny neck. It'd snap real quick. Not much satisfaction in that."

"Then I'll have to think of something else. Can't have revenge without —"

He didn't finish. Two shots fired in quick succession drew his attention, and his demeanor changed to tense alertness, even though the shots had come from a distance. The low rumbling that followed moments later, however, needed no explanation. They had both heard that sound before.

Cassie groaned inwardly. Angel was more vocal. "Let's get the hell out of here," he said as the first stampeding steers came tearing over the distant rise — heading straight in their direction.

Cassie didn't even consider taking his advice. "That's my father's herd," was all she replied before she set her horse to a gallop to intercept the cattle.

Angel couldn't believe his eyes. "Lady, you're

going the wrong way!" he yelled after her, but she didn't stop.

For two seconds he thought, To hell with her. The area was wide open, with ample room to get out of the way of the oncoming herd. Then he let out a foul expletive, dug in his spurs, and followed her.

Chapter 9

Cassie had no fear riding toward that herd — well, not too much. But she knew what she was doing. She'd seen it done before. The animals had been spooked into the wild run by gunfire. Gunfire could turn them back. But as frightened as they were now, she had to wait until she was close before making her move to be sure her shots would startle them into turning back.

So she didn't draw her rifle until she was almost upon them; then she fired off two rounds into the air, only the shots didn't do what they were supposed to. Instead of the cattle veering off so they'd circle around on themselves, the herd split in two with Cassie now dead-center of the two halves. And those two halves quickly closed in on her.

Angel was cut off from reaching her by the terrified cattle rushing past him. He fired off a shot himself to clear a path to her, but he only succeeded in turning a few steers aside. There were just too many of them, and they were moving too fast for him to slip through. Yet she was trapped in the center of that mass, barely above it, and from what he could see, she'd lost control of her horse. Nor did the animal have enough room now to turn around on its own so it could at least move with the cattle. And then it floundered, its hind legs buckling under, and he saw the woman go down with it.

Suddenly Angel was in the grip of a fear worse than he'd felt the first time he'd nearly died. He had an acceptance of his own death now. It came with the job. This was different. This had him circling around far enough behind the herd so that he could ride into it, had him emptying his rifle into the mass, uncaring of what he hit, and yelling at the top of his lungs — and soon had him as enmeshed as Cassie was, with the bawling, pushing animals all around him. But at least he was moving with them, moving toward her, though he could no longer see her.

He heard another shot, but wasn't sure if she'd fired it or if one of the two cowboys had finally shown up, racing along the outer edges of the mass to attempt to stop it. But after a moment Cassie's horse appeared again, just up ahead, only Angel still couldn't see her.

By the time he reached it, his heart seemed lodged in his throat. Finding Cassie on the other side, clinging to the saddle horn and using the horse as a shield, didn't rid him of his fear, either. Until he got her off the ground . . .

He did that, reaching over her horse to yank her across the saddle. His instinct was to keep pulling until he had her safely on his own mount, but she was already bringing her leg over to sit up, so apparently she wasn't too injured. He took her reins instead, and managed to get her horse turned so they could continue moving with the herd, gradually working their way to the edge of it.

Fortunately, most of the cattle were beyond them now, so it didn't take that long to reach clear ground. But Angel didn't stop until he came to a lone tree at the base of the hill the cattle had come over. There he dismounted and carefully lifted Cassie into his arms, carrying her under the tree to set her against the trunk.

She was as pale as death beneath the layer of dust they were both wearing now, which was why his voice was so sharp when he demanded, "Where are you hurt?"

"I'm all right," she got out before a few seconds of coughing took over. "I just got my foot stepped on, but I don't think anything's broken. I could use some water, though. I feel like I've eaten half the dirt in Texas."

That was *not* what he was expecting to hear. He was hunkered down beside her and didn't move for several long moments as he stared at her. It took that long for it to sink in that she wasn't hurt at all, was no more than shook up. And then his anger rose in proportion to his relief. But he kept it to himself. He felt like throttling her for the scare she'd just given him, but he reckoned she'd been through enough already. She didn't need . . .

"Damn fool woman! Haven't you got a lick of sense?"

He stood up as he shouted it, and didn't wait for an answer, but marched over to get his water canteen from his horse. This he dropped carelessly in her lap when he returned. She didn't reach for it immediately. She was too wary of his angry expression to move at all.

"Well?"

"I reckon I don't," she said appeasingly.

"Damned right you don't! That was a stampede out there, lady. You don't deliberately put yourself in the path of something like that."

"I thought I could turn them. They were heading straight for the MacKauleys' grazing land, and any of my father's steers that they've been finding lately, they haven't been giving back. We're already missing about thirty head. I've tried to keep the herd contained because of it."

"Which is likely why they were so easy to stampede," he said in disgust. "So which side do you suppose we have to thank?"

She visibly relaxed now that he wasn't shouting at her. She even washed out her mouth, then took a long swallow from his canteen before answering. "This has the mark of the Catlins on it. And the shots came from their direction."

"The other side could have come around so you'd think so," Angel pointed out.

"True, except the MacKauleys just threatened me straight out, but the Catlins don't let a week go by that they don't do *something* to hurry me on my way home. And neither side has tried to conceal what they're doing or place the blame on the other. They want me to know it's them."

He thought that over while he watched her try to untie the knot on her bandana with shaky fingers. He finally hunkered down next to her to do it for her. She flinched as his hand came near, then just stared at him as he worked the knot loose and slipped the cloth from her neck.

94

"You should have put this on," he said gruffly as he doused the red cloth with water and handed it back to her.

"I know, but there wasn't much time to think about things like that, and, contrary to what you might think, they don't come natural to me. I may have grown up on a ranch, but I've never worked with cattle the way my mama does."

He said nothing to that, so she took a moment to scrub the grime from her face with the wet cloth. When she was done, he took it from her and rubbed a few places she'd missed. She stared at him in bemusement then.

"Why are you being so nice?"

His black eyes met hers with a frown. "So you don't look so pitiful when I beat you."

Cassie's mouth dropped open. He reached over and lifted her chin to shut it. Then he doused the red cloth again and used it on his own dusty face. He'd had enough sense to cover his face with his bandana before riding into that cloud of dust the cattle had created, so he didn't have as much to wipe off.

Cassie was testing her foot when he finished. "You want me to have a look at it?" he offered.

She gave him a sharp look after his last crack, but he appeared sincere. Yet to have his hands on her bare foot? The thought made her shiver. "No, thanks. My toes all move, so it's no more than a bruise."

His frown got darker as he stared at her foot. "It shouldn't be even that, so I'll ride over and pay 'em a visit if you'll point me in the right direction."

"Them" had to be the Catlins. "Oh, no." She shook her head emphatically. "Absolutely not."

He stood up to growl at her. "Lady, that was a stampede we were just in. Someone could have got hurt, including me — in particular me. And *especially* you."

"That wasn't their intention."

"To hell with their intention!" He was back to shouting. "You should have put a stop to this thing a long time ago. You didn't break any laws that I can see. They got no right trying to drive you off."

Cassie sighed when it occurred to her that he was angry now on her behalf, rather than at her. That was much easier to deal with.

"At home when folks get mad at me, my mama has always taken care of it," she admitted ruefully. "She protects me something fierce, I guess because I'm her only child. But her always dealing with my problems hasn't let me gain much experience in handling them myself. I guess I'm not doing too well at my first attempt."

"I noticed."

She bristled at that quiet rejoinder. "Don't think I couldn't have done some threatening of my own and backed it up. I don't wear a Colt just to shoot snakes. I know how to use it, probably as well as you do." She ignored his snort. "But that's not my way."

"Maybe not, but it's mine. And it's things like this that I get hired for, so let me do what I'm good at."

"What you're good at is killing people, but I won't have anyone killed because of something

96

I started. Haven't I made that clear yet?"

"When it just involves you, I'll listen. When it involves me, I'll damn well do something about it. Am I making *myself* clear, lady?"

"Now just a damn minute," she said angrily as she scrambled to her feet. "No one around here has done anything to you. Don't you dare make this personal."

"It became personal when I realized who you are. You're Colt's neighbor, and he happens to be about the only man I call a friend. That makes it personal."

She had no answer for that, since it hadn't occurred to her that he'd see it that way. And it didn't look like he was going to wait around for her further input, either. He was already heading for his horse.

She had to try anyway. "What are you going to do?"

He mounted before he said, "I'll see the sheriff first. If the law will handle it, I'll back off."

That should have delighted her, but had her groaning instead. "Don't waste your time. He's a Catlin relative this year. He'd take care of a complaint against the MacKauleys, but against his own kin he won't do anything."

"Then I'll have to have a talk with the Catlins after all," he replied.

All she could think about then was that story he'd told about the partner who owned the sheriff, and how he'd taken the law into his own hands because of it. "Couldn't you do things a little differently this time?"

"How's that?"

"Guns aren't the answer to everything. Could you maybe *not* shoot anyone around here? I — I would consider it a personal favor."

He didn't answer right away, and those sinful black eyes of his managed to unnerve her before his words did. "You already owe me, lady. I doubt you want your debt any higher — but I'll keep it in mind."

The color came hotly to her cheeks, but he didn't stay to see it. She hoped he wouldn't be able to find the Catlin ranch. She hoped Buck Catlin wouldn't be there if he did, because Buck might not be as hot-tempered as the MacKauleys, but he was twice as arrogant. And how dare Angel make light of her request by reminding her of that ridiculous debt that they both knew he wasn't serious about? It was a joke — with heart-pounding possibilities.

Chapter 10

The Catlin ranch was a Spanish-style hacienda, large and impressive. The high adobe walls that surrounded the house and outbuildings made it a veritable fortress with iron gates at the arched entrance. The gates weren't closed, so Angel wasn't stopped from riding in.

There was a lot of activity going on inside the walls. Three men at a corral breaking in a horse. A servant leaving the storehouse with an apron full of dried apples. Mexican children pretending to ward off an Indian massacre, stirring up dust near a small cemetery plot with three crosses in it. The sound of wood being chopped. A woman singing off-key, then laughing and trying again.

As Angel moved into the yard in front of the house, heads turned his way, movement stopped, the noise at the cemetery died down, the off-key singing sounded louder.

A young man stepped out on the veranda with a coffee mug in his hand. He had blond hair hanging to his shoulders, brown eyes, was of medium height and no more than a year or two over twenty. His chaps were rough hide; his six-shooter rested overly low on his hips to account for a long reach. And he stood with an overstated arrogance, telling Angel he was about to meet his first Catlin.

"Can I help you, mister?" the young man asked in a neutral tone.

Angel didn't dismount, but he rested his hands nonthreateningly on his saddle horn. "I'm here to see the owner."

"That'd be my ma. I'm Buck Catlin, and I do the hiring here."

"I'm not looking for work. I've got a message for your ma, so if you wouldn't mind fetching her, I'd appreciate it."

Buck Catlin didn't move, other than to take a sip of his coffee. "Ma's busy. You can give me any message you got to deliver. I'll see she gets it."

"You're welcome to hear it the same time she does, not before."

Buck's eyes narrowed with a frown at that answer. He wasn't used to being told no. He'd been giving orders to men older than he since he was born. The ranch would be his one day. He was already running it. No one told him no — except his ma.

"Who the hell are you, mister?"

"The name's Angel."

"And who's your message from?"

"Me," Angel replied, then elaborated. "Actually, it's more in the way of a warning. So will you fetch your ma, or do I have to find her myself?"

"I don't think you'll be doing anything but leaving."

Buck had started to draw his gun before he finished that statement. Angel's weapon was palmed, cocked, and pointing at his belly before his hand had even got near it.

"You don't want to do that," Angel said in his slow drawl. "And Miss Cassie doesn't want me to shoot anyone, so back off. This way, you get to live and I don't upset the lady. We both win."

Buck's fingers twitched, then closed on empty air, and the hand slowly lowered. "Who did you say you were?" he asked in a choked voice.

"Angel."

"Angel what?"

"Just Angel."

"Should I know you?"

"No reason why you should."

"But you know the Stuart girl. You said so. She hire you to come here?"

"No," Angel replied. "Fact is, she asked me not to. She had this notion that I might shoot someone. That isn't going to be necessary, is it?"

Buck Catlin turned a little bit pale with that gun still pointed at him and the new expression Angel wore of ominous intent. All he could manage at that point was to shake his head.

"Good," Angel said. "Now, I've allowed you more questions than I usually do, so why don't you return the favor and fetch your ma?"

"His ma is already here, mister," Dorothy Catlin suddenly said behind Angel. "And I've got a rifle aimed at your head, so drop that gun if you want to live to leave here."

Angel's muscles tensed only a little. But his expression didn't change, and it remained on Buck.

"I'm afraid I can't oblige you, ma'am," he said

101

politely, though without looking around. "I'll keep the gun until I do leave."

"You think I won't shoot you?" Dorothy demanded incredulously.

"I don't particularly care whether you do or don't, ma'am. 'Course, your boy here will die, too. If that's what you want, go ahead and shoot."

A long silence followed that had Buck breaking out in a sweat. He was the one to break it when his mother still made no move to lower her rifle. "Ma, if you don't mind, I'd rather not die today."

"Son of a bitch," she cursed then and came around to face Angel. Her rifle was now pointed at the ground. "What are you, a crazy man?"

"Just a man who's lived with death too long to pay it much mind." He tipped his hat at her as he gave her half his attention. His gun, however, remained pointed at Buck.

She was tall for a woman at only an inch or two shorter than her son. And she had the same blond hair and brown eyes. Angel guessed she hadn't reached forty yet. Frankly, Dorothy Catlin was still a beautiful woman, so she must have been stunning when she was younger. And she was soft-looking in her full skirt and lace-edged blouse.

Holding a rifle didn't suit her. Her shooting one seemed absurd. But Angel hadn't survived this long by dismissing innocent-looking people. He'd learned long ago that anyone with the right provocation was capable of killing.

"I heard you mention the Stuart girl," Dorothy said in a highly disgruntled tone. "If you're here to apologize for her, you're wasting your time."

"I'm not. I don't apologize for myself, much less anyone else."

"That's good, because what she's done ain't excusable."

Buck spoke up to second that opinion. "You just look at my sister these days and she starts to bawling. That's all she ever does anymore is cry, and Cassie Stuart and her meddling is the cause."

Angel wondered about that, when it could be just as likely that the girl was crying because she was back home, rather than living with her new husband. But all he replied was, "So I hear."

"Then state your business and get off my property," Dorothy said.

"The Stuart herd was stampeded this morning, the cattle scattered clear to the MacKauley range. The shots that started it came from your direction."

Dorothy's face reddened with indignation. "You're accusing me of starting a stampede?"

"I'm a cattleman, mister," Buck added angrily. "I wouldn't stampede cattle for any reason."

"And the *last* thing we'd do is plump up the MacKauley herd," Dorothy added, "even to get rid of that meddling Northerner."

"But my guess is you've got men who work for you who might not take that into account," Angel said. "And a stampede's too dangerous to fool around with. Men have died in 'em. So if I find who started this one, I'll probably kill him."

"You've made your point," Dorothy gritted out with a good display of rage to accompany her supposed innocence.

"Not quite," Angel replied, and a cold, steely edge entered his voice. "Cassie Stuart happened to be on the range and got caught in that stampede. If that wasn't your intention, I'll call this one an accident. Anything else happens, I won't, and I'll be back to hold him responsible." He nodded at Buck so she wouldn't mistake his meaning. "You don't want me calling him out, ma'am. I don't shoot to wound, so odds are he wouldn't survive it."

Buck swallowed hard. He'd already seen Angel draw. So had Dorothy as she'd come up behind him, but she didn't address that now.

"Was she hurt?"

Angel reserved judgment on the concern that entered Dorothy's expression as she'd asked that. "She could have been, *should* have been, since the idiot woman rode right into that stampede to stop it."

"Don't sound like you like her much," Buck got up the nerve to comment.

"I'm still making up my mind about it," Angel admitted. "But whether I do or don't's got nothing to do with my protecting her. I'll be doing that until she leaves here, and she won't be leaving until her pa gets back. So I would advise you folks to leave her alone from here on — unless you're willing to take me on."

"I don't want her dead, mister, just gone," Dorothy stated, belligerence back in her tone. "The sooner she is, the sooner my girl can forget what happened."

"When she's got a more potent reminder in a husband living only a few miles away?"

"Ex-husband, just as soon as the judge gets back from Santa Fe."

Angel shook his head at that reasoning. A divorce paper wasn't going to make Jenny Catlin MacKauley forget she'd been wedded, bedded, and abandoned.

"That's your business," he replied. "Cassie Stuart is now mine."

"You've got your nerve, coming in here and threatening me, I'll give you that," Dorothy told him. "You'd be easy enough to get rid of, fast gun or not."

"You're welcome to try, if you want bloodshed added to this thing. But for the record, I rarely threaten, ma'am. I state facts as they currently stand. What you do with 'em is up to you."

Dorothy was red-faced with anger again. "All right, you've stated your *facts,* now here's one of mine. You show up here again and you'll be shot on sight."

Angel grinned at that point. "Fair enough, though I ought to warn you that isn't likely to stop me. Good day, Mrs. Catlin."

He tipped his hat to her again, holstered his gun, and turned his back on them. He'd gone several yards before she called out, "If the Stuart girl didn't hire you, what's she to you?"

"A favor."

Dorothy didn't say anything else, just watched him leave without the least concern that he'd be shot in the back. She hated gunfighters, she really did. You couldn't deal with a man who lacked fear.

"Find out who he is, Buck," she said, still bristling. "A man don't talk like that unless he can back it up. And find out which one of the boys is taking matters further than ordered. I want whoever it is gone by sundown."

Chapter 11

Cassie walked from one end of the porch to the other, then back again, her arms crossed tightly beneath her breasts, her eyes anxiously scanning the distant road in both directions. She'd cleaned up after returning to the ranch. She was now wearing a very stylish skirt with three deep flounces in a cream-colored sateen sprigged with tiny flowers. The white silk blouse was trimmed with soft Sicilian lace at the cuffs and the collar, all exposed beneath a thick white shawl. And she'd managed a plain yet becoming coiffure with Maria's help.

The overall effect was not too fancy, not too understated — "armed," as her mama would put it, though unlike her mama, Cassie had always chosen subtlety over blatancy when she dressed for a specific reason. Her reason now was to give the appearance of being calm and collected when she was anything but.

She was waiting for Angel to return to the ranch. She'd been waiting for several hours already. And the things she was imagining happening at the Catlin ranch kept her pacing the front porch.

Marabelle paced right alongside her. Occasionally the panther would nudge her leg and Cassie would drop a hand to absently pet the sleek cat.

107

She'd tried once to put her in the house, but Marabelle had just sat back on her haunches and roared her refusal, so Cassie didn't try again. But then, the feline could always sense when something was wrong with Cassie, and would refuse to leave her side when she did. Appearances couldn't fool the cat.

It was late afternoon when Cassie finally heard a horse ride in, though she didn't know if it was Angel's, since the sound came from behind the house. But she didn't wait to find out, hurrying around the side of the house and reaching the stable just as Angel did.

"What happened?" she asked before he could even dismount.

She was wringing her hands. So much for the effort she had put into appearing calm and collected. And the infuriating man didn't answer immediately — well, possibly because he was having some difficulty with his horse now, since Marabelle had followed Cassie to the stable.

Angel glared down at her from the back of the rearing horse. "I thought I told you to keep that cat away from me."

"She won't hurt — never mind. Don't go away," she added before she ran back to the house.

She entered through the kitchen, waited until Marabelle had followed her in, then slipped back out, closing the door firmly. A roar of displeasure sounded behind her, but Cassie ignored it and ran back to the stable. Angel was dismounting, though his horse was still acting skittish.

"Well?" she demanded, a bit breathlessly.

He started to lead his horse into the stable, and his voice was on the testy side as he tossed back, "I didn't have to shoot anyone, if that's what you're hankering to hear."

Cassie felt like collapsing in a puddle of relief. She followed him into the stable instead, despite the disgruntlement he was displaying over what had just happened.

In her lightened mood, she thought to reassure him. "Marabelle wouldn't hurt you . . . well, as long as you keep your boots on when she's around."

That stopped him. "Why?"

"She's got a real fondness for feet, mine in particular, but anyone's will do when she's in the mood. She loves to rub her face all over them, and occasionally clean her teeth on them."

"Clean her — how the hell does she do *that?*"

Cassie grinned. "Not by chewing, I assure you. She just scrapes the surface of her teeth on you, but that *can* be a bit painful if your feet happen to be bare when she does it."

He didn't look reassured. In fact, he looked even more disgruntled. "I don't intend to find out," he said with finality and led his horse into the nearest empty stall.

Cassie shrugged behind him. She knew from experience that strangers had a hard time getting used to Marabelle, and an even harder time relaxing around her. Angel wasn't proving any different in that respect, though there was one major difference in him. He was more likely to shoot her pet if he felt threatened, whereas most folks would simply run from it. So she wasn't going to give up trying to convince him that Marabelle was harmless, but she let the subject drop for now in favor of her other concern.

"So did you find the Catlins?"

He went about unsaddling his horse as he answered. "I found 'em."

"And?"

"And they didn't take too kindly to the advice I offered."

"Which was?"

"To leave you alone or end up taking me on. I explained why they might not want to do that."

She could just imagine. "You didn't threaten them, did you?"

"Just gave 'em the new consequences of continuing as they have been."

Which still told her nothing and she finally was annoyed enough to say, "I swear, getting information out of you is worse than getting a mule to do what you want. Can't you give it all to me in one dose?"

He gave her a long look. "If anything else happens to you, I'll be calling on Buck Catlin again. He knows it. His ma knows it. Is that what you wanted to hear?"

"To shoot him?"

"Probably."

Cassie groaned. "I wish you would look a little more reluctant when you say that."

He frowned at her. "You think I like killing?"

"You don't?"

"No, I don't."

"Then why don't you change what you do for a living?"

"Tell me what else I'm suited for. I tried ranching and it didn't work. I don't know anything about farming. I could probably open a saloon in some place, but I doubt I'd have the patience to learn the business end of it. The only other thing I know is trapping, but I think I'd rather die than live alone up in the mountains again."

She was amazed he'd said so much, and that he'd obviously considered other means of work. "You'd make a good sheriff," she suggested hesitantly. "Didn't they offer you the job in Cheyenne?"

He went back to tending his horse. "It'd take a couple of years as sheriff to earn what I do now for one job. Can't see as how it'd be worth it when I'm risking my life either way."

He had a point. And she'd had no idea he was so expensive to hire.

The remark stirred her curiosity enough to ask, "You've been doing this for quite a few years. Does that make you rich, or do you spend it as soon as you get it?"

He came out to close the stall, then turned to give her his full attention. There was a slight curve to his lower lip when he replied, "Now, what would I have to spend that kind of money on?"

She knew what most young men spent their money on, all of which could be found in a saloon. If he didn't, he must have a sizable bank account by now.

"Have you thought of retiring?" she wondered aloud, then pressed the point by adding, "Of never killing again?"

"I've thought about it, but retiring wouldn't keep the gloryseekers from finding me and calling me out. I'd have to change my name."

"So why don't you?"

"What?"

"Change your name?"

He was silent for so long, she began to fidget under his direct gaze, and then he said, "The last woman who pestered me with so much chattering, I offered to marry — so I'd have the right to beat her."

Her eyes flared for a moment before she snorted, saying confidently, "You wouldn't do it. You said it disgusted you to see a man treat his wife that way."

"It's not that I wouldn't, it's that I wouldn't want to," he said in his lazy drawl. "There are nicer things to do with a woman — when she's not being a pest." Then with a grin he inquired, "Are you blushing, honey?"

She had to be beet-red, she realized, if he could notice it in the dim stable light. Primly, she insisted, "I'm going to have to ask you to stop saying things like that to me."

He shrugged. "You can ask," he replied, then started to leave the stable.

"Wait a minute!"

Cassie hurried after him, then came around to block his way when he stopped at the entrance to the stable. Unfortunately, she brought her blush with her, which was much more discernible in the chilly afternoon sunlight. But she wouldn't think about that, or his improper remark, which he had probably only made to shut her up. Too

112

bad for him. If he couldn't stand questions, he ought to be more informative to begin with.

"What took you so long to get back here?" she wanted to know. "You were gone more'n four hours."

He tipped his hat back with a sigh. "You should have warned me you were a nag as well as a meddler."

She bristled. "If you weren't so close-mouthed —"

"All right." He gave in. "I took a ride over your neighbors' land counting heads."

That surprised her. "Cattle?"

"Hired hands," he corrected her. "It pays to know what you're up against. I counted twelve hands on the Catlin side."

Cassie agreed with his reasoning, so decided to be helpful. "They've got more'n that. Some must be in town today."

"And about fourteen on the MacKauley side."

"Whatever the number's up to, it's guaranteed to be the same. Whenever the Catlins hire a new man, the MacKauleys do, too, and vice versa. It's like they want to be assured of even odds for the day it comes down to outright war."

"Has it ever?"

"No. But every time I went to church with the MacKauleys on the one side and the Catlins on the other, it seemed like it would at any moment, so many hateful looks kept crossing the aisle. It was experiencing that unpleasant tension every Sunday that put the idea in my head to ease it, especially after I noticed that the looks passing between Jenny and Clayton weren't hateful at all."

"If you ask me, you only hurried things along a mite."

"Now why would you say that?"

"We'd already heard that Clayton is having second thoughts. Appears Jenny might be, too, since, according to her brother, all she does is cry these days."

"But that's terrible!"

Angel shrugged. "Depends on what she's really crying about. Could be those two young 'uns might have got together eventually without your help. If their kin would leave them alone, they still might." That brought a thoughtful frown to Cassie's brow that was easy to interpret. "Don't even consider it, lady. Hell and your mama should have broke you of that meddling habit of yours."

She gave him a sour look. "It's just not fair that Clayton and Jenny are caught up in that feud, that it's keeping them apart. Do you know, they don't even know *why* their folks despise each other."

"But it's not your business, *they're* not your business, and you aren't going to interfere again, are you?"

His expression was so intimidating, Cassie said, "Well, when you put it that way, I guess not. But tell me, after meeting her, do you think Dorothy Catlin might be willing to talk to me now?"

"Not a chance. But I did tell her you wouldn't be leaving until your pa returns. I don't think you'll be having any more trouble from that side."

Cassie smiled slightly. "I guess it didn't hurt

114

for you to pay them a visit after all. Thank you."

"Don't mention it."

"Well, I'll let you go." She started backing away from him toward the house, but added before turning around completely, "Since the other two hands have been staying out on the range, you're welcome to have dinner at the house." Emanuel had brought his meal to the bunkhouse last night.

"Is that an invitation?"

His surprised tone flustered her. "No — I mean — yes, it is, but not the way you're implying."

"You mean you haven't started liking me yet, honey?" he asked with a grin.

That teasing question didn't deserve an answer, but it did get another blush out of her as she whipped around to hurry from his sight. She was beginning to wonder if Angel didn't have as bizarre a sense of humor as Frazer MacKauley.

Chapter 12

Cassie didn't change her clothes again for dinner that night, which she would have done if her papa had been there, since both he and her mama adhered to the more formal proprieties of the East, even though they'd lived more than half their lives in the West. If she did change, she was afraid Angel wouldn't see it as a mere formality and might think she was trying to impress him, and that was the last thing she wanted him to think.

But she really wished she'd kept her mouth shut. Maria noted her nervousness and reminded her that Angel could eat in the kitchen with her and her son. That had actually been the idea when Cassie had made the offer. But after Angel's misinterpretation, real or feigned, he'd think she was still frightened of him if she refused to eat with him. Whether that was true or not, she'd prefer he didn't think it. And after all, he wasn't a hired hand. He was a guest — uninvited, but still a guest.

And he was late. Maria had been holding dinner for fifteen minutes when Angel finally showed up at the front door. But Cassie didn't mention his tardiness, even though Emanuel had been sent to tell him what time dinner was usually served. She was too surprised by his appearance to say

116

much of anything at first.

He wasn't wearing his mackintosh. He'd exchanged it for a black jacket that revealed a sinewy musculature previously hidden by the shapeless yellow slicker. His clean black shirt was buttoned to the collar with a string tie instead of his bandana. He removed his hat immediately. His black hair was still damp from a bath, thick and parted to fall near his shoulders, though there was a perfect neatness to it. But like most men who spent a lot of time outdoors, he was obviously letting it grow long for the winter, to protect his neck and ears from the cold.

There was no overlooking his handsomeness this time. It was blatantly there, and it flustered Cassie as much as his dangerous reputation did. She caught herself simply staring at him. Fortunately, he didn't notice. He was too busy looking around him.

"You locked her up?" he asked after she closed the door behind him.

"Who — oh, you mean Marabelle? She's in the kitchen. Don't worry, I've asked Maria to keep her there while you're in the house."

"Appreciate it," he replied.

His wariness of her large pet should have amused her, but she was too cognizant of the fact that the man wore his gun even to come to dinner, so Marabelle, despite her lack of aggression, wasn't safe around him.

With visions of a disastrous evening ahead of her, Cassie led Angel down the hall to the double doors on the right. The long, formal table held two place settings. Seeing them together, Cassie wished she had thought to tell Maria to arrange them at opposite ends of the table, rather than both at one end as was the custom when she dined with her papa. It seemed a much too intimate arrangement under the circumstances, but she'd insult Angel now if she tried to change it.

She stepped toward one chair and was surprised to feel him behind her, moving the chair out to seat her. She hadn't expected refined manners from him.

"Thank you," she said, feeling even more flustered when he made no reply but took the seat directly across from hers.

Maria, having heard Cassie's voice, stuck her head in the side door, then moments later began serving. Angel made some remark about the room's fine furnishings, and Cassie was relieved to have something neutral to converse about. She explained how every piece in the house was the same as in her home in Wyoming, how her papa had gone to the same store in Chicago where all the original pieces had been bought. Some had no longer been available, so he'd commissioned to have them replicated.

"Why?" Angel asked when she had nearly depleted the subject.

"I never asked," she admitted. "There are certain things I don't discuss with my papa. Anything that has to do with my mama, or what I even suspect might have to do with her, isn't broached."

"Why not? Just because they're divorced —"

"They're not." When he lowered his fork to

118

just stare, she added, "I guess most folks assume that, but neither one of them ever got around to it. Living at different ends of the country seemed to satisfy them both."

"What if one of them wants to get married again?" he inquired.

Cassie shrugged. "Then that person will probably do something about ending the first marriage."

"Would that bother you?"

"In my whole life, my parents haven't spoken directly to each other. Why should it bother me if either one of them wants to have a *normal* marriage?"

Angel shook his head before continuing his meal. "I don't think I really believed that they hadn't said a word to each other in all these years. That must have been difficult for you growing up."

She grinned. "Actually, I was seven before I found out that everyone's parents didn't behave that way. I thought it was normal. Now why don't you tell me something about yourself, Angel?"

She blushed the moment she said his name. It was the first time she had, and it hadn't occurred to her how intimate-sounding it was, especially with a woman saying it.

He noticed. "What's the matter?"

"Is there — ah — something else I can call you?"

He didn't actually smile, but she could tell he was amused by her discomfort. "You were doing fine with 'mister,' " he told her.

But that was hardly appropriate at this point, and "Mr. Angel" didn't work, either, since "Angel" wasn't his surname. He appeared indifferent to resolving the problem for her, which annoyed her enough to ask, "Whatever made you pick the name Angel?"

One black brow went up. "You think I would pick a name like that?"

"Didn't you?"

"Hell, no. It happens to be the only name I remember my mama calling me, so it's the only name I could give the old mountain man who raised me when he asked. *He* thought it was hilarious, as I recall."

It took her only ten seconds to think about that and remark, "But that was probably just a pet name your mama used, like 'precious' or 'honey.' "

"I finally figured that out, but by the time I did, I was stuck with the name. And it didn't matter all that much to me. When you go as long as I did thinking that was the name I was born with, you get used to it. Anything else wouldn't sound right to me now."

What about folks who weren't used to it? she wanted to ask, but was more curious about what he'd inadvertently revealed. "Had your mother died? Is that why you were raised by a mountain man?"

"He stole me."

Cassie was the one to lower her fork this time. "I beg your pardon?"

"Right out of St. Louis," he continued as if she weren't sitting there with her mouth open.

"I was five or six at the time. Don't remember which."

"You don't? Are you saying you don't know how old you are now?"

"I don't."

That seemed so sad to her, she automatically reached out to pat his hand in sympathy. She snatched her hand back when she realized what she'd almost done. He noticed, and that flustered her so much, she took three quick bites of Maria's spicy chicken so she couldn't say another word.

But after she had swallowed, she did speak. "How could a child be taken from a town that large? Wasn't any effort made to find you?"

"Since I wasn't found, I couldn't say. And I spent the next nine years so high up in the Rockies, we never saw an Indian, much less another white man."

"Didn't you ever try to escape?"

"A few months after we got to that cabin up in the mountains, I wandered off too far from it. When Old Bear found me, he chained me out in his yard for three weeks."

Cassie was having a difficult time accepting what she was hearing. The last appalled her. "He left you out in the elements?"

"I guess I can be grateful it was summer at the time," Angel said offhandedly, as if the subject weren't bringing back terrible memories. "But I didn't wander off again after that. And it was nearly five years before he let me go with him to the settlement where he sold his furs. It took a week just to get there."

"You didn't tell anyone there?"

"He'd cautioned me to keep my mouth shut. By then I was used to obeying him. Besides, those folks knew Old Bear. Wasn't anyone there who would have gone against him to help me get back to St. Louis."

Cassie wished she'd never asked him about his name, yet she couldn't seem to drop the subject it had opened up. "Do you know why he took you? Did he want a son?"

"No, just company. Said he got tired of talking to himself."

Just company. A small boy had been taken from his family in order to keep an old man company. She'd never heard of anything so pathetic and sad — and outrageous.

"Where is he now?" she asked.

"Dead."

"Did you — ?"

"No," he replied, explaining, "He got his name because there was always one or two bear hides in the furs he sold. He loved pitting himself against bears, the bigger the better. But he was getting too old to go after 'em anymore. The last one survived, he didn't."

"And you left?"

"Soon as I buried him," Angel said. "I was fifteen — or thereabouts."

"Did you go back to St. Louis to find your folks?" Cassie asked next.

"First thing. But no one remembered my mama, or anything about a missing boy. 'Course, St. Louis wasn't my real home. I remember a train ride to get there, and Old Bear took me soon after that."

"You don't mention a father."

"Don't recall much about one. There was a man who called himself my pa, but I only remember seeing him once or twice. Whatever job he had, it kept him away from home for long stretches at a time."

"But didn't you ever find them?"

"Didn't know where to look."

He said that so indifferently, like it no longer mattered. Cassie was having as much trouble with his attitude as she was with his tale.

"Chase Summers never knew his father, either," she told him. "But he knew his name, which made him easy to find when Chase went to Spain to search. But there are men trained to find people, who know how to go about sifting through clues long buried or thought forgotten. We could hire one to find your folks, if you'd like."

"We?"

She blushed and reached for the wine bottle to refill their glasses. His had hardly been touched. She should have had Maria try to locate a bottle of whiskey for him, she supposed, if there was any in the house — her papa didn't drink — though the thought of Angel intoxicated was a frightening one to contemplate.

"I guess my meddling instincts are showing," she admitted, hoping her pink cheeks weren't showing, too. She didn't think she'd ever blushed so much in her life as she had since he'd shown up. "You'll have to forgive me. I can't help it if I like to help people."

"Even when they don't want it?"

That should have shut her up, but she wasn't done making excuses for her irritating habit. "Sometimes people need a little help figuring out what they really want."

Angel conceded that point by saying no more. He wished he could find his folks. He'd never had anyone love him, and they were about the only two people who might. Love was something he'd missed in his life, and not just the parental kind. Since the time he'd seen Jessie and Chase Summers together, the way they touched frequently and looked at each other, the way their love blazed between them, he knew he'd like to have that for himself, that closeness with another person, the caring, the tenderness, things he'd never had, or had experienced so long ago he had no memory of it.

But he had given up finding it for himself. Good women shunned him because of his reputation. Bad women liked his reputation and welcomed him to their beds, but got scared at the first sign that he might want something more serious than a good time.

Now, what was it about Cassandra Stuart that made him think of that? No, not her, but her dredging up all his years of loneliness.

"I'm sorry," she said, drawing his eyes back to her. "I think you just — well, *surprised* me with your revelations. I thought I knew a lot about you, but I'd never heard anything about your early years before."

He'd told Colt about Old Bear, but he'd never told anyone else — until now. And for the life of him, he couldn't figure out why he'd told her.

Possibly because she was disconcerting him, sitting there looking so prim and proper, and prettier than she'd looked at any other time. And that didn't make sense, because there was nothing different about her. She was even wearing the same clothes she'd been wearing earlier.

However, it was the first time he was seeing her without a coat, jacket, or shawl covering up her figure, and he had been somewhat surprised to find that she had a nicely shaped body, with well-rounded breasts that would be a handful, and a sharply curved waist. In the candlelight, she was soft and creamy-looking, her gray eyes like liquid silver. And those lush lips . . .

He couldn't count how many times tonight his eyes had kept returning to that mouth of hers as she talked and ate and pursed her lips to sip her wine. He'd barely had a taste of her when she'd bestowed that kiss on him, but what he had tasted had been so incredibly sweet.

There was no use denying it any longer. He wanted another taste. And as his eyes dropped down to her breasts, then slowly lifted to her soft mouth, his body started telling him he wanted more than that.

Angel's unexpected reaction to her so startled him, he reached for his wineglass and drained it. When he lowered the glass, he saw Cassie staring at his scarred jaw. He knew she'd seen the scar before, though she hadn't asked about it. It ran just under his jawline, so you saw it only when he tilted his head back or at a certain angle. And the way she quickly looked down at her plate told him she wasn't going to ask now, either.

He wondered why not, when every other subject seemed fair game for her. Perhaps it was seeing the result of actual violence that intimidated her. But her squeamishness annoyed him for some reason . . . no, it was his suddenly wanting her that annoyed him, and the urge he had to reach over and haul her onto his lap for a more thorough taste of her.

So he volunteered an explanation. "A man thought to sneak up on me from behind and cut my throat. His aim was off."

Her eyes came up to lock with his dark ones. "Is he still living?"

"No."

Angel tossed his napkin on the table as he said it and abruptly stood up. He had to get out of there, away from the candlelight, the wine, and her looking prettier to him by the second.

"Thanks for the dinner, ma'am, but don't feel obliged to repeat the invitation. Truth to tell, I'm more comfortable eating alone, I'm so used to it."

He wished he hadn't added the last. The sympathy that suddenly entered her expression twisted at his insides something fierce. He left before he was tempted to accept what she had to offer. Whatever it was, he didn't need it. He didn't need anyone.

Chapter 13

Sleep seemed to elude Cassie that night. She tossed and turned in her bed. She got back up and tried to walk herself into exhaustion. The exhaustion didn't come, but she managed to agitate Marabelle so much that she finally had to put the cat out of her room and hope her prowling through the house wouldn't wake Maria downstairs.

Her own room was upstairs at the back corner of the house. One of the windows overlooked the bunkhouse, and each time she passed it in her pacing, she saw a light still burning. She wondered if Angel was having the same problem she was. Uncharacteristically, she hoped so, since her problem was because of him.

That wasn't fair. It was her own fault that she knew what she did about him now. She'd pried and poked and got him to admit things she would have been better off not knowing. She had liked it better when he was just the Angel of Death. Now he was also Angel the little boy, and Angel the man who was more comfortable eating alone.

More than once tonight she had wanted to wrap compassionate arms around him. She could be grateful she wasn't the spontaneous sort to act on impulse, or she'd be mortified now if she'd done so. She would have been abruptly rejected, of course. He wasn't the kind of man who would take to being comforted, no matter the reason.

It was absurd to want to comfort a man like him, a ruthless gunfighter, a killer . . . She wasn't being fair again. Angel wasn't just a killer. He helped people in what he did. He also had a profound sense of justice. It might be only barely inside the law, but he still felt he was on the side of right, and maybe he was. Who was she to judge?

When she finally saw his light go out, she tried her bed again and surprisingly went right to sleep this time. It seemed only moments before she was awakened by a hand pressing firmly over her mouth.

The terror of those first moments abated somewhat when Cassie realized it must be Angel. Why he hadn't knocked to wake her, instead of frightening her by just suddenly being there, she couldn't guess. It was too dark to see his face; the small fire she had started earlier had burned down too low. So he couldn't see, either, that her eyes were open, which was probably why he still hadn't let go of her mouth.

"You awake yet, little lady?"

That voice didn't belong to Angel, it belonged to Rafferty Slater. And Cassie's terror was back and debilitating her.

"Just nod if you are."

She couldn't. She couldn't move at all, her limbs seemingly weighted to the bed. She'd sworn she wouldn't let him touch her again, but she didn't sleep with her revolver. She had no way to stop him . . .

She moaned as his other hand found one of

her breasts beneath the cover and squeezed. "That's better," he said with a low laugh. "Playin' possum, was you? Or just plumb worn out from chasing down them cattle I scattered? But you ain't gonna sleep through this."

It was the laugh that made her suddenly come alive, her arms flaying, her legs kicking to get the cover off. One fist got lucky and cracked against his face.

"Stop that!" he growled.

She didn't. And trying to subdue her arms with only one hand wasn't working too well for Rafferty. The hand over her mouth slipped enough for her to start a scream, only it was cut off too quickly, his fingers smashing her lips against her teeth.

"You ain't too smart, girlie. You ought to think about bein' nice to me 'fore I have to hurt you."

He leaned close to her face to utter that warning. His liquor-soured breath gagged her, but she couldn't turn her head away from it. It occurred to her that he might be drunk, that it was the liquor that had given him the nerve to come here and accost her, but she was too frightened to think how she might take advantage of that.

"I shoulda come to visit you sooner'n this, seein' as how your only protection was so easy to bribe."

He found that so funny he was laughing again, while Cassie couldn't make sense out of what he'd said. Angel bribable? She'd stake her life that wasn't true. But Angel was sleeping, and she'd barely been able to make a sound when she'd tried, so she knew she hadn't awakened him. Her windows might be cracked open, but unless she could manage a good scream . . .

Rafferty's mouth suddenly changed places with his hand, too quickly for Cassie to do more than draw a breath. With both hands free now, he swiftly gathered hers together to hold in one of his, then began yanking on the high neck of her nightgown with the other. The small pearl buttons popped off one by one, the chill December air now touching her breasts. Then he was.

"Shoot, I shoulda brung a light. But feelin's as good as seein'."

Cassie started to whimper. The stench of his mouth was choking her; his hands were hurting her. He had one leg thrown over hers so she couldn't move them, either. And then Marabelle roared, the sweetest sound she'd ever heard — only it came from outside.

"Damn cat. Shoulda shot it instead of —"

Rafferty forgot about keeping Cassie's mouth covered, long enough for her to get out one piercing shout; "Angel!"

"Shut up, damn you!" His hand clamped back over her mouth. "If that Angel's the new man they're talkin' about in town, you better hope he didn't hear you."

Cassie was hoping just the opposite, and when a door slammed downstairs, she prayed it wasn't Maria or Emanuel. Rafferty must not have thought it was, because he bolted toward her door to lock it.

"That won't stop Angel," she taunted now that she was free, though she took the precaution of slipping out of bed to duck down on the other side of it before she added, "He'll kill you if you're still here when he comes through that door."

She could barely make out that Rafferty was looking frantically around her room. If he thought he was going to hide, he'd better think again. But it was another exit he was searching for, and he found it in the double doors that led out onto the upper balcony. He ran toward them and tried to open them, but all they did was rattle.

Cassie had locked the doors for the night, but she didn't particularly want a dead man in her room, so she said, "Turn the key, you idiot."

He did, and as soon as he swung the balcony doors open, she was running for the door to the inside corridor to unlock it.

Behind her, she heard him mumble, "Bitch won't even give me a head start."

He *had* to be kidding. He was lucky she didn't run for her gun instead of Angel's assistance because she could have shot him before he got off the balcony, whereas Angel probably wouldn't get the chance to. And, in fact, Angel was just reaching the top of the stairs when she got her door open and stumbled over Marabelle, who'd been leading the way.

"What is it?" he asked as he helped her up off the floor.

"It was one of the Catlin hired hands."

Surprise showed in his voice. "After the warning I gave 'em?"

"Rafferty Slater acts on his own, but I don't think he'd been told about your visit yet. I doubt he's even been back to the ranch since he stampeded the cattle this morning, which he just owned up to. He mentioned hearing about the 'new man' from the folks in town. He hadn't even heard your name. And from the stench of him, I'd say he spent most of the day in town drinking."

Angel was heading toward her balcony doors before she had finished talking. Cassie didn't try to stop him, since Rafferty had likely reached his horse by now. She moved to light a lamp instead. Her fingers were almost trembling too much to accomplish that. The physical threat had been too close. It was over, but her relief was slow in coming.

Marabelle was weaving around her legs. She wasn't purring; she was making low growling noises.

"It's all right, baby," Cassie said. "But you're right. I shouldn't have put you out of my room. Next time —"

"There won't be a next time," Angel said behind her. "I'm going after him."

She was putting the chimney back on the lamp, so didn't turn toward him. "You'll never find him in the dark."

"I'll find him."

But in the dark, Angel was as likely to get shot as Rafferty was, and that thought prompted her to say, "The man will still be around come morning, but it's not really a killing matter, Angel. He didn't get a chance to seriously hurt me."

"You know how I feel about intentions, lady. And my debt doesn't get canceled if you get hurt."

She wished he were concerned about her, rather than his debt, but she still didn't want him taking unnecessary risks. And Rafferty was an unknown factor. He didn't have a reputation, but that was no guarantee when he wore a gun as if he knew how to use it.

She heard Angel take a step to leave. She turned to stop him, completely forgetting about the condition of her nightgown. But Angel couldn't very well overlook it with the room lighted now. His eyes went right to the long rip down its center that exposed half of one breast and a portion of her belly. She gasped and yanked the material closed when she saw where he was looking. His face turned as red as hers.

"That son of a bitch," he growled in a low, fury-tinged voice. "Are you all right?"

"No. My hands won't stop shaking." Nor would they if she didn't change the subject real quick. "How — how did Marabelle get outside?"

Mention of the cat brought his eyes to it, and Marabelle chose that moment to saunter toward him. Understandably, Angel didn't answer Cassie's question just then. He didn't so much as move a muscle. But Marabelle merely rubbed her body against his legs as she passed him on her way to investigate the balcony, an area of the house she used to have free access to before the trouble began.

Angel was quick to close the door behind the panther. Cassie heard him sigh before he turned back toward her. His reaction to her pet was still a problem, obviously, no matter what she said about Marabelle's tameness. She supposed time and familiarity would have to take care of it.

Angel finally answered her question. "There was a haunch of raw beef on the back porch with an empty sack next to it. Slater must have used it to lure your Marabelle out of the house."

"She would have sniffed her nose at that. He probably had to push her out."

Angel was impressed, actually more like incredulous. "Now, that took nerve."

"Not really. When I first came here, I had to let everyone know that Marabelle was harmless. Folks tend to get angry when they get scared and find out after that there was no reason to be scared."

"Now that you mention it, it didn't look like she even touched the meat. She came scratching at my door instead, and like to scare me to hell when I opened it and she let out a roar before she bolted back to the house. I wouldn't have thought anything of it, except she passed by a horse tied up at the back porch that wasn't there when I turned in."

"I'm glad you noticed."

He nodded uncomfortably. Situations like this were beyond his experience.

"If he's as drunk as you say, he'll be easy to catch up to," Angel said.

"He wasn't that drunk, but I wish you wouldn't go. I'll never get back to sleep unless I know you're nearby."

"Sure you will. Just —"

"Please, Angel."

She had started crying before she got his name

134

out, and it wasn't all feigned for effect. She really was beginning to panic at the thought of him leaving.

"Now don't do that."

She wasn't listening. Her unbound hair fell forward to hide the part of her face that her raised hands didn't cover. She'd forgotten about her nightgown again, but the edges stayed closed from being overlapped.

"Come on now, cut it out." He had tried again, but she simply cried harder. "Ah, hell."

Cassie was surprised to feel his arms suddenly come around her. That wasn't what she'd been after, but she couldn't deny it felt nice.

Angel didn't say any more, just held her awkwardly. But that was all right. At least he wasn't going off to shed blood — or get his shed. And after a while her hands dropped to rest on his sides, and she laid her wet cheek against his chest.

Until that moment she hadn't realized his shirt wasn't buttoned or tucked into his pants. She'd been too upset to really notice. But it was bare skin she was pressing her face against.

She should have pulled back immediately. That would have been the proper thing to do. But that was the last thing she wanted to do when she felt so utterly content exactly as she was. And that was amazing, since she was usually so nervous around Angel.

But she couldn't stay like that without an excuse, and hers was gone, her tears dried up, just a few sniffles remaining. So she remained still for only a few moments more before she sighed and looked up at him.

"I'm sorry," she said softly. "I haven't cried since this thing started. I suppose I was overdue."

Their eyes locked for long moments, his so dark and inscrutable, hers glistening bright silver. A tension suddenly filled the air that had Cassie holding her breath as his eyes moved slowly, so slowly, down to her parted lips and stayed there.

"You apologize too much," he replied in his slow drawl, just before his mouth closed over hers.

It was completely unexpected. It was also nothing like the kiss she had instigated yesterday. Then she had been in a panic and fearful of being rejected. Now she was relaxed and open to a wealth of discovery.

He began tentatively, as if he were the one anticipating rejection this time. She had no thought of that, was too busy savoring the niceness of it. But with not even a whimpered protest out of her, he quickly deepened the kiss, parting her lips, sliding his tongue inside for a tantalizing exploration. New feelings arose, almost frightening in their strangeness and intensity; deep, swirling, hot sensations. And it wasn't just the kiss anymore. It was also the tightening of his arms that drew her closer, flush with him, her nightgown too thin to resist the details of his body.

Languor spread, a contradiction to the pounding of her heart. She felt weak all over, unable to end the kiss even if she wanted to. She didn't. He didn't. And that was the most amazing discovery of all.

She had noticed him staring at her lips during

dinner, but she hadn't thought anything of it. She certainly hadn't thought he might desire her. She just wasn't the desirable sort. But Angel was kissing her as if there was nothing else he'd rather be doing, and Cassie wasn't merely flattered that he'd want to, she was liking it too much.

When his mouth turned in a new direction, she was surprised that he wasn't finished but was, in fact, tasting her skin in other areas. His tongue moved slowly up her neck to flick at her earlobe.

"Honey all over," he breathed in her ear. "That's what you taste like."

Shivers spread in all directions. Cassie was almost trembling now, and getting weaker by the second. And then he leaned back to look at her as his hand slipped between the ripped edges of her nightgown to move slowly, carefully, over her bare, sensitized skin.

It was the most sinfully erotic experience of her life, his hand on her breast, his eyes holding hers with smoldering intensity. It was too much all at once, the feelings he aroused far beyond her experience. Cassie became frightened and stepped back, out of his arms, away from his thrilling touch.

"You — you shouldn't."

She didn't recognize her own voice, nor could she get out more than that. But he just stared at her, and for so long, she thought she'd faint, the tension was so unbearable.

Finally he let out a sigh and said, "I know. Guess it's my turn for apologies. It won't happen again."

She watched him leave, frustrated by the urge

to call him back and by a returned sense of what was proper behavior. Kissing Angel certainly wasn't, nor was liking it so much. So why was there so much regret at the thought that it would never happen again?

Chapter 14

Angel wasn't surprised that they'd set a watch on those high walls that surrounded the Catlin ranch. Someone had to have spotted him a far ways off, because Buck Catlin and two cowboys rode out to meet him before he even got close to the place. And they weren't taking any chances. The two hired hands had their rifles drawn, their fingers on the triggers.

He wondered if there were more rifles lining those walls. He didn't bother to look, since being lean of frame had its definite advantages. He was a somewhat smaller target, and this allowed him to move with a swiftness that could get him out of the path of long-distance bullets. Of course, the odds were about half that he'd be moving into the path of a badly aimed bullet that would have missed him if he'd stood still, but he judged folks by his own standards, which were high, so he attributed most of them with at least a halfway decent chance of hitting their target.

He pulled up and waited for the three riders to reach him. He supposed he could take them if he had to. He was simply that fast, and he never missed at showdown range. He might take a bullet in return since two of them were ready for him, but what the hell. His mood this morning was dangerous in that it included a heavy dose of self-loathing as well as the feeling that his stupidity last night deserved some sort of retribution. He should have taken precautions so Slater couldn't have broken into the house so easily. He should have followed him immediately after he had.

He should never have touched Cassandra Stuart.

Therein lay his greatest misery and confusion. That woman. That irritating, meddling, rarely quiet woman — and her man-eating pet. What was there to like about her? She wasn't even pretty — actually, last night she had been damn pretty, but last night he and that wine she'd served him obviously hadn't mixed well together. Why else would he have given in to that incredible craving to taste her again?

The cowboys drew up abreast of him, Buck slightly in the lead. The rancher took off his hat and slapped it against his thigh, a nervous gesture, Angel supposed. The young man did look slightly harassed.

But arrogance was well and truly ingrained in Buck Catlin, so his tone was still damn close to offensive as he said, "Thought my ma told you what would happen if you showed up here again."

Angel didn't answer right away. It was times like this he wished he smoked. Rolling a cigarette right now would be a good way to ignore the young rancher and find out if he was willing to back up that threat, or if it was just bravado.

"As I recall, I told her it wouldn't matter — if I had a good reason to return."

Buck chuckled. "Mister, you gotta be either

140

the craziest or the bravest man I ever met. Ain't you realized yet that one word from me and you're dead?"

"Not dead, Catlin. Wounded, maybe. But I'll give you three guesses who *will* be dead, and you'd be right on any guess you make."

"You can't be that good."

"You don't want to find out."

Buck glanced to each side at his two men to make sure they were still prepared for any move. Seeing that they were didn't reassure him as much as he'd hoped.

"Look, Angel, you got no call to come back. We get rid of our own bad apples around here."

"I'm here for Slater."

"And I just told you, you're too late," Buck said. "When I questioned the men, Rafferty's friend, Sam, confessed that Rafferty had planned to stampede the cattle. And he wasn't around yesterday, which verified Sam's tale as far as I'm concerned. I don't know what time Rafferty crawled into his bunk last night, but I hauled his ass out of it this morning and fired him. He lit out before sun-up."

"Where to?"

"He didn't say, I didn't ask."

"Then I'll talk to his friend, Sam."

"He'd be out on the south range today. You're welcome to go find him — but it's a big range, about two thousand acres. A man can easily get lost on Catlin land."

The arrogance was back. Angel didn't feel like putting up with it. "Then *you* find him and send him to me. It's not just the stampeding now.

141

Slater showed up at Miss Cassie's last night, broke into her house, and scared her something bad. I want him."

There was so much menace in that statement, all three men were glad they had other names. But Angel didn't wait for a reply. He yanked his horse around and rode back toward the Stuart ranch.

Buck released a silent sigh and turned to his left. "Yancy, maybe you ought to ride south and see if you can locate Sam. I don't want that man to have another excuse to pay us a visit. I wouldn't even wish him on a MacKauley." But then he pictured his sister's red eyes and added, "On second thought, maybe just on Clayton MacKauley."

Cassie found one excuse after another not to leave the house that day. She instigated a spring cleaning in December that had Maria clucking her tongue and mumbling under her breath. She took stock of their supplies. She wrote another long letter to her mother to tell her about Angel, then tore it up. Her mother did *not* need to know that a notorious hired gun was living within shouting distance of her daughter. Nothing would get her down here quicker. And although her mother's stern, no-nonsense approach to problems was probably just what was needed, Cassie was determined to get through this mess on her own.

Added to the mess, however, was the new predicament she'd allowed to develop last night — her own behavior. Her own *wanton* behavior. In the bright light of day, she was mortified that she had simply stood there and let Angel take such liberties with her. So she had been flattered that he might want her, extremely flattered, actually, since he'd candidly mentioned that he and ranching didn't suit. So for once the Lazy S had nothing to do with a man's being attracted to her.

That was no excuse. Neither was the fact that she had derived so much enjoyment out of the experience. She knew better, knew what was acceptable behavior and what wasn't. Besides, it was absurd to even think of Angel as someone she might have a future with. He was unpredictable, dangerous, a loner. If he wanted her, it was only for the moment, and Cassie knew how that sort of thing ended up. Saloons all across the South and the West were filled with women who had given in to passions of the moment.

She couldn't imagine what he must think of her now, after she'd acted like an old maid starved for the tiniest crumbs of affection. She supposed the best thing she could do was to pretend nothing had happened. And he'd said it wouldn't happen again. He probably wanted to forget about it as much as she did — but she knew she never would. When she was old and gray and had grandchildren about her — hopefully — she'd still remember Angel's hand on her breast.

Staying in the house worked well to avoid Angel, until he showed up at the door late that afternoon with his saddlebags slung over his shoulder.

"I've thought it over," were his first words as he walked past her into the foyer. "I'm moving in."

She stared after him incredulously. "What?"

He kept on walking, stopping only when he reached the bottom of the stairs to glance back at her. And as if he weren't shocking the hell out of her, he said, "Put me in whichever room is closest to yours."

Cassie didn't move from the door. She'd thought this first meeting with him again would be awkward, but he'd managed to make her completely forget about last night.

"That's out of the question," she told him emphatically. "You can't —"

"Just do it," he cut in just as emphatically, but relented enough to explain. "Slater has left town. Until I hear he's out of Texas or dead, I'm not taking any chances. I want to be able to hear you snore."

"What?"

His lips twitched slightly because her eyes had grown so round. "Just a figure of speech, lady, but you catch my drift. If you need me, any time of the night, I want to be close enough to know it."

Her face brightened at the double meaning she heard in those words, unintentional on his part, she was sure — which made it all the more embarrassing. "This is highly improper," she felt compelled to point out.

"Proper doesn't come into it when protection is called for. If I didn't think you'd faint at the suggestion, I'd be moving right into your room. So don't mention proper to me again, all right?"

Embarrassment turned to anger as she nodded curtly and headed for the stairs. "Follow me," she said, passing him, her voice as stiff as her back was, her hands fisted on her skirt to raise it the bare minimum so she could mount the stairs.

She led him to the room next to hers, which did happen to be empty. She'd been using it as a sewing room.

"Maria is an excellent housekeeper, so the bedding should be clean. If you need anything, you can usually find her in the kitchen. I'll inform her now of your move."

"You're taking this too hard, lady," he said in an agreeable tone, now that he'd gotten his way. "You won't even notice I'm here."

Like hell she wouldn't.

Chapter 15

Cassie wasn't taking any chances on having another carriage ride with Angel like the last one. Having the supplies she needed to buy delivered would require paying extra, but that was a minor irritation compared with enduring Angel's proximity again. Telling him there was no need to accompany her to town had been a waste of time. He took his role as her self-appointed protector very seriously.

Riding her horse, of course, required wearing the durable divided skirt that she used on the range, as well as the short, shapeless deerskin jacket that went with it. Her stylish Eastern clothes didn't suit a Western saddle, nor did hairpins. Her gun belt did, though. For once it didn't look quite so ridiculous resting on her hip.

She hadn't given her casual appearance a thought, however, until she found the folks of Caully staring at her as if they didn't recognize her. Having Angel at her side drew even more attention. And she got to see firsthand how people reacted to him. They gave him a wide berth. Whatever premises he entered quickly vacated. Store owners and clerks wouldn't meet his eyes, hoping if they ignored him he'd just leave.

Cassie shouldn't have been surprised. Despite what had happened the other night, Angel still made her uncomfortable, too, particularly when he was silent, which he'd been since they'd left the ranch this morning. She'd left her carriage at home for that very reason. Yet she still found herself embarrassed on his account at the way folks treated him.

Upon leaving the general store, she got up the nerve to broach the subject. "Does it bother you that you make people nervous, Angel?" It was getting easier to say his name without blushing.

He was scanning the street in both directions, so he didn't look at her. "Why should it?"

"It must make it hard for you to get to know people."

He glanced down at her then, his black eyes revealing nothing. "Who says I want to?"

She shrugged, letting it rest. But his answer left her unaccountably sad, which in turn made her annoyed with herself for trying once again to discern his feelings. He probably didn't have any. He was probably as stone-cold dead inside as his eyes made you think he was. And why should she care if that was so?

His eyes were scanning again, a habit she associated with his profession. But she noticed they stopped more than once on the Last Keg Saloon down the street. He probably wanted a drink, but wasn't willing to leave her alone long enough to get one. Or maybe he wanted something else. Most of the saloons in Caully had a number of women who worked both upstairs and down.

The thought put a dour expression on Cassie's lips and made her tone excessively prim. "I'm finished for today. I'm sure I can get home without being ambushed or anything like that if you have some things you need to do in town."

"I did want to ask around about Slater, since his friend, Sam, couldn't say where he'd head to, but it can wait till I'm alone."

He looked at her again to say it, so he didn't see the man who rode around a corner behind him just then. Cassie did, and her mouth dropped open. Speak of the devil, and he was riding right in their direction.

"Actually — I forgot something — in the store," Cassie said quickly. "We need to go back inside —"

"Go ahead. I'll get the horses."

"No!" She grabbed his arm and tried to pull him back into the store. "I need your help to pick —"

She was cut off again, but this time by the shout that came from behind them. "Hey, you!"

Angel turned so fast, Cassie was jerked around with him. And there was nothing she could do now to keep him from noticing Rafferty Slater, who was stopping his horse only a few feet away from them.

"You Angel?" Rafferty asked once he had dismounted and stepped up onto the boardwalk. Angel just nodded. "I heard you was lookin' for me."

"And who might you be?"

"Rafferty Slater."

Had Cassie thought Angel's eyes never showed emotion? Now they blazed with such satisfaction that she was filled with dread, knowing why. But unexpectedly another, more powerful feeling joined it, a need to prevent and protect. She'd never experienced anything like it, and it was utterly ridiculous. There was no one less in need of protection than Angel. But her emotions didn't take that into account.

For someone who wasn't the impulsive sort, Cassie let her emotions guide her right into the fire. "I'm challenging you to a gunfight, Rafferty," she said, moving forward. "I believe you know why."

Angel let out an expletive. Rafferty stared at her blankly for a moment before he started laughing. Cassie really wished people would take her and her Colt a little more seriously.

"You got one second to make yourself scarce," Angel told her.

She spared him the briefest glance just to determine if his expression was as furious as his tone. It was, so she looked back toward Rafferty while she tried reasoning with Angel.

Amazingly, under the circumstances, she did it with calm and logic. "I think you should let me shoot him. I swore I would if he ever touched me again."

"So swear something else. This one is mine."

"But I'm the one he accosted the other night," she reminded him.

Angel didn't address that; he just said, "Go back in the store, Cassie."

"You aren't listening to me."

"Damned right. Now get!"

With an order like that, and with an arm shoving her behind him to help her on her way, she should have gone, but she didn't. She wrung her hands, racking her mind for another way to prevent the showdown that was coming, but Angel wasn't going to oblige her with enough time to think of something.

"I don't usually do this, Slater," he said as he tucked his slicker back out of the way, "but for you I'm making an exception. Where do you want it, out in the street or where you're standing?"

Rafferty didn't look impressed or the least bit intimidated. He grinned and spit out a sliver of wood he'd been chewing on.

"I'd a stuck around the other night if I hadn't had a belly full of rotgut. But I'm sober now, and don't much like the idea of you doggin' my trail. The street's fine with me, friend, but you ask me, the little lady ain't worth your dyin' over."

"So who asked you?"

Rafferty merely chuckled and extended an arm, indicating Angel should precede him into the street. Cassie found Rafferty's confidence appalling. She'd been right to worry about him, and as Angel stepped off the boardwalk, she saw why. Rafferty had had no intention of facing Angel in a fair fight. He went for his gun the second Angel's back was to him.

Cassie drew her gun but shouted, "Look out!" just to be safe. She still fired. Angel also fired. Rafferty's bullet hit the dirt at his feet as he dropped facedown in the street.

At such close range, smoke from the three discharges stung Cassie's eyes. And she realized, as she watched Angel shove the downed man over with his foot, that she could have kept her own gun holstered. Angel had turned and shot Rafferty before she'd even finished her warning.

She came up beside Angel to stare at the two bullet wounds, one in the shoulder, meant to immobilize, and one directly over the heart, meant to kill. Both had done as intended, and the results were quite sickening.

"You should have let me face him," she said in a small voice. "I would only have wounded him. You would have killed — *did* kill — him."

Angel gave her a sharp look. "You going to tell me he didn't ask for it?"

"Well . . . no, but — but the dying part could have been avoided if you had let me face him instead."

"Don't kid yourself. The same thing would have happened — that is, if he could've stopped laughing long enough."

His derision had her bristling. "That isn't funny."

"He thought it was. But that's beside the point. You won't ever participate in a gunfight while I'm around, lady. I don't care how good you think you are —"

"*Know* I am," she retorted.

His tone softened somewhat, probably with condescension. "Practice isn't the same as facing a man who's going to try and kill you, Cassie. You don't want to find out the difference."

"That might be so," she allowed, "but you're missing *my* point. Rafferty shouldn't be dead. A wound would have sufficed —"

"This is the result of shooting to wound," he

cut in, jerking a thumb toward the scar on his jawline. "The guy healed up and came after me again. He wanted me dead, but he was too afraid to face me in another fair fight, so he came at me from behind. I'm here only because his aim with a knife was as lousy as with a gun — and because I don't shoot to wound anymore."

"You're right."

"I'm what?"

Cassie squirmed inwardly. "Don't look so surprised. What you just said reminded me of the number of gunfights I've heard about where one man gets wounded and then a few days later the other man is found in some alley with a bullet in his back. I'm not saying that always happens, but it happens enough that — that your way makes sense, for you anyway."

"All right, what happened here?"

Cassie turned to see the sheriff pushing his way through the dozen or so people who were edging forward, all trying to get a closer look at the dead man without getting too close to the one who'd shot him.

Frank Henley was on the short side, not much taller than Cassie. He wore boots with three-inch heels, which didn't make much difference, but he had a very forceful personality, which did. He'd been known to intimidate men much larger than he was, which was why he made a good sheriff — or he would be if he didn't tend to mix family business with official business.

Just now, he took one look at Slater, and Cassie knew this was going to be one of those mixing times. "Hey, I know this man. He works for —"

Frank paused and narrowed his eyes on Angel. "I'm going to have to take you in, mister."

Cassie barely managed to keep from snapping, "The hell you are!" She stepped between the two men instead to say calmly, "That won't be necessary, Sheriff. Ask around. You'll find a witness or two who saw Slater try to shoot this man in the back. I saw it, which is why he's got my bullet in him, too. And for the record, Slater was no longer employed by your aunt. Your cousin Buck fired him yesterday morning."

As his expression indicated, that last bit of information was all that changed Frank's mind. Cassie had no doubt that Angel would have been arrested, without cause, if Slater had still been a Catlin employee. It could even have come to a bogus trial and hanging if Dorothy Catlin decreed it, such was the domination of that close-knit family. But Cassie didn't think the Widow Catlin was that vicious, and besides, she wouldn't have let Angel be arrested for a justified shooting. She would have drawn on the sheriff herself if she had to.

Which was why Cassie was greatly relieved to hear Frank say, "I'll take your word for it, Miss Stuart. He's with you, then?"

The lie came easily this time. "He's my fiancé."

The sheriff was surprised. "Thought you and Morgan — well, never mind. Just keep this one out of town. Gunfights we don't need, and I damn well hate the paperwork involved."

Cassie nodded and hooked her arm through Angel's to lead him away before Frank changed his mind again. Angel's silence continued until they had reached their horses and he'd given her a boost up onto hers.

"Why do I have the feeling you would've taken on that sheriff if he hadn't backed down?"

Cassie flushed slightly at his discerning question. And he didn't sound all that pleased by the notion, either, so she said, "I don't know what you mean."

He merely grunted before mounting up. "Your lying is improving — some."

Chapter 16

Angel ordered another whiskey and turned to survey the room. The Last Keg Saloon was quiet for a Saturday night, but then, it wasn't the only saloon in town, and Angel had avoided the more lively ones out of habit.

A couple of tables had card games going, but he didn't feel like trying to join one. He felt like getting drunk and taking one of the three girls who worked the room upstairs for the night. One was even pretty, and he couldn't deny he needed a woman, especially after spending the past three nights with only a wall separating him from a woman he was increasingly finding too damn desirable.

He wouldn't get drunk, however, at least not in a public place. That would be careless, and Angel was rarely careless. And he hadn't made up his mind yet about buying a woman for the night. The need was there, but his interest in what was available didn't remain for long.

That was surprising in itself. He wasn't usually discriminating where women were concerned. A warm, soft body that was willing had always been enough to satisfy him. Now he was devoting too many thoughts to one particular woman, something else he'd never done before, and it was starting to irritate the hell out of him. That, among other things.

He didn't like what he was feeling lately. What he'd felt after shooting Slater the other day was a prime example — too much satisfaction. He'd never experienced actual pleasure in killing a man before, and he wasn't sure why he had this time. It had been primitive, what he'd felt. He really hadn't liked it that the man had attempted to bed Cassie. He *really* hadn't liked that. But the only reason he could figure that that had been part of the satisfaction was because she was under his protection. Nothing else made sense.

Angel was on his third and last drink when Morgan MacKauley walked in. Stumbled in, was more accurate. He'd obviously hit the bottle himself tonight, and pretty heavily. And he wasn't alone. He had one of his brothers with him, the second oldest by the look of him. Angel couldn't recall what name Cassie had given that brother, but he supposed he might be finding out, since both men headed in his direction as soon as Morgan spotted him at the bar.

"Well, if it ain't Miss Stuart's fiancé," Morgan sneered. "Brown, was it?"

Angel set his glass down to free both hands. The brothers were crowding him, and Morgan's expression contained an emotion resembling pure dislike.

"The name's Angel."

"Yeah, so I been hearing. Angel Brown."

"Just Angel."

Morgan rocked back on his heels. Angel didn't think the action was intentional. The man ought

156

to be in bed, sleeping it off, instead of looking for trouble.

"You saying Cassie lied?"

"No, only that I go by Angel and nothing else."

"Ah, hell," Richard MacKauley said at that point. "Let it go, little brother."

"Stay out of —"

Morgan was abruptly cut off when the older MacKauley hauled him aside to whisper furiously in his ear. There was a slight grappling as Morgan chose to ignore what his big brother had to say.

He was actually being restrained in a bear hug when he looked at Angel and bellowed, "Is that right? They call you the Angel of Death?"

If everyone's attention hadn't been on them already, it was now. Angel didn't move a muscle. "Some folks are foolish enough to do so."

Morgan was apparently too drunk and too riled up to take the hint. "What the hell's a killer like you doing asking a lady to marry him?"

A damn good question. It wasn't something Angel would do under any circumstances. The very idea was ludicrous. No lady in her right mind would have him, and he had a bit too much pride to leave himself open to that kind of humiliating rejection. But because this particular lady was a meddler who told outlandish lies that *some* idiots actually believed, he was stuck with answering the question — or not. He opted for not, to save both himself and Cassie embarrassment.

"How's it any of your business, MacKauley?"

Someone else in the room was drunk enough to call out, "He was gonna marry her hisself!"

157

Morgan swung around, taking his brother with him, since Richard was still holding him. But he couldn't locate the culprit who'd turned him red-faced with that bit of information. And it was still Angel he wanted to fight, so he swung back again and in the process put some serious effort into breaking his brother's hold.

Angel braced himself. He debated whether to draw and end the coming fight before it started. But the feeling he'd had earlier in the week, that he deserved some sort of retribution, was still with him. He hefted his gun and handed it to the man behind the bar.

"Can you manage to keep it fair?"

The barkeep didn't need to be told what "it" was. "Won't be nothin' fair about it if you take on Morgan," he said with a complacent nod. "I'd be appreciative, though, if you'd take it outside."

"I'm willing, but I don't think he's open to the suggestion."

At the moment, Morgan was telling his brother, "Let go, damn you, Richard. I'm not going to shoot him, I'm just going to break some of his bones."

He ended with a mighty heave that gained his release, only to send him stumbling forward. Having decided after what he'd just heard that it wouldn't be in his best interests to wait for Morgan to throw the first punch, Angel lifted his knee to meet him. And while the larger man was doubled over, Angel followed with a down-swinging right.

That should have put Morgan on the floor. With anyone else it might have, and ended it right there. But Morgan was over six feet tall with a hell of a lot of muscle to go with it. He was barely dazed. He was also too drunk to notice if any pain had been left behind. Angel wished he could say the same when Morgan came up swinging.

Ten minutes later he was wishing it again, though he was glad that Morgan *had* had too much to drink. He never would have beaten him otherwise, and he was kind of amazed that he'd managed to in the end. He'd merely gotten lucky with that last punch. Of course, it was only by dint of will that he was still standing himself.

Angel put out his hand to the barkeep to retrieve his gun. The man handed it over, along with a bottle of whiskey and a grin.

"On the house, mister. It was a pure pleasure, watchin' Morgan lose for the first time. And never you mind the damages, either. I'll take 'em up with his pa."

Angel just nodded. Behind him, Richard MacKauley picked up a glass of beer from one of the tables that were still upright and was about to dump it in Morgan's face. Angel took the bottle and left.

As much as he hurt, he actually felt better. He might even ask Miss Cassie to patch him up.

Chapter 17

It was the whistling that woke Cassie. It took a moment for her to realize it *was* whistling, strident, tuneless, and sounding like it was coming from just outside her door, or close to it. She didn't bother to wonder who might be making that god-awful noise, but she certainly wondered why someone was.

Without looking at the clock on her bureau, she knew it had to be midnight or later. She'd stayed up late herself, waiting to hear Angel return, worrying, because he'd told her where he was going. To town, on a Saturday night, the one night set aside for hell-raising by the local cowboys, the one night almost guaranteeing some sort of trouble. What was it about men that made them court disaster?

She'd imagined the very worst thing happening, of course, a shootout, another death — ultimately her fault, because Angel wouldn't be here if she hadn't written to Lewis Pickens for help. She'd imagined him thrown in jail this time, and her arguing with Frank to release him, and, failing that, breaking him out of jail and sending him on his way, a free man, but now a wanted man. And it would all be her fault because she hadn't been able to deal with a few stubborn Texans on her own.

It was incredible that she'd gotten to sleep at all, and she was certainly wide awake now. But she didn't move from her warm bed. She listened instead, waiting to hear some silence to indicate he'd found his own bed. She'd ask him tomorrow about his whistling. It was the first time in the four days since he'd moved himself into the house that he'd been this discourteous. Usually, she had to strain to hear the tiniest sound from his room.

But the next sound she heard, a dull thud, as if he'd fallen to the floor, had her out of her bed in a flash and throwing the door open. She stopped short, however, upon finding him still standing, though just barely. The light she'd left burning in the hall for him revealed him leaning, with his back against his door, at such a tilted angle that his feet were probably going to slide out from under him at any moment. And he was still whistling.

Understandably, Cassie became annoyed at that point. "Just *what* is your problem?"

His head came away from the door, only to immediately drop back against it instead of turning toward her. "Can't get my door open."

"Did you lose the key?"

"Ain't locked."

She frowned. "Then why won't it open?"

"My hand's too swollen to turn the handle."

"Both of them?"

"No."

"Then why didn't you use your other hand?"

"Didn' think of that. 'Preciate it."

At that moment she realized he was drunk, seriously drunk, and alarm bells went off. She

161

didn't want to deal with a drunken Angel. She ought to go right back into her room and let him muddle his way to bed — or not. But then he turned and she saw his face.

She gasped. "What happened to you?"

One eye was so discolored and swollen it wouldn't open. A patch of skin had been scraped raw high on his cheek with other abrasions around it. Twin trails of blood ran unchecked from his nose, though it had at one point been smeared across the other cheek. She now saw the open bottle of whiskey in his hand, and blood on all four of his fingers. They did happen to look swollen, and that happened to be his gun hand.

His one good eye didn't exactly focus on her; he merely looked toward the sound of her voice. "Had a li'l run-in with your beau."

"What beau?"

"Morgan."

For some unaccountable reason, she blushed. She wasn't sure why she would have preferred he not find out about Morgan having paid court to her. But fortunately, Angel wasn't paying attention to her reaction. He'd turned a bit more to try the door handle with his other hand. The door opened this time, but he'd still been leaning on it, so he went inward with it, flat on his face.

Cassie rolled her eyes, staring at his legs sticking out of the doorway. She was no longer the least bit concerned that he might be dangerous in his present condition. He was obviously quite harmless and definitely in need of assistance.

When she peered into his room, she saw his head was cradled on both arms. Miraculously, the bottle of whiskey hadn't spilled, and he was still holding it, rather protectively, in the crook of one arm, even though he'd passed out.

She thought briefly of leaving him right where he was, merely removing his boots and throwing a blanket over him. She couldn't do it. He was battered enough. A night on the hard floor wouldn't help. So with some pushing, pulling, and a good deal of vocal prodding, she managed to get him into bed. He barely woke up for it. And as long as he was unconscious, she fetched some water and cloths to clean up his face.

No doubt about it, he was a mess. She wondered what had started the fight and what condition Morgan was in. Mostly she wondered why Angel had let it happen to begin with when he'd worn his gun to town. That just didn't seem like something he'd do.

"You have a soft touch, honey."

Cassie jerked, lifting the damp cloth from his chin. He hadn't opened his eyes to say it. In all likelihood, he wasn't quite awake and didn't even know whom he was talking to. Still, it made her feel strange inside when he called her honey, kind of warm and mushy.

"Can't say the same for other females who've patched me up," Angel continued, still without looking at her.

Cassie would have let him ramble, assuming that was what he was doing, except her curiosity was aroused. "What other females have patched you up?"

"Jessie Summers, for one."

That jarred her memory. "That's right, I recall hearing something about you being shot by some rustlers on her land. How badly were you wounded that time?"

"Bad enough."

"Then possibly it's the wounds you remember, rather than the fixing of them."

"Could be — nah, I could count on two fingers the women I know as gentle as you . . . make that one finger."

She smiled at that point. "Are you trying to flatter me, Angel?"

He finally cracked one eye open. "Is it working?"

Yes. "No."

"That's too bad."

"Just what were you angling for?"

"For you to lie down with me. I could use some soft cuddling about now."

Her mouth dropped open, then snapped shut. "You could probably use a doctor," she said tartly, amazed that he would suggest such a thing. It had to be the drink . . . hell, he was probably so far gone he really *didn't* know whom he was talking to.

She continued to think that, even when he replied, "A doc can't fix what's ailing me now — unless it's a female doctor."

"Ours isn't, and I suggest you try sleep as a second option."

"Sure you won't accommodate me on the first?"

"Quite sure."

"You might like it, Cassie."

She drew in her breath sharply. He knew who she was after all, and that simple fact had an amazing effect on her. She actually reconsidered. What harm could it do to lie down next to him? The man was certainly in no condition to do more than cuddle, despite the improper remarks he was making, and . . . She must be mad!

Cassie shot to her feet and hurried out to the balcony, where she'd placed a wet cloth to chill for his eye. Angel let out a sigh behind her. Even drunk, he couldn't get her off his mind.

She was wearing the same kind of white cotton nightgown she'd been wearing the other night, long-sleeved with ruffles at the wrist, high-necked with more ruffles and a bit of lace, totally without shape — and this one wasn't ripped up the front. There was certainly nothing there to tempt a man beyond the fact that she was in her bedclothes, which wasn't about to make a difference to a man in his present condition.

God, he liked seeing her with her hair down. It flowed about her like rich mahogany, looking so soft he ached to bury his hands in it. Didn't suppose she'd stand for that. She was the very proper Miss Cassandra tonight, though for a second there she'd looked like she might devour him. Had to be the drink making him see what he wanted, not what actually was.

She came back with her lips pursed tightly. "This might help the swelling." For all her stiffness, she was very gentle in placing the cold cloth over his eye.

He caught her hand before she drew back. "One kiss to put me to sleep."

"I'm not so sure you're awake even now. More likely you're having a dream that you won't remember come morning."

"Then make it a pleasant dream, honey."

For a moment he thought he had her as she glanced down at his lips. But then she jerked her hand away and he sagged into the mattress, suddenly feeling every single ache he had.

"You're being highly improper," she told him as she headed for the door.

"I'm allowed, after your ex-beau tried to kill me with his bare hands, all because he thinks I'm your fiancé."

"Good *night*, Angel."

"It could have been," he grumbled.

Chapter 18

A storm blew through that Sunday, severe enough to keep Cassie home for the day. Church had been a difficult experience anyway these past weeks with all of her former friends not talking to her. And Jenny hadn't shown up for one service since the elopement. After what Buck had told Angel about his sister, Cassie figured that it was probably because she couldn't stop crying long enough to make the trip to church.

She was glad of the emotional reprieve, but didn't appreciate Angel telling her she wouldn't have gone anyway, because *he* wasn't up to escorting her. Baldly, he told her that he didn't trust her out of his sight. She didn't appreciate that, either, but the man was in a testy mood, so she didn't argue about it.

In fact, he didn't leave his bed that day or the next. The one time Cassie stopped in to see how he was faring had been too unpleasant to repeat, so she left him alone with his hangover, sending Emanuel with his meals.

However, when he didn't come down to breakfast on the third day, Cassie began to worry that he might have some serious injury that he hadn't mentioned and she hadn't noticed. But when she knocked on his door and got permission to enter, she found him up and dressed — and practicing drawing his gun. He didn't stop just because she was there, so she patiently waited for him to give her his attention. He dropped the gun twice, swearing foully each time, before he finally did.

"Well?"

His angry tone should have turned her about without a word. Instead she asked, "Is it broken?"

"What?"

"Your hand."

"No, just a couple of busted knuckles. Mac-Kauley's got a rock for a jaw."

She didn't comment on that. "Shouldn't you let it heal before you attempt to use it?"

"With neighbors like yours?"

That derisive question proved he was most definitely still in a lousy mood. "They've been quiet since you talked to the one side and I was able to talk to R. J. — at least they're leaving *me* alone." That last got her a dark look that she gave right back when she added, "I thought I expressly asked you not to kill any of them."

"I don't aim to kill 'em, but you still need protecting. I can't do that without my gun."

"Oh, I don't know. Mabel Koch — she's one of Caully's biggest gossips — stopped by yesterday to mention you won that fight with Morgan, just in case I wasn't aware of it. Seems to me you do all right without a gun."

Her smug tone, obviously on his behalf, got her an even darker look. "I'm not about to take on another MacKauley without one. Once was enough. And I don't reckon the rest of 'em are too happy about the outcome of that fight, so

168

I'm expecting more trouble from that quarter. It's just a matter of when it'll come, and how."

Cassie frowned. "Now that you mention it, you're probably right. R. J. has always been real proud that no one around here has ever come out ahead in a fight with one of his boys. I'm surprised Frazer didn't come over to tell me his papa has had another fit of ranting and raving. R. J.'s really good at it, you know. I thought someone was going to die the first time I witnessed him in a temper. But he's more bluster than not. Just like Frazer implied, his papa seems to enjoy blowing off steam."

"All the same, I'd as soon you didn't leave the ranch for a while."

"Are you asking this time?"

"Cassie —"

She cut off his warning. "Never mind. I suppose you aren't any good with your left hand?"

"I can hit what I aim at, but my draw is slow."

"Then I don't see a problem, since you won't be participating in any more showdowns that would require speed."

"There's rarely much choice about show-downs," he replied. "But when's it going to sink in that I'm not taking chances where you're concerned? So stay home, and yes, dammit, I'm telling you to."

She stiffened up real quick. "I don't know why I bother talking to you at all. You're not only aggravating, you're — you're —"

He interrupted her before he had to listen to what would undoubtedly be a very prim, lady-like setdown. "Are you here for a specific reason,

169

or did you just feel like annoying me?"

Pink cheeks clashed with her saffron blouse. "I was wor— never mind. It's no longer important."

She turned to leave. He stopped her at the door, and there was a difference in his tone, a definite hesitancy. "Do I — ah — owe you another apology?"

Her back got even stiffer, if that were possible. "Right now you most certainly do."

"To hell with now. What about the other night?"

She glanced back, giving him a doubtful look. "You don't remember?"

"Would I ask if I did?"

The possibilities that came with an answer to that question were numerous, and each one flitted across her face, making Angel groan inwardly.

"Actually," she began, only to pause, obviously changing her mind. "No."

Wondering what he had done to her the other night was going to drive him crazy now because he really didn't have much memory beyond opening that bottle of whiskey the barkeep had given to him to deaden his pain on the way home. And he wasn't going to call her on that lie. He didn't like apologizing anyway, especially for something he couldn't help, which was her fault in the first place. If she'd just stop getting prettier every time he saw her . . .

He wished to hell he knew how she did that. Even now, as irritated as he was with her and her bull of an ex-beau, he wanted to take her in his arms and kiss her. But there were a number of good reasons why he wouldn't give in to the urges she stirred in him. They were getting harder to keep in mind, though, and right now he was in a mood to forget them entirely. He indulged the mood.

"You really ought to stop doing this, Cassie," he said in his lazy drawl as he slowly closed the space between them.

She immediately backed up until the door wouldn't let her go farther. "What?"

"Seeking me out for no good reason."

That took the wariness out of her expression, replacing it with indignation. "I had a reason. I foolishly thought you might be injured worse than you appeared to be."

He reached her, deliberately crowding her against the door. Surprise was written all over her face now, and he heard her gasp when his hands cupped her cheeks to tilt her face up to him. He couldn't resist smoothing his thumbs over her lower lip. It was such a soft, supple lip. He wanted to suck on it — and her tongue — and her nipples, if she'd let him. Hell, he'd like to lick every inch of her. Too bad she wouldn't let him.

But while he had her confused, he continued. "Concern, Cassie? For a hardened killer like me? I'm touched."

Cassie didn't know what was happening. They'd just been snapping at each other, but now he was using those husky tones to mesmerize her. In the dazed recesses of her mind, she thought he didn't look touched. He looked hungry, and she was apparently on his menu for the day.

171

She had to stop him. But as his mouth came slowly toward hers, giving her ample time to do so, she couldn't think of a single thing to say that would. The fact was, "had to" wasn't a priority at the moment, having taken second place to anticipation. Just the thought of tasting his mouth again was incredibly exciting.

But that was nothing compared with the actuality, which stole her breath and seemed to be melting her bones. She braced her hands against the door to hold her up, but that wasn't working, so she reached for his shoulders instead. Better, but she still felt like she'd fall on her face if she were left to stand there alone, especially when her lower lip was drawn gently into his mouth.

A sound purred in her throat; her fingers dug into his muscles. He must have sensed her problem because his hips pressed forward, pinning her to the door, offering support, and she needed it when his thumbs worked her mouth open. It was her tongue he was after now, and he coaxed it, teased it, until she innocently gave it to him.

What she got back was heat, spreading rapidly, and so many other sensations and yearnings she didn't understand. Fear was there, too, because she had no control over what was happening, nor over what she was feeling. Then he groaned, and she was being lifted, her feet dangling, her breasts crushed against his chest, and the kiss took on a savage intensity that she wasn't experienced enough to meet.

Her fear got the upper hand and she pushed at Angel. He let her go immediately. She slumped back against the door, breathing hard. He stared at her for the longest time, and she knew he was debating, fighting something powerful, primitive even, and she held her breath, waiting, not even sure she wanted him to win the fight.

Finally he said, "I'm not apologizing this time. You come in here again, I'm going to think you want me to finish this, and I'll damn well oblige you."

She didn't pretend to misunderstand. There was a moment of struggling to open the door with trembling fingers, but then she was gone.

Angel stood there for a moment more, staring at the closed door, before he released the urge and slammed his fist against it, then swore a blue streak as the already swollen areas of his hand began to throb. But that wasn't all that was throbbing.

Why did he keep letting her arouse him like that? Letting her? Hell, there didn't seem to be anything he could do about it, and he finally admitted it. He'd like to teach Miss Cassandra Stuart how to be not so proper. If he stuck around here much longer, he just might.

Chapter 19

She worried about it for a week, but Cassie finally came to the conclusion that Angel had kissed her again because Angel had been angry with her. He'd been frustrated over his inability to use his gun hand. And he probably blamed her for the fight he'd gotten into with Morgan.

It really made sense, and it went hand in hand with that threat he'd made the day she'd stomped on his foot. She hadn't taken him seriously then, but he'd said she owed him for it, and he'd implied he would collect by kissing her. Being angry with her again had probably reminded him of that other time, and he'd decided to go ahead and get even that way. After all, how else could he retaliate against her? He wouldn't call her out. He wouldn't even leave, because he wasn't here for her, but for Lewis Pickens.

It made sense. What didn't make sense was that he could want her. Men just didn't — want her, that is. Even those two who had semi-courted her at home had never even bothered to act like they wanted her. It was the ranch house that had interested them, and the number of cattle on the range. Morgan had been different, but she'd found out quick enough that his feelings had been a sham, too, that he'd just been after her wealth like the others.

But with Angel, well, they'd been at odds from the beginning. There was no getting around that. And he had no interest in ranching, so there wasn't even that to tempt him. And, giving it more thought, she had to discount the night Slater had broken in. Then she'd been in a shameful state of disarray. She'd also been pressing herself against Angel. He'd probably assumed she was asking for it, and he'd been kind enough to oblige. Hadn't she called her own behavior that night wanton? She had also discounted his silliness the night he had got drunk. The man simply hadn't been right in the head that time.

To support her conclusion, ever since that last kiss had happened, Angel hadn't said a word about it, had been acting like it had never happened. He'd been his curt, surly self whenever she came upon him, which wasn't often, since she'd gone out of her way to avoid him, even changing the hours when she ate so she wouldn't pass him in the hall as he headed for the kitchen and she for the dining room.

The trouble was, Cassie caught herself more than once wishing she were wrong. Pure foolishness, but she couldn't seem to help it. She couldn't stop thinking about that last kiss, either, and regretting that it had frightened her there at the end. If she hadn't pushed him away . . .

A confused jumble of mixed feelings was pulling at her. What she needed was someone she could talk to, someone who could help her sort through the mess. At home she would have gone to see Jessie Summers. Here her only close friend had been Jenny, but even if she could get to speak to Jenny somehow, Jenny was too young to offer mature advice. Hell, Jenny needed more help than Cassie did.

It would have been nice if that weren't so, because to Cassie's surprise, Jenny Catlin showed up that afternoon. To her further surprise, her young friend looked like a disaster blowing in, her blond hair a tangled mess, as if she'd raced to get there, her clothes rumpled, as if she hadn't changed them in a week. And Buck hadn't been exaggerating. Jenny's blue eyes were bloodshot and puffy.

Cassie ushered her into the front parlor and tried to get her to sit down, but that didn't work. Jenny bounded back up after a few seconds and started pacing around the room like a cornered animal.

Frankly, Cassie didn't know what to say to the girl after all the trouble she'd caused. "I'm sorry" seemed so trite. She tried it anyway. Jenny just waved a dismissive hand as she stopped by the window to glance nervously out.

Cassie guessed, "Your mama doesn't know you're here, does she?"

Jenny shook her head as she started another round of the room. "I waited until she and Buck went to town today."

"Is she giving you a hard time?"

"You mean aside from the fact that she looks at me like I've stabbed her in the back?"

Cassie winced, reminding her, "You knew that part wasn't going to be easy."

"I know."

"Then what is it?"

Jenny put her hand on her stomach and then burst into tears. Cassie wasn't very good at that kind of addition or at charades.

"Tell me, Jenny."

Jenny hugged her stomach now and wailed, "I just did! I'm havin' his baby!"

Cassie's mouth dropped open. It took her a few moments before she could manage to say, "Are you sure?"

"I've been sure more'n a month now. What am I gonna do? I can't tell my ma. It's bad enough I married a MacKauley behind her back, but this . . . she'll probably kick me out."

"She wouldn't —"

"She would!"

"No, she wouldn't — but if she does, you can come live with me."

That didn't dry up Jenny's tears. Actually, her crying got louder. "I don't want to live with you. I want to live with Clay, but he won't have me!"

Cassie sighed inwardly. At least she hadn't been wrong about Jenny's feelings, and according to Morgan, she'd probably been right about Clayton's, too. That was slim consolation when it didn't matter to the parents how their children felt, but it still relieved Cassie of some of her guilt — though that didn't solve a single thing. The girl might truly care about her husband, but the situation was hopeless when her husband was too immature to stand up to his father.

Cassie sighed again, aloud this time. "Jenny, how did everything go wrong? You and Clayton were so happy and excited when you left for Austin."

Jenny finally slumped down in a chair to admit, "We somehow got to talking about who loved each other first. He said he wouldn't even have noticed me if you hadn't told him I was in love with him. That made me mad, so I told him the truth, that I hadn't even thought of him in that way until you told *me* that he loved me. He blew up then. Said he'd been tricked. I think he was just already scared about what his pa was gonna say when we got home."

Cassie wouldn't be surprised if that was exactly the reason. She wondered if she ought to tell Jenny that Clayton was probably regretting abandoning her. It certainly couldn't make things worse.

"If it's any consolation, I think Clayton is as unhappy right now as you are."

Jenny sat up instantly, her eyes wide and hopeful. "How do you know?"

"I had an unpleasant run-in with Morgan a couple of weeks ago. He said his brother hasn't been working, that he 'hasn't been right in the head since he came back from Austin.' Morgan also said that Clayton was talking about 'rights' and that he might just go over and collect you, but that R. J. whipped the notion out of him."

Jenny shot to her feet again, but in a burst of anger this time. "I really hate that old man!"

Cassie couldn't argue with that, but she pointed out, "Your mama's just as bad, but you don't hate her."

"Who says I don't?"

"Come on, Jenny, hate's what started this thing. Love was supposed to end it."

Jenny stopped to stare at her. "If that's what you thought, you were dreaming. But I don't blame you for playing matchmaker. Before we fought on the wedding night, it was wonderful. I don't regret that I'm having his baby, either. I just don't know what to do about it." Tears started gathering again. "I don't want to be a divorced mother."

"Then don't be. Your mama can't sign those divorce papers for you, Jenny. So don't you sign them."

"She'll make me."

"Maybe not. Or haven't you considered that the baby might change everyone's thinking on the matter? It'll be your mama's first grandchild, after all. R. J.'s, too."

Jenny sighed. "You still don't get it, Cassie. Their hate runs too deep. The only way those two will bury the hatchet is in each other's breast."

Cassie's optimism couldn't hold up to that. "I haven't been much help, have I?"

"I know you can't do anything else for me, Cassie. And I've got to get back before I'm missed and Buck sends every hand out looking for me. I just needed to talk to someone. Thanks for that."

Cassie nodded, understanding too well. Her own troubles seemed like nothing now. At least she wasn't pregnant and hopelessly in love with a man her mama would never approve of. But she couldn't bear that she'd be gone and out of this mess in a week or so, while Jenny would be left behind with the turmoil Cassie had created.

As she walked her friend to the front door,

she said, "I wish I could sit your mama and R. J. down in the same room to talk some sense into them."

"They wouldn't stay in the same room together."

"Then I'd lock them in."

Jenny actually laughed. "Wouldn't that be something — no, they'd kill each other for sure."

"Or be forced to settle this thing between them."

"It's a nice thought, Cassie, but it'd take a miracle to see it happen."

Cassie was fresh out of miracles, but she did have a tarnished Angel living under her roof. As she closed the door behind her friend, she wondered —

"Don't even think about it."

Cassie started at that deep voice and swung around. She located Angel sitting at the bottom of the stairs. His hat was on and tipped low. He was wearing his yellow slicker, too, and the black bandana tied at the side of his neck. He'd obviously been on his way out, or in. How much had he heard?

She crooked a brow at him, playing dumb. "Don't even think about what?"

The look that came back at her said he didn't appreciate her innocent act. "Meddling. I catch you at it again in these parts, I'm liable to do what your papa should've done years ago and whip your bottom. And don't go getting all huffy, or I'm liable to anyway. I swear, you don't know when to quit while you're ahead."

"What makes you think I'm ahead?"

180

"We'll both be out of here in a few days, this ranch is still standing, you're still in one piece, and I've had to kill only one man. In my book, that's way ahead. So you wait to start meddling again until you get home, where your mama can take care of the trouble you cause. Hell and I bet she's used to it."

Cassie marched toward him, her fingers itching to slap him, but all she did was stop near his feet to glare down at him. "I didn't ask you here, if you'll recall. Fact is, I remember asking you to leave. And since my neighbors have been quiet, I don't see why you're sticking around any longer. They're obviously allowing me to wait until my papa gets home."

"Your point?"

"I'd say you've done what you came to do, and you ought to be thinking about leaving — preferably today."

"So who asked you?"

He growled that as he stood up, which forced her to back up if she wanted to keep eye contact. She didn't at the moment, since there was no mistaking that she'd pushed him beyond his mild annoyance. And he wasn't finished.

"I'm staying, Cassie, not until your father gets here, but until I see you packed and out of this county. That can't happen soon enough for me, but until it does — *no more meddling*. You got that?"

She was surprised that she could do more than nod. "Yes, quite perfectly. I should have known better than to expect you to sympathize with my position or to feel one ounce of compassion for those two young people who happen to love each other. You'd have to have a heart . . ."

She left it at that, marching off to disappear down the hall. He stared after her, amused at her gumption. Her courage kept popping up when he least expected it. Damned if he didn't like that about her.

"Oh, I've got one, honey," he said softly. "Fortunately, it's wrapped in rawhide too tough for you to crack."

Chapter 20

Cassie had put off making another trip to town with Angel for as long as she could, but the fact was, her papa wasn't one for surprises, so he should have let her know by now exactly when he'd be arriving. A telegram would have been delivered, but a letter would sit in town until she got around to picking it up. That meant going to town, and Angel still wouldn't let her go alone.

With Christmas just short of a week away, she also had some shopping to do. That was a cheerless thought. It was a holiday she'd always looked forward to. This year was going to be an exception, because if there'd been no further delays and her papa returned in the next few days, she couldn't take the chance of extending her visit even for the holidays. It'd be the first Christmas that she didn't spend with at least one of her parents. She'd be spending it alone on a train or a stagecoach heading north.

That wasn't what she was thinking about, however, that afternoon on the way to Caully. After she and Angel had had those last unpleasant words following Jenny's visit three days ago, it had struck her, forcefully, that he'd be out of her life soon, very soon, and she'd probably never see him again. They might hail from the same area of Wyoming, but look at all the years he'd been in and out of Cheyenne and she'd never crossed paths with him. She had no reason to think it'd be any different when she returned home.

And even if she did happen to see him some-day in Cheyenne, Angel would probably cross to the other side of the street to avoid her. And why not? It wasn't exactly as if they'd become friends during his time here. Just the opposite. He couldn't wait to leave, and she — she'd felt like crying these past three days.

Surprisingly, Cassie had no misgivings this time about riding with Angel. In fact, by taking the carriage today, she was sort of daring him to endure her company and conversation. He must not have been up to the challenge. He rode his horse, and kept it just far enough ahead to rule out talking while on the road. And he didn't even notice that beneath her fur-trimmed coat she had on the very latest in Chicago finery in lavender-and-white lace. So much for spending half the morning agonizing over her appearance.

There was indeed a letter from her papa wait-ing for her in town. He didn't give her an exact day of arrival, but he promised to be home before Christmas.

When she informed Angel of that, he greeted the news with his usual inscrutability, which told her nothing of his feelings. But she could guess. He had to be delighted it was almost over.

At least they had no trouble in Caully this time. Richard was there with a couple of the MacKauley cowboys, but all he did was stare at them a bit on his way out of town. Cassie stayed no longer than she had to, though it was getting on toward evening by the time she rolled the carriage into the barn. Angel followed her in and began un-hitching the horse before she'd even alighted from the carriage.

"Emanuel will do that," she informed him dully, her mood sunk to the dregs.

He didn't stop what he was doing to reply, "I don't see the kid about, do you?"

Cassie's head snapped up at the surly tone he'd used. She was the one in the rotten mood. What did he have to be testy about?

"Considering the hour," she said stiffly now, "I suppose he's having his dinner. But I can take care of the carriage horse. You have your own horse to —"

"Don't push it, Cassie," he cut in, still with-out stopping what he was doing. "Go on to the house —"

"Now that's a right fine idea," a new voice interjected. "Why don't we all do that?"

Three guns cocked simultaneously. Cassie stared wide-eyed as Richard MacKauley stepped out of the shadows at the back of the barn. From the sides, Frazer and Morgan came forward. Each of them held his gun pointed at Angel.

A trap? Richard must have raced home to fetch his pa the same as Morgan had that other time. Only this time it wasn't just to confront Cassie.

"Don't move, Angel, or your name will take on new meaning," Richard said as he came up behind him and carefully lifted Angel's Colt out of his holster.

Angel let him. He didn't have much choice,

185

Cassie supposed, though she was surprised that he didn't say or do something before he lost the opportunity. In his line of work he had to be familiar with this type of situation, must have a few tricks or moves that he could have already used to turn the tables on the MacKauleys. Of course, she hadn't yet seen the fourth gun trained on herself.

Not that she paid much attention to it when she did turn to the man who'd originally spoken. R. J. stood in the wide entrance to the barn, grinning broadly. That grin should have warned her she wouldn't like hearing what this was about.

She still had to ask, "What are you up to now, Mr. MacKauley?"

"Just here to do you a favor, Miss Stuart, a sort of thank-you for all you've done for my family. Couldn't let you return home without a proper show of . . . appreciation."

Cassie looked around her. Frazer had gotten a kick out of his father's choice of words. Richard wasn't amused, however, and Morgan didn't look like he wanted to be there at all. Clayton was conspicuously absent. And Angel, he was as inscrutable as ever.

The thought ran through Cassie's mind that today, of all days, she had decided not to wear her own weapon to town — and for what? Stupid vanity and trying to look her best for someone who hadn't even noticed. But then, R. J. couldn't be planning anything of a serious nature. He wouldn't be standing there grinning if he meant to do any real harm. Would he?

"I'd just as soon you didn't do me any favors,

Mr. MacKauley," she began cautiously, then suggested, "Why don't you simply think of me as already gone? I will be in a matter of days."

"I know it. That's why I'm here now, to help you out before it's too late."

Cassie frowned. "Help me out how?"

"We're gonna get you hitched up nice and proper, before that young fella of yours just happens to disappear on you again."

Hitched up? It was too incredible for her to grasp immediately, but when she did, Cassie started to laugh. "You're joking."

"No, ma'am." R. J. shook his head. "Got the preacher waitin' in your parlor to say the words. He was happy to oblige when he heard you two've been livin' under the same roof all this time without a proper chaperone."

Hot color flooded her cheeks at the insinuation R. J. was making, only to have every speck of it desert her as the greater implication hit her. They were going to force Angel to marry her. But no one could do that to a man like him. He'd be so furious, he would kill every one of them without a qualm the very second he got his gun back.

Damn Frazer. He'd said his pa would get a kick out of this idea, and he'd probably made sure that it occurred to him. She gave him a glare worthy of a lightning bolt. He grinned back at her unrepentantly.

"It came out of your own mouth, Miss Cassie," Frazer said, rubbing it in. "And gettin' married is what engaged couples do, ain't it?"

Her own lie, and coming back to haunt her

in a monstrous way. Frazer knew it was a lie. R. J. probably did, too. They were only using it to get revenge — "just deserts," as Frazer had called it. But she couldn't let them go through with it. For their own sakes, she couldn't.

Cassie was afraid to look at Angel to see how he was taking this new dilemma, but she knew he wouldn't say anything. That wasn't his way. Afterward he'd deal with them, and feel justified, since they weren't exactly lawful in what they were doing.

Still, she couldn't allow it to go that far. She'd have to lie some more. And if that didn't work, she'd have to flat out refuse to cooperate.

She turned back to R. J. "I appreciate your concern, Mr. MacKauley, but my mama's already planning a big wedding for the end of January. Hundreds of guests have been invited. She'd never forgive me if she had to cancel it."

The old man chuckled. "No need to disappoint your ma. Ain't no law says you can't get married twice — leastwise to the same man."

Cassie gritted her teeth. "Then I'll wait until my papa gets here so he can give me away."

"You can have yourself even another wedding when Charley gets here, but we ain't gonna disappoint the preacher on this one, since he come all this way to do the right thing. I'll give you away, little girl. It'd be an honor."

At which point Cassie got angry. "The hell it would. I'm not getting married to suit your misplaced sense of revenge, R. J. MacKauley. If you'd just open your eyes, you'd see that Clayton and Jenny want to be together. It's your orneriness that won't let them, and the same thing's brought you here today. So what are you going to do now? Shoot me?"

"Well, now, I can do that," he said with some careful thought before nodding in the direction behind her. "But I'd probably shoot him instead."

"Him" was Angel, and the very thought of him being shot turned Cassie's blood cold. He still hadn't said anything, and she could no longer avoid looking at him. But that was a mistake that gave her the jolt of fear the MacKauleys hadn't been able to. Angel was furious, all right, and for some reason, the full blast of it was coming her way. No, not *some* reason. This was her fault, too, and he was putting the blame right where it belonged.

She swung back around again, frightened enough now to plead with R. J. if she had to. Angel didn't give her the chance. He came around and yanked her down from the carriage. No one tried to stop him.

"Let's get this over with, Cassie. One wedding or three won't make any difference at this point."

His tone was as smooth as his expression now was, but she wasn't fooled. She'd seen the fury, and her feet dug in as he started pulling her toward the house. They got there anyway, with the MacKauleys following close behind. And the preacher was indeed waiting.

Her last hope. All she had to do was tell him that she and Angel were being forced to marry . . .

"Not another word except 'I do,' " Angel hissed in her ear. "You got that?"

Cassie stared at him, uncertain why he was giving in. Possibly because the sooner it was over, the sooner he'd get his gun back, and then all hell was going to break loose. She hoped he'd let the preacher leave first. The MacKauleys she had no sympathy for at the moment. Poor Maria was going to have a fit at all the blood . . .

"You got that?" Angel repeated.

She nodded. What did she care if she had a bloodbath in her parlor? First she was getting married, and that was accomplished quite painlessly, actually. There was even a small, crazy part of her that regretted that it wasn't for real. Crazy was right. When she thought about what her mama would do when she heard about this shotgun wedding . . . of course, she'd have to be alive to tell her, and she wasn't at all certain she was going to survive the night.

R. J. was laughing as he walked the preacher out. Morgan hadn't come into the parlor to listen to the vows, though Cassie heard his disgruntled voice in the hall before he left with his father. Richard looked no more amused now than he had earlier. In fact, he seemed kind of uneasy now. Smart man. He'd be smarter still if he took Angel's gun with him, but he was already removing it from his belt as he left the room, obviously to leave it on the hall table. Cassie hoped he would change his mind before he left.

But Frazer, that bizarre miscreant, was still standing there grinning at the newly wedded couple as if they ought to share in his delight. Fortunately, Angel was ignoring him. He'd moved to the window to watch the others ride off. Cassie

190

couldn't ignore him. The man's flashing teeth irritated the hell out of her at that point.

So she marched over and literally shoved Frazer out of the room and toward the front door, saying in a furious whisper, "Are you happy now? If Angel doesn't kill you for this, I think I will."

"What's the big deal, Cassie?" he had the gall to reply. "Pa's satisfied now, and you'll just get it annulled. So what's the harm done?"

"The harm is that Angel might not see it that way, you jackass. Now get out of my house."

It was very satisfying, slamming the door behind Frazer, but a glance at the hall table proved Richard wasn't as smart as she'd hoped. He'd left Angel's gun. She picked it up, looking for a place to hide it, but there was nowhere in the hall, so she slipped it inside her coat and felt it lodge against the form-fitting waist. Suddenly she realized that she hadn't even thought to remove her coat for her wedding.

A laugh bubbled up in her throat. She swallowed it down with a silent groan.

"Cassie?"

Her head snapped up at the sound of his voice coming from the parlor. She wasn't ready for this. Tomorrow they could discuss the annulment. Tonight, his gun wasn't the only thing that needed hiding.

Without answering him, she raced up the stairs and locked herself in her room.

Chapter 21

When Cassie didn't come down for her dinner that night, Emanuel was sent up with a tray. Maria had outdone herself in preparing several of Cassie's favorite dishes. Well, she'd had the time, since she hadn't had to clean up any blood yet. And the housekeeper had either been listening to or guessed what had happened. But Cassie barely picked at the offerings.

She did a lot of pacing, with Marabelle prowling right alongside her and nearly tripping her a half-dozen times. As usual, the panther sensed her upset and wouldn't settle down until Cassie did. But Cassie was a bundle of nerves, wondering if Angel had left the house, wondering what he was going to do — and to whom. It was impossible for her to sit down, much less think of going to bed yet.

When the knock came at the door, she was so deep in thought she didn't think twice about opening it, assuming the person was Emanuel returning for the tray. It wasn't.

"Didn't think you'd open up to me," Angel said.

She wouldn't have if she'd known it was him. And she would have immediately closed the door again if he hadn't taken a step forward so she'd end up smashing him if she tried it. She didn't.

She started backing up instead. She seemed to do a lot of that when he was around.

He must want his gun. No, he couldn't know she had it. He probably wanted hers. She had to talk him out of whatever he was going to do — somehow.

"You must have been hungry."

She followed his gaze to the empty tray. "Marabelle was," she replied, not trusting for a minute the mellow tone he was using. "Look, can we talk about this?"

"Sure — after you get rid of the cat."

Marabelle was sitting on her haunches next to Cassie. The last thing Cassie wanted to do, knowing Angel's wariness of the panther, was to send her out of the room. But she supposed a peace offering would be more appropriate now, so she led the big cat to the door and shooed her off. Angel had stepped farther into the room to get out of Marabelle's path.

Cassie closed the door, but stayed near it. Angel had been in her room only once before. She remembered that night and felt flutterings in her belly. And he was staring at her bed. Why was he staring at her bed?

She took a deep breath and began to speak conversationally, hoping to set the tone at a rational level. "You know, you really don't have to kill anyone over this. I'll get an annulment. It will be like it never happened."

His eyes came to her, briefly meeting her gaze before dropping to her mouth. "You'll have to make that a divorce instead."

"No, you don't understand. An annulment will

193

be much easier to obtain."

His gaze locked with hers now. Cassie became slightly breathless with the intensity of his stare.

"Not after tonight it won't," he said in his slow, mesmerizing drawl.

"Why?" She barely got the word out.

"Because I'm in the mood to play husband."

"You're *what?*"

He started toward her. She was too stunned to move, so he was there and reaching for her before she had time to even think about running.

"We're having a wedding night," he said as he lifted her off her feet.

"Wait — !"

"Not this time, honey. I didn't ask you to marry me. You would have said no if I had. Yet we're married, and right now I want you bad enough to take advantage of that."

Cassie wasn't given another opportunity to protest, not for a while anyway. Angel no sooner laid her on the bed than his body came down to pin her there, and his kiss captured her full attention, fiercely taking, tenderly giving. Pleasure came swiftly, aided by his weight pressing her in intimate places. She was helpless to resist it or him, and then she didn't want to.

It was a magical word, "married." It gave permission to enjoy, taking away the guilt and most of the fear. It also removed inhibitions, so that she could hold him and kiss him back. And when she did, she reveled in the sound of his groan as he understood she wouldn't be stopping him this time.

He wanted her, for whatever reason, revenge

or desire, she didn't care. Nothing mattered then except the need they shared, and Cassie definitely shared it. Like fire it was, the feeling that grew inside her. It was so consuming she barely noticed when he started undressing her, until his hands were reaching bare flesh, and she couldn't help noticing that, it was such a sensual shock. But there were more shocks to come, for he was soon touching her everywhere. And then the warmth, skin on skin, and his lips suddenly closing on a turgid nipple to suck it deep into his mouth.

Such incredible heat in contrast to the silky coolness of his hair as it trailed over her skin. Her back arched off the bed. Her breath was coming in short bursts. She held his head in her hands, his waist between her legs, and the intensity of what she was feeling now made her want to scream. She didn't, not yet. But something continued to build deep in her loins, something hot and achy and out of control.

Then suddenly he was slipping out of her hold. His hands molded to her breasts as his tongue licked a path straight down her belly to — no, he wouldn't. Oh, God, he did. The protest came and died on the same breath, because in the next instant there was an explosion of pulsating pleasure that reared her off the bed, leaving her caught in a realm of pure sensation. It was beyond reality, beyond comprehension, and she was helpless to do anything but ride it out to the last blissful pulsebeat.

She was wrapped in his arms by then, his sleek musculature molded to her, his weight a surprising comfort. But a new sensation intruded on her languor, an invasion that had her tensing. Yet fear didn't have time to take hold. She was warm and wet, and his entry was so smooth, there was only the tiniest bit of pressure to denote the breaking of her maidenhead before he was filling her fully, deeply.

He reared back then, straightening his arms to brace them on either side of her, embedding himself even deeper inside her. But when she opened her eyes, it was to find him staring down at her, just staring, his eyes so dark, so intense.

"You can't imagine how much I've wanted this — wanted you."

No, she couldn't. She could still scarcely believe it. And she couldn't reply. She held her breath, watching him look his fill. He didn't move, only his eyes, and a tingling returned to her breasts as he stared at them, the fluttering stirred in her belly when he looked there, and where they were joined, the heat came back in a rush.

"Oh, God," she gasped.

He smiled, and began a slow, sensuous thrusting. He lowered his head to kiss her. Her lips clung to his, her arms wrapped tight around his neck, and tighter still as the tension mounted again. And then the throbbing was back, bursting over her senses, surrounding him, and he plunged deep, grinding into her, enhancing it, his own head thrown back to emit a low, animal sound of pure pleasure.

Chapter 22

Waking up with a man in her bed was a unique experience, one Cassie wouldn't half mind if the circumstances were other than what they were. As it was, she didn't know whether to get up or go back to sleep and hope he'd be gone by the time she woke again. Of course, she couldn't fall back asleep with reality intruding. Reality was such an ugly word this morning. It had been suspended for a while last night, but now it was back with a vengeance.

Married. And not by choice, though if she'd had a choice — no, her own wishes didn't count. But she'd had a wedding night. And Jenny had certainly called it right, wonderful — actually, that was too mild a word to describe what Angel had given her. But it shouldn't have happened, not with Angel. And it had happened for the wrong reasons.

It was laughable, really. She'd been so sure he was going to go after the MacKauleys, that he'd want his revenge in blood. But he hadn't faulted them for something she'd instigated in the first place. No, he'd put the blame smack where it belonged and reserved his revenge just for her. And that was so like him, to be fair in that way. She didn't know why she hadn't guessed what he'd do sooner. After all, if he got even for minor things with kissing, it stood to reason that he'd go for the whole works for something as serious as a forced marriage.

She wondered if she was supposed to have enjoyed it so much. Probably not. Or maybe that didn't matter to him, since the divorce he was forcing on her was the true revenge. Although more and more people were ending marriages these days in that way, it was still a scandalous thing to do, so much so that whatever hopes Cassie had of one day marrying, she might as well bury. No man with decent morals would consider a divorced woman for his wife.

That was a really rotten thing for Angel to have done to her, now that she thought about it. Had she really deserved that because he'd been a little inconvenienced? She didn't think so, when an annulment would have served *and* saved her reputation. He was damn lucky she wasn't the vindictive sort, or she'd do some getting even of her own and not divorce him at all. It would serve him right to be stuck with her. But she couldn't do that to him, since none of this was his fault.

He stirred just then, drawing her attention. He was sleeping on his stomach, with his face turned away from her. Only the arm thrown up over the pillow and his bare shoulders were visible, because at some time during the night they'd both gotten under the covers. Yet he was naked beneath them. So was she.

After last night, that thought shouldn't make her blush, but it did. And her curiosity added even more heat. She hadn't gotten a good look at his body last night. She couldn't deny she'd like to. But she wasn't daring enough to throw back the covers. Besides, she didn't want to have words with him while they were still in bed. That would put her at a distinct disadvantage, and she had so few advantages — none, actually, that she could think of at the moment. But at least putting on some clothes before she had to face him would make her more comfortable.

With that decided, she carefully sat up, and immediately noticed Marabelle's tail swishing the floorboards at the end of the bed. It came to her then, a vague memory of the panther scratching at the door in the middle of the night to get in. Cassie must have got up to let her in, then gone right back to sleep. And obviously Angel hadn't been disturbed by it, or he wouldn't still be there.

But she had to put Marabelle out before he woke up. His finding her there would almost guarantee his starting the day in a rotten mood. Yet Cassie didn't move immediately to do so. And suddenly she smiled to herself.

So maybe she could be a little vindictive just this once. After all, Marabelle had more right to be there than Cassie's soon-to-be divorced husband did. And why should she worry about his mood anyway? He ought to be worried about hers after what he did to her — making love to her for revenge. She wouldn't have thought him that cruel, but it just went to show that you couldn't trust a man who went around killing people for a living.

She wouldn't remove her pet. She'd like to

remove her husband. She settled for getting dressed, and so inched her way out from under the covers and tiptoed to her wardrobe. But by the time she got there, Cassie was cringing. She'd never realized how many loose floorboards she had that creaked, and for God's sake, why had she never noticed that the hinges on her wardrobe needed oiling? She was making enough noise to wake the dead, and a glance over her shoulder proved that Angel didn't fall into that category. The first creak on the floor had brought his eyes open, and those eyes were now fixed on her naked backside.

Her modesty scandalized, Cassie managed to gasp, "Close your eyes!"

"Hell, no," he replied, and he actually grinned. "You're a damn pretty sight to wake up to, honey. Why don't you turn around so I can have a better look?"

"Why don't you go to hell?" she retorted and grabbed the first thing at hand, a voluminous petticoat, and whipped it over her head to wiggle into.

"Aren't your drawers supposed to go on first?"

That was laughter in his voice, she'd swear it was. "Just shut up, Angel."

"You are going to pull that down, aren't you?"

She'd let the petticoat catch on her breasts so her torso was at least covered. "Not on your life."

She heard him sigh. She gritted her teeth and pulled out a camisole. But after a moment of trying to get it on, she found it wouldn't fasten over the thick petticoat.

"You're taking modesty too far, Cassie. Your back is to me. Go ahead and drop it."

He meant the petticoat, and she was being ridiculous. There was nothing left for him to see. Even her back was covered by her hair. So she yanked the petticoat down, adjusted the lacy camisole over her breasts, and quickly fastened it. But when she reached for a dress, she caught Angel's reflection in her vanity mirror, which sat at a cross angle from her wardrobe. He wasn't staring at her, he was staring at the mirror, and if she could see him clearly, he had a good frontal view of her . . .

She whipped around to face him. "You sneaky son— !"

"What are you getting all fired up for?" he interrupted, sounding absurdly reasonable. "For the time being, I've got a right to look."

"The hell you do. We're getting divorced, and it can't be soon enough for me."

He'd been leaning up on one elbow. With her last statement, he dropped back on the bed to stare up at the ceiling.

Cassie took that as a sign that she'd made her point and he was done provoking her.

She let it go at that and quickly wiggled into a dress, but she was still simmering. Rights! He'd dared to mention rights *for the time being,* when he knew full well their marriage wasn't legal — or it wouldn't have been legal if he'd stayed out of her bed.

It struck her then that he was right. He'd made their marriage legal by bedding her, and it would remain legal until they signed the divorce papers.

So — legally he did have certain rights.

To hell with legal. She hadn't asked that he complicate matters with his revenge. He'd already overstepped the bounds of decency. So he had no rights as far as she was concerned, and she'd back that up with her gun if necessary.

"Cassie?"

The note of panic in his voice made her turn to him instantly, everything that had just run through her mind as quickly forgotten. And the problem was revealed in the first glance.

Marabelle's attention had been caught by the movement of the covers above Angel's toes. She'd come half up on the bed to investigate, and was now rubbing her face against the small tent his crossed feet made out of the covers. Cassie had been awakened in the morning dozens of times in such a way. But those weren't her feet her pet was drooling over, they were Angel's. Marabelle hadn't noticed the difference.

"How did she get in here?"

His voice was whisper-soft, and he wasn't taking the chance of moving the slightest bit. But Cassie's concern had left as soon as she saw there was no danger, and that put her back in the mood that wasn't inclined to take pity on Angel.

"I vaguely recall letting her in in the middle of the night when she scratched at the door," she answered with blatant nonchalance. "After all, she's *allowed* to sleep with me."

He wasn't about to touch that remark. "Get her out of here."

"I don't think I will. You made me your wife last night instead of your bride. The bride was

202

willing to oblige you. The wife isn't."

"Cassie," he began with clear warning, but ended on a startled note. "She's biting my feet!"

"No, she isn't. She's cleaning her teeth. I told you she likes to do that."

"So make her stop."

Cassie sighed at that point and moved to the foot of the bed to run a hand down Marabelle's back. "Honestly, Angel, you've been around her long enough now to know she's harmless."

He still wouldn't take his eyes off the panther — or move. "I don't know any such thing. A bullet is one thing. I can handle going by a bullet. But the thought of going by being that cat's dinner . . ."

"Marabelle doesn't even like raw meat. She prefers it cooked, but she's actually more partial to biscuits and flapjacks."

"Biscuits?" he choked out.

"And flapjacks."

He gave her the briefest glance that said clearly she was crazy before his eyes were back on the panther. But after another moment of thinking about it — biscuits — he yanked his feet out from under Marabelle's purring adoration. And when the cat just looked at him without moving, he went one further and leaped out of the bed.

Cassie wasn't expecting that. Her eyes rounded. Her breath caught. But she didn't even think about looking away. Lord love him, he had a fine-looking body, all sleek grace and subtle strength — like her panther. She noted old bullet wounds, three, four, but it was all that male skin that fascinated her. Broad shoulders, flat belly, long legs — which he was stuffing into his pants. He was angry. She could see it in every line of his body. And she was the cause.

He confirmed it. "That was a rotten thing to do."

She knew full well he referred to her lack of help with Marabelle. "Then that makes us two of a kind, doesn't it?"

"Lady, when I get even, it's with lasting results."

She sat down on the bed, looking away from him. Her voice was exceptionally quiet. "I know."

He was suddenly there in front of her, despite the fact that Marabelle was right next to her. He hadn't found his shirt yet. His pants weren't fastened, were barely clinging to his hips. Nothing but skin, only inches from her face — and the crazy urge to lean forward and press her lips to it.

"Last night wasn't 'getting even,' Cassie. It was a temptation too great for me to resist. For your sake, I'm sorry it happened. For mine — I'm damned if I am."

She hadn't expected him to attempt an explanation. He could have saved his breath, though, since she didn't believe a word of it — except that he wasn't sorry for his sake. Why should he be? It hadn't cost him anything and certainly wasn't going to damage *his* reputation.

She didn't answer, and wouldn't look up at him. But she was startled when his hand came toward her cheek. It stopped short of touching her, however, hesitated there, then dropped away. And why did she suddenly feel like crying?

She wouldn't. She pushed herself off the bed to squeeze past him. "Find your boots and leave," she told him on her way to her bureau. There she opened a drawer and pulled out his gun. "And you'll need this." She turned and tossed it to him. "You never know if you'll have to shoot someone today."

He'd caught the gun, but he didn't move other than that, just stared at her for a long moment. She could almost see it happening, the change in him, the hardness coming to the surface, taking control.

"Yeah, you never know."

Cassie cringed inwardly. Standing before her was the man who'd arrived three weeks ago, a man of violence, ruthless when necessary, conscienceless — heartless. She'd caused that with her own coldness. But it was just as well. This was the man she was more accustomed to, not the one who was afraid to touch her cheek.

Chapter 23

Angel sat in the parlor with the bottle of tequila Maria had fetched for him, her own private stock. Charles Stuart didn't drink hard liquor, so there hadn't been a single bottle of whiskey in the house. And Angel didn't feel like riding to town to get some. In his present mood, there would definitely be trouble if he did.

He hadn't seen his *wife* since he'd left her room — the second time that morning. The first time he'd been angry enough to leave without his boots. He'd even gotten halfway to the stable before he realized he had nothing on his feet. He'd had to go back. He only had the one pair. But he'd waited until he cooled off some before he knocked on her door again.

She'd calmed down some herself by then. At least she'd used a civil tone when neither of them could find his boots right off. "With Marabelle in the room, you might as well look under the bed," she'd suggested. "That's where she stashes things she wants to keep."

"Wants to keep?" The tug-of-war that had come to mind had him frowning. "I'm not going to fight your Marabelle for my boots."

"You won't have to. In case you haven't noticed, she's not here."

He hadn't noticed. It was hard to notice anything else when he could barely take his eyes off Cassie. Even with her hair tightly coiled again, her dress properly fastened — undoubtedly she'd put some drawers on by then, too — he kept seeing her as she'd been last night, lying beneath him, her long brown hair spread out on the pillow, her breasts full and pouting — and no drawers on.

It was happening again. He'd lost count of how many times he'd gotten hard today from remembering how she'd been last night. He stretched out his legs and took another swig of the tequila, but it wasn't helping him to forget.

He'd gotten down on his knees to look under the bed. She'd gotten down on the other side. The boots were there, all right. So were a lot of unrecognizable things — and Cassie's lavender-and-white lace dress. He'd pulled the dress out first and held it up.

"It made a fine wedding dress, Cassie. You should have removed your coat."

She didn't reply, just stared at him wide eyed. He didn't know why he'd said it, and added uncomfortably, "It doesn't look like the cat ruined it."

"She wouldn't. She knows better than to chew on my clothes."

"What about boots?"

"That's another story. Marabelle goes crazy for them."

"The smell of leather?"

"Sweat, actually."

He'd wanted to laugh at the way she'd said it, as if he should have known. She made him

207

want to laugh at the strangest times, and usually over nothing that was funny. He didn't laugh. He fetched his boots and got out of there before he gave in to the urge to make love to her again.

He never should have gone up to her room last night. He'd known that. It had been a really stupid thing to do. Yet through no fault of his own, he'd been given the legal right to make love to the very woman who'd been driving him crazy with lust.

There was no way he could ignore that once the notion took hold. No way he could fight a temptation that powerful. He hadn't lied to her this morning. But she wasn't interested in his reasons, or that she had become his weakness. She was still too upset that he'd made their forced marriage into a temporary real one.

R. J. MacKauley was an ornery cuss, but what he'd done was no big deal. They'd all known that — except Cassie. She hadn't wanted it to happen for any reason. Angel was still infuriated over how hard she'd fought to prevent it from occurring. And that was stupid, too, his taking that rejection so to heart when he'd already known that he didn't stand a chance with a woman like her.

He couldn't remember ever having his emotions this tied up in knots. And he didn't know what he could do about it — except leave. That he could do in just a few more days. That was all he needed, to remove himself from the temptation. Distance would take care of what he was feeling, get his thoughts straight, get him back on his solitary path, and end these foolish yearnings for something different.

And he'd be leaving with a clear slate. He owed no one now . . .

The hell he didn't. He'd known last night that if he went up to her room, he'd end up owing Cassie. She wouldn't have given him her innocence if she'd had a choice. She'd stopped him every other time he'd come close to tampering with it. But how did he pay back a woman for something like that?

The answer came rather quickly, since the tequila wasn't helping to dull his thoughts yet. He knew what Cassie wanted. Her meddling had made a bad situation worse, and as a result she would be leaving some pretty unhappy people behind. She'd like nothing more than to turn that around so she could go home with a clear conscience. Angel didn't operate that way, but he knew he could probably accomplish that for her. She wouldn't like his method — hell, none of them would — but it could be done.

He started to take another swig, then tensed, hearing *her* coming. Hell, purring that loud went through the walls. He watched the open doors, his fingers tightening around the glass in his hand. She didn't usually bother him. He'd come across her in the house before, but she'd just stared at him with those huge golden eyes.

She did that now as she appeared in the doorway and sat back on her haunches. But when she made no move to enter the room, he relaxed somewhat.

"Smart girl," Angel said with a nod. "After those teeth marks I found on my boots, I'm your

209

worst enemy. Just keep your —"

Marabelle was at his feet in a couple of strides, gave them a few sniffs, then plopped down on the floor to literally curl around them. One large paw flipped over Angel's ankles, as if to keep him from moving. He wasn't about to budge.

"You start cleaning your teeth on me and I'll shoot you," he warned the cat.

She didn't look in the direction of his voice. She started rubbing her face on the edge of one boot. Angel didn't reach for his gun.

"Hell, you're as bad as she is. You don't know when to quit."

The panther kept on purring. Angel watched closely, and damned if her teeth didn't scrape across the top of his boot. He shook his head, deciding the tequila must have been stronger than he'd thought. Why else would he be sitting there letting a full-grown panther gnaw on his feet?

Chapter 24

Cassie opened her eyes to find it hadn't been a dream after all. Angel had come to her room again last night. Only this time it had been really late. She'd already been sleeping. Not for long, though.

She woke to his kiss, his body half covering her, and to the husky words "We're not divorced yet, honey."

That was perfectly true. They would be, but they weren't yet. And she simply hadn't cared to remember that she'd promised herself she wouldn't let him exercise any more temporary rights. At least last night she hadn't wanted to. But the bright light of morning had a way of putting things in their proper perspective, whereas the dull glow of a dying fire didn't lend itself to clear thinking.

She wasn't sorry he'd come to her. She couldn't say that. But she couldn't let him continue to do so. Granted, he'd be there only a few more days, and if there weren't any other consequences to consider, she'd give anything to spend every minute of the remaining time in his arms.

But Jenny would be the first to tell her it didn't take a lot to get pregnant. And as much as Cassie wanted to have her own children someday, she didn't want to be caught in the same predicament as Jenny — being a divorced woman having a baby.

Actually, if it came to that, she'd take her own advice and not sign any divorce papers. Of course, that wouldn't gain her a husband, at least not one who would live with her. Angel wanted his freedom. He fully expected to get it back. A little thing like a paper that said he was legally married wouldn't make him stick around.

"Such serious thoughts so early in the morning?"

She turned her head to find those black eyes on her. She'd thought he was still sleeping, which was why she hadn't even tried to get out from under the arm draped across her chest. That arm moved now as he brought his hand up to trace the frown on her brow.

"I can give you something more pleasant to think about," he added, and rose to lean toward her.

She almost let him kiss her. He was so damn enticing with his hair all tumbled, his eyes slumberous, his expression so sensual. Angel bent on lovemaking was devastating to every one of her newly awakened senses. Just one more time. What could it . . . ?

Her hand shot up at the last moment to hold him back. Inwardly she was groaning over the loss. Outwardly she schooled her features to show her determination.

"Last I heard, this is how babies get made," she said, trying not to sound too accusatory. "Is it your intention to leave me with one before you take off?"

He said nothing for all of five seconds, then he dropped back on the bed to stare at the ceiling. "You don't pull any punches, do you?"

"It's a reasonable question."

"I know." He sighed. "And no, that isn't my intention. Truth to tell, that's not something I've ever had to consider, not with the kind of women I usually . . ."

He left that open, but she got the drift easily enough. He was used to paying for his pleasure, and men took it for granted that their soiled doves knew how to prevent such things from happening. Likely they did, since they'd be out of business otherwise.

Suddenly he rolled toward her, though he was careful not to touch her. And there was an expression of keen interest on his face.

"Do you want a baby?"

Cassie's eyes flared wide. "What kind of question is *that?*"

"A reasonable one."

"The hell it is," she grumbled, and sat up to glare at him, wrapping the sheet tightly over her breasts. "I need a husband before I start having babies, a real husband, one who'll be around to help raise them. Then I'd like to have lots of them — but not until then."

The resentment was heard, loud and clear. It had slipped in because she didn't think she'd ever find that husband now. He took it as another rejection, that she didn't now, and never would, consider him for that position.

He sat up also, but to leave the bed and get dressed. She wouldn't watch this time. She

213

wrapped her arms around her upraised knees and turned her face away so she couldn't be tempted. She was annoyed with herself, but what else could she have said to him? That she wouldn't mind having *his* baby. And why had he even asked?

"I should've shot that vindictive old coot Mac-Kauley when I had the chance."

Cassie's head whipped around at that low-voiced mumble. Angel was dressed, and strapping on his gun.

"That's not funny," she said tersely.

"Am I laughing?" he shot back just as tersely.

"I don't know what the hell you're doing or thinking, but you can't go shooting R. J. He didn't push you into my bed, Angel."

"No, he just figured out my only weakness. Why the hell do you think *he* was so amused?"

"What weakness?"

He didn't get a chance to answer. The click of the door latch sounded as the door started to open. Angel turned and drew his gun in the same instant. And the greeting Charles Stuart had been about to make never got out.

Cassie gasped. "Papa!"

Angel took one look at her horrified expression and said, "I suppose I can't shoot him, either?"

He had said it softly enough, but Cassie was afraid her father had heard him, so she quickly assured Charles, "He's joking, Papa. He didn't mean it the way it sounded."

Angel refrained from saying, "The hell I didn't," as he put his gun away. He didn't know what it was about conversations with his "wife," but they frequently ended with him feeling like

214

shooting someone, anyone, it didn't matter who. Too bad it wasn't MacKauley who'd come through that door. Charles Stuart was another matter entirely.

The man was younger than Angel would have expected, probably in his early forties. His hair was as dark and lustrous as Cassie's, his eyes a chocolate brown. He had a slight crook in his nose that testified it had been broken at some time. He was presently leaning on a cane to favor his injured foot. That got him down to Angel's height, since Charles would have had an inch or two on him otherwise.

Her papa.

Angel had never had to deal with an enraged father before. And because he *was* Cassie's father, he couldn't shoot him, couldn't call him out, couldn't fight him. Hell, this ought to be interesting.

Charles was tired, his foot was paining him, and although he did have a formidable temper, he'd never once lost it where his daughter was concerned. Besides, he was still too incredulous to show anger.

"Cassie, what is this man doing in your bedroom?"

Cassie had been sidetracked by Angel's "shooting" crack, but it came blaringly now, the thought of how it must look to her father, her in bed with nothing on beneath the sheet, her nightgown on the floor by Angel's feet. Angel was dressed, but only barely. His black shirt was tucked into his pants, but it wasn't fastened. He hadn't put his boots on yet. This wasn't how

215

she had imagined explaining things to her father, and her cheeks got so hot they stung.

"It's not what it seems, Papa — well, it is, but — we're married — at least for the time being we are — oh, damn, a lot has happened since you left!"

"Obviously," Charles replied, and said in the same breath, "Married? For God's sake, I haven't been gone *that* long. You couldn't wait until I got home?"

"I tried to get R. J. to consider that, but he wasn't inclined to be reasonable."

Charles looked at Angel. "Are you another R. J.?"

"No, sir. Name's Angel."

"Angel what?"

"Just Angel."

"Does that make you Mrs. Angel, Cassie?"

"I guess so, or —" She suddenly blanched, turning to Angel. "They could have used 'Brown.' Did you look to see which name was put on the marriage paper?"

"With that many witnesses, it doesn't matter what name was put down. The thing was done legal, no matter how you look at it."

Charles glanced back and forth between the two of them, then settled his gaze on Cassie. "If he's Angel, what's R. J. got to do with this?"

"It was his idea," Cassie explained. "The truth is, R. J. sort of insisted at gunpoint." Then she sighed loudly. "It's going to take a while to sort it all out for you, Papa. Why don't you wait for me downstairs? I'll join you as soon as I get dressed."

216

Charles didn't move for a moment. Finally he looked pointedly at Angel. "Are you coming?"

There was another long moment of silence while Angel debated how much argument he'd get if he refused. He took the chance that for the time being, the father would give way to the "husband."

"In a minute," Angel said.

It was a few more seconds before Charles nodded and left the room. Angel immediately looked toward Cassie, and they ended up staring at each other for nearly a full minute, both poignantly aware that their time here was at an end.

She finally glanced away to say, "He won't like it none, but there's nothing he can or will do about it at this point. He's not a violent man. My mama would want to go over and cut R. J. into little pieces if she knew about it, but that's not my papa's way."

Angel accepted that. She knew her parent better than he did. "Hold off on filing for that divorce, Cassie, until you know, one way or the other."

It was as if her father hadn't intruded. They were both still attuned to the last subject they'd been on before the interruption.

"I'll wait until I get home before I do anything," she assured him.

"And you'll let me know?"

"When you get the divorce papers, you'll know," was all she said.

"Fair enough."

Her eyes swung back to him, wide, almost glassy. "Are — are you leaving now?"

He didn't notice the catch in her voice. He'd already turned toward the door. "I've got one more thing to do before I head out. I'll see you tonight."

The door closed on him, but she had a reprieve. A few hours more. Time enough for her to think seriously about burying her pride and asking him to stay.

Chapter 25

It was approaching the hour for turning in, but Cassie made no move to leave the parlor. She hadn't seen Angel again that day, but he'd said she would tonight, and she wasn't going to bed until she did.

Her father sat with her in companionable silence. It had taken most of the morning to explain everything to him. He'd been shocked and amazed by turns, then had gotten furious at R. J. for coming down on her so hard. He'd told her she didn't have to leave, that he'd take the Mac-Kauleys on, and the Catlins, too, if it came to that. Of course she couldn't let him. She'd already caused enough trouble.

Thankfully, he hadn't asked again what Angel had been doing in her bedroom that morning once he'd learned the marriage was only temporary. But she knew what he was doing, sitting up with her. He might not have said anything about it, but he had no intention of leaving her alone with Angel again, much as she wished he would. And he'd been tired that morning, after riding on ahead of his men, who weren't expected to arrive until tomorrow with his new bull. But he'd slept all afternoon, so exhaustion wasn't going to get her a few minutes alone with Angel, either.

Cassie tensed when she heard the front door open and close. She'd have to ask her papa for a few minutes of privacy. He probably wouldn't allow it, but she'd ask anyway. Only it wasn't Angel who was drawn to the lights and warmth in the parlor. Looking even more exhausted and bedraggled than Charles had that morning, Catherine Stuart appeared in the doorway.

"Am I in Texas, or did that storm I left up north blow me back to Wyoming?"

Catherine was referring to the house, which she hadn't seen before, and how closely it resembled the house on the Lazy S. But she didn't get an answer. Cassie was temporarily speechless. Charles wouldn't have answered in any case, but all he could do at the moment was stare.

Catherine did some of that herself as soon as her eyes lit on him. They each had ten years of changes in their appearances to take note of, and they did so with blatant curiosity.

They were still staring at each other when Cassie finally found her voice. "Mama, what are you doing here?"

"You must be joking," Catherine replied, and came over to give her daughter a hug. "After you practically dared me to come?"

"I did no such thing," Cassie protested, trying to remember what she'd put in that last letter to her mother. "I invited you, didn't I?"

"In such a way that would guarantee I wouldn't accept. But you forget I know you better than anyone else, baby. And I wasn't going to wait until you got home to find out why you *didn't* want me down here."

220

Cassie winced. So much for attempting deviousness that wasn't in her nature. And she should have figured this would happen when her mama hadn't written back or telegraphed again. She'd hoped that meant she wouldn't come, but she should have known better. And now she also remembered what her mama had threatened to do.

"You — ah — didn't bring an army with you, did you?" Cassie asked.

"Just a few hands."

"How many's a few?"

"Fifteen," Catherine said as she moved closer to the fire. She took off her hat, then gave Charles a brief glance before she whacked it against her riding skirt, creating a small cloud of dust that settled on his Oriental rug. "I left them in town for the time being."

Watching her mother, Cassie groaned inwardly. It was starting already, the little things her parents did to irritate each other. They didn't even try to be subtle about it because they knew neither one would say anything — at least not to each other. After ten years' separation, you'd think they would have forgotten about that particular aspect of their rift. But no, it was as if they'd never been parted.

"I'm sorry to say you've come all this way for nothing, Mama. I was leaving tomorrow."

"Then your problem did right itself?"

"With a little help from my guardian angel."

"Well, I'm sorry I didn't arrive in time, but at least Mr. Pickens did. And I'm delighted to have you come home — but why are you cutting your visit short?"

221

"You could say I've worn out my welcome in these parts," Cassie replied, trying not to sound dismal about it. Explaining about Lewis Pickens's substitute could wait.

"If you want to stay, baby, I'll see to it," was Catherine's response.

Cassie quickly shook her head. "Papa already offered, but I don't want to cause any more trouble. It'd be better all around if I go home."

"Your papa actually offered to do something?"

There was too much derision in that question, not to mention feigned incredulity, for Charles to remain quiet. "You can tell your mama, Cassie, that I can take care of my daughter's problems just as well as she can."

"And you can tell your papa I said, 'Ha!' " Catherine shot back.

Cassie looked at her parents with exasperation. When she was ten years old, their talking through her had seemed like a game. Now it seemed pretty ridiculous. Why hadn't she ever tried to do something about it?

"Hell and you weren't kidding, were you, honey?" another voice asked.

Cassie turned to see Angel in the open doorway, leaning against the frame, his arms crossed, his hat pushed back from his forehead and hooked on at the neck. He had on his yellow slicker. She was dying to know where he'd been, but . . .

"This isn't a good time," she was forced to say instead.

"This is the only time," he replied. "Fact is, your reunion will have to wait."

"Don't I know you, young man?" Catherine asked.

Angel nodded. "Yes, ma'am. We met a few years back. Name's Angel."

Catherine's surprise was evident. "That's right, you worked on the Rocky Valley spread for a while, didn't you? But what brings you this far south?"

Angel's eyes met Cassie's briefly before he answered, "Looking after your daughter as a favor to Lewis Pickens."

Catherine glanced at Cassie. "But I thought —"

"Mr. Pickens couldn't make it, Mama, so he sent Angel — and what can't wait?"

The question was for Angel, and he abandoned his casual pose to reply, "You need to come with me."

"Where?"

"Out to the barn."

That wasn't exactly what Cassie was expecting — hoping — to hear. "What's in the barn?"

"Some friends of yours, prepared to listen to you meddle one more time."

Her eyes flared wide in understanding. "You didn't! Both of them?"

"And then some."

"Could you two maybe talk in plain English?" Catherine interjected at that point.

"Angel has managed to bring some MacKauleys and Catlins together under one roof so I can talk to them," Cassie explained, and to Angel she added, "That *is* why you did it, isn't it?"

"Figured I owed you that," was all he said.

Cassie blushed and smiled at the same time

— until another question occurred to her. "Did they come willingly?"

"I wasn't going to waste my time asking."

"Now just a minute," Catherine demanded. "Are you saying you brought these people here — at what? — gunpoint?"

Angel shrugged. "With this bunch, there wasn't any other way, ma'am. You folks can come along or not, but Cassie has to come with me. And I reckon this is going to take some time, so don't expect her back for a while."

Charles finally spoke up. "You're out of your head if you think I'm going to let you go off alone with my daughter, for whatever reason. Besides, I've got a thing or two to say to R. J. myself. Cassie, tell your mama there's no need to wait up for us. She can make herself at home."

"Cassie, tell your papa *he's* out of his head if he thinks I'm staying behind," Catherine retorted.

Cassie didn't follow either order, but Angel issued a warning. "You enter that barn, folks, you'll be playing by my rules. There won't be no leaving until I say so. And I'll take your gun, Mrs. Stuart. Mine is the only one that will be needed tonight."

Catherine conceded that much, handing her weapon over, but she whispered in an aside to Cassie, "Just what does he think he owes you that he's breaking the law for?"

"It's personal, Mama."

At which point silver eyes the same color as Cassie's narrowed. "Am I going to have to shoot him before we leave here, baby?"

224

Cassie wished her mama weren't serious, but she knew she was. "Please don't go jumping to conclusions," she told her. "I'll explain everything once this is over."

"It better be good, because I don't think I like that young man."

Cassie wished she still felt that way, too.

Chapter 26

Angel handed Cassie a knife as soon as they entered the barn. With several lanterns burning, she saw at a glance why a knife was needed. The look she gave Angel was definitely full of reproach.

He merely shrugged indifferently, saying, "Did you really think they'd be sitting around chewing the fat, just waiting for you?"

"I suppose not, but this isn't going to make them very open-minded."

"They won't be leaving until they are."

"Do you expect me to shove common sense down their throats?"

He actually grinned at her. "I expect you'll give it a good try."

She grinned back, because she would. But first she had some neighbors to cut loose. Her mother helped, since Angel hadn't taken her only weapon. She still had a hunting knife she wore strapped to her boot, and she used it to release the Mac-Kauleys. Cassie went straight to Jenny.

"I'm sorry about this," she told her friend as she cut through the rope on her wrists.

"What's going on?" was the first thing Jenny asked as soon as she pulled the gag out of her mouth.

"Angel heard me make that wish the other day

and decided to grant it for me."

"It won't work, Cassie."

"Let's hope you're wrong. Do you want to do the honors?" Cassie nodded toward Dorothy.

"I'd better. She's liable to come loose taking a swing at you."

Dorothy wasn't quite that enraged, but she was definitely put out at being there. Embarrassment had a great deal to do with that, however, since Angel had collected her right out of her bed. She was in her nightgown, her blond hair loose and flowing around her. She actually looked years younger, and to a woman like Dorothy, who was used to wielding complete authority, that put her at a disadvantage and she knew it. But there was another consequence she hadn't even noticed yet. R. J. couldn't seem to take his eyes off her.

He'd also been taken from his bed and was in his long underwear, red in color, but that wouldn't bother a man like R. J. It was getting caught so unawares that had him steaming, and the fact that he was without a weapon, while Angel stood in front of the closed barn door, arms crossed, looking relaxed and removed from what was going to happen, but with his Colt in plain view to say otherwise.

The only MacKauleys and Catlins not present were Buck and Richard, who'd both been inaccessible due to having bed companions whom Angel hadn't wanted to involve. Frazer came loose laughing, and was in fact the first one to say anything.

"I gotta hand it to you, Miss Cassie. Things

sure have been interestin' since you showed up this time."

His humor, as usual, got her dander up. "It wasn't my intention to entertain you, Frazer."

"Guess you just can't help it, huh?"

She ignored that. R. J. didn't. "Close it up, Frazer," his father ordered, and said to Cassie, with all the belligerence he was capable of, "What in hell's tarnation are you up to this time, little girl?"

Catherine, just finishing slashing through Morgan's bonds, looked up to say, "Watch your tone when you talk to my daughter, mister."

"*Your* daughter? Well, don't that beat all. You're a mite late, lady, in showin' up to take your girl in hand. You damn well shoulda —"

R. J. didn't get any further. "You'll watch your tone when you talk to my wife *and* my daughter," Charles said as he stepped up to R. J. and planted a fist in his mouth.

The larger man staggered back two steps, shook his head once, then eyed Cassie's father with surprised reproach. "Now what'd you wanna go and do that for, Charley? I thought we were friends."

"After what you did to my daughter? You'll be lucky if I don't tear you apart."

"What'd I do except hurry along what she was plannin' anyway?"

Hearing that, Frazer fell back onto a bale of hay, giving in to silent laughter. Only Cassie noticed, but didn't have time to spare him a look of disgust. She thought she'd talked her papa out of taking on R. J. Apparently not, and their fighting wasn't what she'd wanted to accomplish here.

"Papa —"

He didn't hear her because he said at the same time, "What she was planning doesn't matter, R. J., and you damn well know it."

R. J. held up a hand when Charles took another step in his direction. "Now, come on, Charley. I don't want to have to hurt you."

It was indicative of R. J.'s confidence that he'd put it that way, and of Charles's anger that he didn't care. Charles raised his fist again, R. J. took a stance to block him, and Angel fired a shot into the roof above their heads.

A cloud of dust and wood splinters filtered down on the two men as they and everyone else turned toward the entrance. Angel was calmly slipping his gun back into its holster.

"I'm right sorry to spoil your fun," he said in his slow drawl, "but if any violence is going to be committed here, it'll come from me." He looked directly at Charles to add, "If what MacKauley did was worth a fight, I'd have killed him already, so let it go, Mr. Stuart. For the time being, Cassie's my responsibility, not yours, and all she wants is to say a few words to these folks."

Charles lowered his fist and nodded grudgingly, though he gave R. J. a this-isn't-finished look before he turned away. In the meantime, Catherine came up beside Cassie. "It appears something important didn't get mentioned to me before I was invited to join this little party," she said. "Would you mind telling me what your papa is so riled about, and why that hired gun thinks you're *his* responsibility?"

"He's my husband," Cassie said in a whisper.

"He's your *what?*" Catherine shrieked.

"Mama, please, this isn't the time to explain."

"Like hell it isn't!"

"Mama, please!"

Catherine would have said more, a lot more, but Cassie's expression stopped her. It wasn't a pleading look she was getting, but one of stubborn determination that Catherine wasn't used to seeing in her daughter. Cassie simply wasn't going to discuss it now, no matter what Catherine said.

She wasn't used to giving in, either, but in this case she did — for the moment. "All right, but as soon as you're done here, we talk."

"Fair enough," Cassie replied, and turned to look at R. J. and Dorothy. She took a deep breath before she said to them, "I tried to apologize before, but I won't again, because my intentions were good whether you think so or not. I thought a marriage between your two families would end the animosity you've been living with for so long. It should have — but you won't let it, will you? And what's ironic is you've both raised your children to hate and they don't even know why. Why don't you tell them why?"

R. J. went red in the face to be put on the spot like that. Dorothy turned her face away, refusing flat out to discuss the feud or anything else.

Cassie sighed. "You're mighty stubborn, both of you, but haven't you realized yet that that stubbornness is now hurting your children — at least Jenny and Clayton? If you folks would just leave them alone, they could end up with a happy marriage. Haven't you figured out yet that they're both miserable right now?"

"My boy ain't miserable," R. J. blustered. "And you ain't got nothing to say that I want to hear, little girl, so tell that husband of yours to open up that door."

"Not yet, Mr. MacKauley. You forced a wedding on me. I'm just forcing a little conversation on you."

R. J.'s answer was to turn his back on her, making Cassie grit her teeth in exasperation. But she'd known what she was up against. She'd never met anyone so bullheaded, so unreasonable, so plain-out ornery. But before she could even think of what to say that might break through his obstinacy, Dorothy Catlin spoke, and there was no doubt that she'd been caught by surprise from what she'd just heard.

"R. J., you didn't. Again? You made the same stupid mistake again?"

"Now, Dotty," R. J. began in what was clearly an attempt to placate, but he didn't get far.

"Don't you 'now, Dotty' me, you sorry son of a bitch. Tell me you didn't arrange another wedding with a gun in your hand. Go on, tell me."

"It wasn't the same, dammit," R. J. protested. "She claimed he was her fiancé."

"And you believed that?" Dorothy exclaimed incredulously. "An innocent thing like her and a ruthless killer?"

Angel winced. Cassie cringed. The MacKauley boys were staring at the arguing pair in wide-eyed amazement, including Frazer, who couldn't find anything funny about *this* — yet. But Jenny Catlin was getting mad, as certain things she'd heard over the years started clicking together.

"What do you mean *again*, Ma?" Jenny asked as she left Clayton's side — no one had got around to untying him, so she had done it — and confronted her mother. "Who else did he force to get married?"

Dorothy's fury was quickly replaced with defensiveness. "It's not important."

"Isn't it? It was you, wasn't it?"

"Jenny —"

But Jenny was standing her ground for once. "I want to know what's keepin' me from my husband, Ma. You've put me off every time I've ever asked, but not this time. It *was* you, wasn't it? Is that what started this feud?"

Dorothy actually looked to R. J. for help. When Jenny saw that, she exploded. "Dammit, I've got a right to know! My *baby* has a right to know!"

"Your baby?"

Three people said it. Clayton added a whoop to his and rushed forward to swing Jenny around in his arms. She hadn't meant to tell him this way. Actually, she hadn't thought she'd get a chance to tell him. And his happiness dissolved some of her anger with their parents.

"A baby," R. J. repeated and sat down on a wooden crate to digest the news. "If that don't beat all." And then he caught Dorothy's shocked expression and grinned. "Did you hear that, Dotty? We're going to share a grandbaby."

Dorothy gave him a narrow-eyed look. "Who

said anything about sharing? Your boy can come and live at my place."

"Like hell!" R. J. shot back onto his feet. "Your girl will be havin' that baby at my place, or I'll —" He had to stop, since there simply wasn't a threat appropriate to this particular situation that he could think of.

Dorothy took advantage of his pause to advance on him. "So *now* she's welcome?"

R. J. ignored that and stubbornly insisted, "A wife's place is with her husband."

Dorothy reached him and poked a finger so hard in his chest that he was pushed back down on the wooden crate. "Not if she's divorced it ain't."

"Oh, hell, Dotty, you can't still —"

"Can't I?"

"Both of you stop it," Jenny said as she pushed back from Clayton, though he retained an arm around her waist, clearly indicating they were a united front. "Where I have this baby is up to me, and I might not be having it in Texas at all if I don't get some answers. The truth, Ma, and no more sidestepping 'round it."

Dorothy had turned around to face her daughter. R. J. grumbled behind her back, "Where the hell did she get so much gumption?"

"Where the hell do you think?" Dorothy replied for his ears only, before she squared her shoulders and started the explanation her daughter was demanding. "We were in love, that old coot and me."

It was too much for Frazer, whose humor returned with a vengeance. Morgan leaned over to shut him up with a kick. That didn't work, so Clayton went over and socked him one.

That got the quiet back, long enough for Jenny to express everyone's amazement. "Not you and R. J.!"

"Yes, me and R. J.," Dorothy said in pure disgruntlement. "Now, do you want to hear this or not?"

"I won't interrupt again," Jenny assured her.

"We were supposed to get married —"

"You and *R. J.?*"

"Jenny!"

"Well, I can't help it, Ma. You hate that man."

"I didn't always," Dorothy said defensively. "There was a time when I would have shot the son of a bitch if he even looked at another woman. Trouble was, he was more crazy jealous than I was. And one day he came by and saw me sitting on the porch with my pa's foreman, Ned Catlin. I was patting his hand in sympathy 'cause he'd just had word that his ma had died and he was real broke up about it.

"R. J. jumped to the wrong conclusion, though, and went off and got drunk, so drunk he came back that night and took me and Ned to the church, where he forced us to marry. He had some crazy idea about making me a wife and a widow in one day, only he passed out before he got around to the widow-making part. And Ned wasn't exactly as honest as the day is long. He didn't mind marrying me at all, not when it promoted him from foreman to boss, giving him a share of the profits from the ranch. He wouldn't give me a divorce even though he knew

234

I didn't love him and never would.

"It didn't end there. R. J. stayed drunk for a couple of months, and he started taking potshots at Ned whenever he saw him. 'Course drunk, he can't even hit the side of a barn. But Ned got annoyed enough to start shooting back. He was a bit luckier and hit R. J. once."

"You call shootin' me in my foot lucky?" R. J. interjected.

Dorothy ignored that, continuing. "That's when R. J. started sobering up and got serious about killing my husband. Ned figured since I didn't want him around anyway, it'd be healthier if he took off. Only he got my pa all fired up before he left, enough for him to file charges against R. J. But all that did was embarrass R. J. and turn him meaner.

"That's when he married my best friend, thinking that would hurt me. I'll admit it did, particularly when she got pregnant so fast. I had a husband I couldn't get a divorce from, and R. J. was starting a family. I started hating him then.

"And Ned, he only came home when he ran short of money. But he never stayed long because as soon as R. J. found out he was back, the damn shooting would start up again."

"I know Pa was never around," Jenny said, speaking quietly now. "But how come you never told us he was such a bastard?"

"Because I had reason to be grateful to him, Jen. He didn't come around often, but each time he did, he left me with a baby. And the ranch and you children were all I had to live for. Besides, he never would have got so greedy if R. J. hadn't shoved temptation his way. Ned was a hard worker and a good foreman before that."

A heavy silence followed. R. J. was the one to break it. "Christ, that ain't the way I remember it, Dotty."

She turned around to give him a level look. "I'm not surprised. You were never sober long enough back then to remember much of anything."

"If that's the way it happened, I think maybe I owe you an apology."

She wasn't impressed. "Is that right?"

He looked distinctly uncomfortable. "Do you — ah — suppose we might put all that behind us and start over?"

"No."

He sighed. "I didn't think so."

"But you can take me to town tomorrow night for dinner and we can discuss it."

Frazer couldn't let that one pass. His laughter started up again. R. J. took off one of his boots and threw it at his eldest.

Dorothy remarked, "That's a strange one you got there, R. J."

"I know it," R. J. grumbled. "Dumb shit would laugh at his own funeral. Come on, Dotty, and I'll escort you home like I used to — that is —" He turned to Cassie. "You got any more conversation to force on us, little girl?"

Cassie was grinning. She couldn't help it. "No, sir. I don't believe there's anything left for me to meddle with in these parts."

Angel had already opened the door and was

standing to the side of it. The chill night air that rushed in wasn't conducive to lingering. R. J. led the way, minus his boot, but stopped next to Angel to give him an appraising look.

"I think you and me can call it even," R. J. said.

"Looks to me like you came out ahead," Angel replied.

R. J. grinned. "Guess I did at that. But satisfy my curiosity, son. How come they call you the Angel of Death?"

"Probably because no one has ever survived a fight with me."

R. J. found that amusing and left chuckling. His sons didn't, and gave Angel a wide berth as they exited. Jenny stopped by Cassie to give her a hug.

"I can't believe this really happened, but thank you," Jenny said.

"You know what they say about love and hate. Half the time you can't tell them apart."

"I know, but Ma and R. J.?"

Both girls grinned. "Take care of yourself, Jenny, and your new family."

"I will. And now that everything's changed, you don't have to leave."

"Actually, with my mama showing up, I do. You can't imagine how unpleasant it can get with her and my papa living in the same house."

"But you've got a pocket full of miracles tonight. Why don't you pull another one out?"

"I wish I could, but I just don't have the nerve to meddle in my parents' problems."

"Well, you take care of yourself, and write me."

"I will."

Jenny ran to Clayton, who was waiting for her at the barn entrance. They left arm in arm. Cassie sighed, thinking about what she still had ahead of her. She looked around to find her mama just getting up from a bale of hay. Her papa was leaning against Marabelle's transport cage, but he pushed himself away from it and came toward her now.

"It's nice to know I'm not the only one with dirt in the closet," Catherine remarked snidely as she started toward Cassie, too.

"Your mama has no sense of compassion, and you can tell her I said so," Charles said.

Cassie did no such thing. All she wanted to do was escape to savor her triumph for a while before she had to placate her mama's formidable temper. With that in mind, she didn't wait for her parents, but hurried toward Angel.

"Thank you —" she began, but he cut her off.

"You're not finished yet."

"I'm not?"

"No," he said, and moved to block the entrance just as her parents got there. "You called a cease-fire on your private war twenty years ago," Angel told them. "Maybe you should've fought it out. Would you like to remain in here a little longer?"

"Hell, no," Catherine replied.

"Yes," Charles said, drawing a shocked gasp from his wife and a grin from Angel before he shoved Cassie out the door and shut it behind them.

Of course, Catherine immediately started shouting and banging on the door. Cassie stared at Angel in horror as he dropped the wooden bar into place, locking them in.

"You can't do that," she said.

"I just did."

"But —"

"Shut up, Cassie. There's something about being locked up that brings out the worst — and best — in folks. Let your parents experience it. It could do them a world of good."

"Or they could kill each other."

He chuckled and pulled her into his arms. "Where's that optimism that lets you meddle in everyone's life?"

She didn't get to answer. He kissed her, long and hard, and she was so bemused when he finished, she didn't even notice that the shouting inside the barn had stopped.

"Go on up to the house, honey." Angel pushed her in that direction. "You can let 'em out in the morning."

She went, but only because she expected him to follow. He didn't. He rode out of her life that night.

Chapter 27

Cassie didn't leave Texas the next day as she'd planned. She'd spent the night in a parlor chair, where she'd fallen asleep waiting for Angel to join her. When she woke up with sunshine pouring in through the windows, she first went up to his room. There she found the bed unslept in, his saddlebags missing from the corner where they'd been stacked, and nothing else in the room to say he'd ever been there.

She rushed out to the stable next, but she'd found what she expected to by then. His horse was gone. He was gone. And Cassie sat down and cried.

When she got around to wiping her eyes dry, she decided she wouldn't have had the nerve to ask Angel to stay even if she'd gotten the chance to. Rejection was a horrible thing, after all. She ought to consider herself lucky that she'd avoided it. So why didn't that make her feel better?

She was dragging her feet by the time she reached the barn, though she didn't particularly care what kind of temper her mother was going to be in. She just didn't want to have to talk about Angel again, not now. And she got a short reprieve, but only because her parents were still sleeping — side by side on a bed of hay.

Cassie didn't think anything of their proximity.

She just left them there with the doors unlocked and went back to the house. But by the time she'd bathed and changed into fresh clothes, her mother was knocking on her door.

"That was a rotten thing to do to your mama, Cassie," were Catherine's first words.

"I know," Cassie replied dispassionately, and dropped into her reading chair. "I should have locked me and Angel in the barn instead."

"Oh, no. Your papa has the right idea. You're not going to be left alone with that man again."

"You don't have to worry about it," Cassie said in a quiet voice, raising her knees to rest her chin on. "He's already left."

"Good."

"Why 'good'? You don't even know him, Mama."

"Of course I do," Catherine replied. "Who in Wyoming doesn't know him?"

"You're talking about his reputation. You don't know what he's really like."

"And I don't intend to find out. Your papa told me what happened. I just —"

Cassie looked up in surprise. "You and Papa talked to each other?"

"Don't change the subject," Catherine replied sternly. "I just have one question for you. Why on earth did you tell those people he was your fiancé?"

"Because he was about to tell them who he really was, and tempers were too high at the time. I was afraid they'd get the wrong idea, and think I hired him to fight them."

"Which is what you should have done. That's

what he does, after all."

"Mama, I started the whole thing," Cassie said in exasperation.

"And from what I heard last night, you patched it up nicely. Well, never mind about why you ended up getting married. It'll be an easy enough thing to dissolve, and we'll take care of that before we leave Texas."

"No."

Catherine came to stand before her daughter. "What do you mean *no?*"

Cassie dropped her head back on her knees. "I promised Angel I'd wait until I got back home — in case there's a baby to consider."

"A — oh, God, why do I suddenly feel like that poor woman from last night — what was her name? Dotty?"

"Dorothy Catlin," Cassie said. "But it's only a possibility, Mama."

"Only?" Catherine bent over until their heads were touching and she could get her arms around Cassie, knees and all. "My poor baby. You're so brave not to cry about it. And why didn't your papa mention that part — or doesn't he know that the man raped you?"

Cassie pushed herself back to say indignantly, "Mama, he did no such thing."

"He didn't?" Catherine said in confusion, then quickly changed her tone. "Well, why the hell not?"

"Obviously because he didn't have to."

Catherine digested that, as well as the dryness it was uttered in, and admonished, "Cassandra Stuart, don't you dare sit there and tell me —"

242

"Mama, it's too late for a lecture, don't you think?"

Catherine was forced to concede that point. "I suppose it is." Then she sighed. "Oh, baby, what possessed you to make such a fool mistake?"

"He wanted me," Cassie said simply. "And that's all that mattered to me at the time — well, there was the little fact that I wanted him, too."

"I don't think I want to hear this."

"I'd rather not talk about it myself," Cassie said dismally. "I can't even figure out *why* he wanted me."

Catherine took exception to that. "Nonsense. You're a beautiful girl. Why wouldn't he want you?"

Cassie waved a dismissive hand. "You're my mama. Of course you'd say that. But I'm well aware that men don't find me very attractive."

Catherine grinned. "And that bothers you?"

"It's not amusing, Mama."

"Actually, it is, because when I was your age I thought the exact same thing. I didn't have a single suitor, even though there was no end of eligible young men in my town. Then suddenly I had, not one, but three suitors who were so serious in their efforts to win me that it became embarrassing. I couldn't go anywhere that one or two of them didn't show up, sometimes all three.

"There was a lot of bickering and jealousy, even though these men happened to be lifelong friends. It finally escalated into an actual fight, with one of them taking on the other two — at the same time. He just barely won, but I

243

thought it was so romantic, I accepted his proposal that very day. That was your papa."

"That's hardly the same thing as my case, Mama. You happen to be a beautiful woman."

"And you still think you aren't? Well, let me tell you a secret, baby, a confession your papa once made to me. He said that I grew on him, that one day he noticed that I was prettier than he'd thought. You see, we'd known each other for years, and he'd never paid any attention to me before then. He also said that every time he saw me after that, I kept getting prettier, until finally he thought I was the most beautiful woman he'd ever seen."

"Are you pulling my leg, Mama?"

"I wouldn't do that. I'm trying to tell you that your looks are just unusual and take a bit of time getting used to, same as mine used to be. As I got older, my features filled out and sort of settled into more traditional lines. I expect yours will, too, and it won't be much longer before men find you lovely when they first meet you, not weeks later."

Cassie couldn't help laughing. "That's a nice story, Mama, but I'm not buying."

"No? Well, I reckon that gunfighter was around you long enough for you to start looking mighty pretty to him. You can't figure out why he wanted you? My guess is the man couldn't help himself."

Cassie blushed at that, but only because she so wished it were true. Of course it wasn't, and it didn't matter now anyway.

She said as much. "It doesn't matter now. He's gone and he expects me to divorce him."

"And we certainly won't disappoint him," Catherine said firmly.

It was obvious her mama didn't like Angel, but that last crack rubbed Cassie wrong. She wanted a change of subject, and knew exactly how to get it.

"So what did you and Papa find to talk about after twenty years?"

"None of your business," Catherine replied and left before Cassie could probe further.

Chapter 28

Cassie never did find out what happened between her parents in the barn that night — or if anything *did* happen. Her mama simply wouldn't talk about it. Her papa just teased her, saying they'd stopped acting like children, whatever that meant. But they did seem to have a truce of some sort going on. At least they continued to talk to each other. Nothing of a personal nature, at least not that Cassie heard, but it was communication: cautious, hesitant, as if they'd just met each other for the first time, but definite communication.

Catherine even insisted on holding off her and Cassie's departure until after the holidays, so for the first time in ten years, Cassie got to spend Christmas with both of her parents. And she got to see Jenny once more at church services. Jenny had already moved in with her husband — R. J. had gotten his way in that — and she claimed the MacKauley men were treating her like a queen. It had been quite a few years since a woman had ruled the roost in that household, so things promised to be interesting there for a while.

Of course, R. J. and Dorothy were presently the talk of the town. Mabel Koch stopped by to tell Cassie, in case she hadn't heard, about their being seen having dinner together, and that they'd stayed so late, they hadn't gone home that night. They'd taken two rooms at the hotel, but Mabel insinuated only one had been needed.

Catherine had laughed for a half hour after hearing that. With all Cassie had been through, she hadn't found it so funny herself. But ironically, the neighbors weren't mad at her anymore. R. J. even sent by a brief note. "Feel free to meddle in my town anytime." Cassie didn't find that funny, either. The fact was, she wasn't finding humor in much of anything these days.

She missed Angel.

When Catherine caught her seriously moping about it, she decided they'd go on a shopping spree back east before returning home, maybe all the way to New York this time.

"Let's make it St. Louis instead," Cassie impulsively suggested.

"Whatever you like, baby. And we can see a lawyer about filing for that divorce while we're there. No point in letting all of Wyoming know about it if we don't have to."

Cassie said nothing to that, but she'd felt like asking, "If you're so divorce-happy, how come you never got one for yourself?" But that wouldn't have been very nice — sometimes she wished she weren't so nice. A little mean streak could come in handy when dealing with certain overbearing people.

Her mama meant well, of course; she just had a longtime habit of overprotectiveness and making Cassie's decisions for her. Cassie had never protested because Catherine was happiest when she was controlling things. But it was time Cassie

247

started making a few decisions on her own. Going to St. Louis was one, even if it was spur-of-the-moment.

Sending off a telegram was another, and something she didn't bother to mention to her mama. But she'd had Angel on her mind so much, the idea had just sprung up and wouldn't go away. So she sent off a request to have a Pinkerton detective meet her in St. Louis to find out what, if anything, could be done to locate Angel's parents. She didn't think he'd ever try again himself, after all, and it was just the sort of thing that appealed to her meddling nature, the reuniting of a long-lost family.

Cassie and Catherine left Caully a few days after the new year began. With everything turning out so surprisingly well where Charles's neighbors were concerned, Cassie knew she could come back for another visit next fall if she wanted to. What she hadn't expected was her papa's parting remark, that he'd probably be coming north himself for a visit in a month or two — and her mama's secret smile when she heard him say that.

Obviously, something *had* happened in that barn. And unraveling the mystery of it was just what Cassie needed at the moment to take her mind off Angel. Not that she had been successful so far in getting any information out of her mama. Perhaps she'd just been going about it the wrong way.

She remembered being so amazed when she'd first realized that the Catlin and the MacKauley children didn't know what had started the feud they were so deeply involved in. But Cassie was so used to not meddling in her parents' lives that it hadn't occurred to her at the time that she was just as ignorant of what had caused her own parents' rift. She decided to start with that.

But a crowded stagecoach was no place to have a private discussion, so Cassie waited until they reached the rail lines farther east, which offered much more comfort in traveling and some relative privacy. In fact, she began her conversation in the dining car their first day on the train, deliberately lingering over dessert and coffee until the tables around them had vacated.

By then, more than a week since leaving Caully, Cassie was eager to try out her new strategy. Innocently she asked her mother, "How come you and Papa stopped loving each other?"

Catherine nearly choked on her last bite of cherry cobbler. "What kind of question is that?"

Cassie shrugged. "Probably one I should have asked a long time ago."

"Your little party in your papa's barn that night has made you bold, Cassie — or should I say impertinent?"

"Do you think so? I do try —"

"Don't you dare be catty with me, young lady."

"Then don't be evasive, Mama. It was a simple question, and one I figure I have a right to ask."

"It's too . . . personal."

Catherine was still evading. Cassie knew the signs. She wasn't giving up this time.

"I'm not some nosy neighbor. I'm your daughter. He's *my* papa. I should have been told a long time ago what happened, Mama. Why did you stop loving him?"

Catherine looked out the window at the dull winter landscape that held little of interest. Cassie knew from experience that she wouldn't get another word out of her. That was her mama's way. If she couldn't intimidate people to end whatever they were doing to bother her, she simply ignored them.

So Cassie was amazed when a few moments later her mama said, "I never stopped loving him."

Cassie could have imagined a dozen answers. None of them would have been that one. In fact, she was so incredulous, not a single reply came to mind.

Catherine was still looking out the window, but she could guess at the shock she'd just caused. "I know it probably never seemed that way," she said.

"There's no 'probably' about it. There isn't a single person who knows you, Mama, who ever doubted how much you two hated each other. I don't understand."

"I know you don't. I don't, either, to tell you the truth." Catherine sighed. "Anger can be a powerful thing. So is fear. Both can make you do things you wouldn't ordinarily do. And both had control of me for a long time."

Cassie couldn't accept that, either. "Fear, Mama? We're talking about the woman who stood out in the middle of the street in Cheyenne, without cover, with bullets flying every which way, and shot two out of four bank robbers, one of whom happened to be holding the money they'd just stolen. You can't tell me you're not one of

250

the most fearless women I know."

Catherine finally looked across the table, her lips turned up in a half smile. "I had a lot of money in that bank. I wasn't going to see it ride out of town if I could prevent it. But I never said I was afraid of dying."

"Then what were you afraid of?"

"Cassie —"

Cassie knew that tone and quickly said, "You can't stop now, Mama. It'll drive me crazy if I don't hear the rest of it."

Catherine gave her an exasperated look. "You get that stubbornness from your papa."

"I get it from you."

Catherine sighed again. "All right, but first you need to know how much I wanted children. After your papa and I married, I used to cry every month when — when I knew I wasn't pregnant yet. Then when it did finally happen, I was the happiest woman alive. I think I went around with a smile on my face those whole nine months."

Cassie found *that* hard to believe, too, since it was rare that her mama ever smiled. "What's that got to do with being afraid?"

"That came after. You see, I didn't know what it was going to be like, the birthing. My mama had died when I was young, so she never told me. Your papa and I had only just moved to Wyoming, so I didn't have many women friends who might have warned me. And I'd never witnessed an actual birthing. I was so ignorant, I thought I was losing you when my water broke. But then the pain started.

"You wouldn't know it to look at you, but

the doctor told me afterward that you were one of the biggest babies he'd ever delivered. It took nearly two days. During that time, I thought I was going to die at least a dozen times. Fact is, I wanted to. Even the doc gave up on me at one point, I got so weak. But somehow you got born. I don't remember exactly how. I was out of my mind with the pain by then.

"And there were complications after. I'd been pretty ripped up. The bleeding wouldn't stop . . . now don't look like that." Cassie had gone quite pale. "It wasn't your fault. If you want to know the truth, I wouldn't have fought to recover if it weren't for you."

"But, Mama —"

"No *buts*," Catherine interrupted sternly. "You see now why I didn't want to tell you? But it certainly wasn't your fault, and you have to believe me, baby, I never once blamed you. I did, however, blame your papa. I know I shouldn't have. Things like that just happen. It's no one's fault. But that's not the way my mind was working back then."

Catherine suddenly laughed, though it was a bitter sound. "To this day I wonder if things would have been different if what I'd learned afterward would have come my way just a little sooner. My, how quickly ignorance can end, whether you want it to or not.

"It's amazing. Another woman sees you with a baby, even one who doesn't know you, and they start telling you all about their own birth experiences. All the things I should have been warned about beforehand that might have pre-

252

pared me better, I was told about after, that the first baby is always the hardest, that the pain is soon forgotten, that women with narrow hips like me usually have an even more difficult time of it — things like that, and, unanimously, that it's worth it.

"I agree wholeheartedly with the last. I've never regretted for a minute having you, Cassie. But after what I went through, I wasn't going to have any more children if I could help it, and I could. I told your papa I'd shoot him if he even thought about climbing into my bed again."

Cassie's eyes widened. "I don't suppose he took too kindly to that?"

"I reckon he didn't."

"And that's it?"

"Only what started it. You see, I didn't ask him to give me time. I said flat out never again. And he was extremely patient in the beginning, thinking I'd change my mind. I might have — the memory of that pain really does diminish. But eight months went by and he finally blew up about it.

"I suppose I can't blame him now, though I sure did at the time. I don't know. I guess the way I was thinking was that if I was never going to make love again, he could damn well abstain, too. That was unrealistic of me, I know. But I was young and emotional, and like I said, my mind wasn't working quite right back then."

"Then that's what did it, his getting angry?"

"No, what did it was my finding out he went to Gladis's place."

Cassie knew about Gladis's place. It had burned

down about seven years ago and Gladis had moved on to some other town. But in its day it had been one of the finest whorehouses in Wyoming. To this day men still talked about Gladis's place — and Cassie just couldn't picture her papa going there.

"Are you sure?" she asked.

" 'Course I am. You don't think I'd end a marriage on mere suspicions, do you? There was this man lived in Cheyenne back then. I don't remember his name now, but he'd taken a fancy to me and was always teasing me about when I was going to leave your papa for him. He even pestered me when I was full-blown pregnant. Well, he figured he was doing me a favor by telling me that half the town had seen Charles visiting that brothel."

"Some favor," Cassie remarked dryly.

"I agree. If I recall right, I think I broke two knuckles on his jaw to thank him. And I never did see him again. But anyhow, I was mad enough when I confronted your papa and he admitted it that I told him to get out. He wouldn't. So I told him never to speak to me again."

"And he didn't — nor did you."

"I can't help my temper, Cassie," Catherine said defensively. "I'm an unforgiving woman. I know it. What that Dotty woman said is perfectly true. Your papa's lucky I didn't shoot him for what he did. I did go to Gladis's late one night to find out who he was visiting there. Her I would have shot. But Gladis protected her girls real good. She wouldn't tell me."

"Yet you say you never stopped loving him,"

Cassie reminded her.

"I can't help that, either. And I know that I drove him to it, but I just couldn't forgive something like that. The fear and the anger — they're a terrible combination. Don't ever let them get hold of you like they did me."

Cassie shook her head in bemusement. For it to have been something as simple as jealousy. She wished she didn't sympathize with both sides, but she did. There were simply no winners in that sort of situation. Yet they were talking now, she reminded herself. Something had gotten them beyond that long bout of anger.

"Mama, what happened in the barn that night?"

"None of your business."

After everything Catherine had just revealed, Cassie had to laugh at that answer. And she retained her good humor until a few hours later. It was that evening when she discovered that she had no reason to deny Angel his divorce. She wasn't pregnant.

Chapter 29

With a population of over three hundred thousand, St. Louis was right up there with Philadelphia and New York City in size. Though Catherine preferred Chicago for their annual shopping excursions, they had come to St. Louis twice over the years.

Their last visit had been back in '75, not long after the completion of the East Bridge, which crossed the Mississippi. The suburbs had expanded greatly since then. In fact, the whole city had grown noticeably in the past six years. But Catherine was a creature of habit. Wherever they went, she always stayed in the same hotels, which were usually the best the cities had to offer, not necessarily the newest.

So Cassie had assumed they would be staying at the same hotel as they had before, and that was where she had asked the detective from the renowned Pinkerton agency to find her. She only hoped he could do so without alerting her mama to what she was up to.

Catherine hadn't mentioned seeing a lawyer again, but Cassie knew she would just as soon as she got bored with her shopping. That would give Cassie about a week, maybe two, to decide what *she* was going to do about a divorce. Of course, there was nothing really to decide. She had to get one. She had no reason not to now. Just because she might like to stay married to the husband she'd unexpectedly gotten didn't mean she could.

He'd have something to say about it, and none of it would be nice. Her mama would have a fit, too, if Cassie even hinted that she liked Angel enough to keep him. All the reasons would be trotted out why he wasn't suitable for a husband. Cassie didn't want to hear them. She already knew them, and they had nothing to do with feelings.

The old-timers in the city were predicting snow any day now, but the sun continued to shine. It didn't warm things up much — St. Louis in January was more what Cassie was accustomed to in winter than Texas was — but it made getting around the city much more pleasant than snow would have. And they didn't have far to go. It hadn't been hard to find the most highly rec-ommended dressmaker in town. She still hap-pened to be Madame Cecilia, the same one they'd used before, and her shop was located only a few blocks from the hotel. They'd even walked there a few times when the wind wasn't too brisk.

This afternoon, for the fourth visit and last fitting, Catherine hired a carriage. Cassie would have preferred to walk, since she didn't feel like participating in her mama's usual chatter. She was brooding again. They'd been in the city for five days now, but the Pinkerton man hadn't ar-rived yet. Cassie was already thinking up reasons to delay their departure if he still didn't show up during the next week.

Finding Angel's parents was no longer just a

whim. It had become quite important to her for the simple reason that if she was successful, she'd have a valid excuse not only to see Angel again, but to talk to him. And she wanted that. She could always see him, after all. She imagined she'd be going to Cheyenne a lot more than she ever had before, just to catch glimpses of him. But he wouldn't talk to her unless he had to. She knew that. Even if it wasn't because he wouldn't want to be bothered, which he wouldn't, he'd be thinking of her reputation. They were both well known in their town. There'd be talk of the scandalous sort if she were seen in the company of Cheyenne's notorious Angel.

"You're moping again," Catherine remarked a block away from Madame Cecilia's.

"I'm not."

"You are."

"All right, I miss Marabelle."

The ranch hands whom Catherine had brought with her to Texas, in case she needed a show of force, had taken Marabelle home with them, since fine hotels frowned on putting up pets of that sort. And it was only a half lie of the evasive kind that Cassie had just told. She did miss her pet. She simply missed Angel more.

"I know I wired for our private sleeper car to be transferred here," Catherine said, "but we don't have to wait for it if you want to go home already."

"No!" Cassie said a bit too forcefully. She quickly amended her negative response. "I mean, I can get along without her for a few weeks, and vice versa."

"I'm not so sure about the vice versa," Catherine remarked. "You weren't the one who had to chase her halfway to Denver the first time you visited your papa, and explain to all those good folks along the way that they weren't hunting a wild panther, but my daughter's pet, who didn't know enough to stay home where she didn't scare people half to death."

Cassie grinned, remembering the long, vituperative letter that had accompanied Marabelle to Texas in the large cage Catherine had been forced to have made for her so she could ship her to Cassie. Marabelle had tried to follow Cassie, but had lost her scent after the first train stop across the Colorado border, not halfway to Denver as her mama had exaggerated. But Catherine had most definitely been put out with both daughter and pet at the time.

"She stayed home okay last summer when we went to Chicago," Cassie reminded her.

"We were gone only ten days that time, and she was locked up tight in the barn with a constant companion in old Mac, to keep her from ripping up the walls."

Cassie took exception to that. "She doesn't rip walls, Mama. But if you want to talk about walls and pets, let's talk about Short Tail, your sweet elephant. Do you think the barn will still be standing when we get home?"

Catherine gave her a sour look. "I'm beginning to think that man was a bad influence on you."

"What man?" Cassie asked innocently.

"You know which one," Catherine admonished sternly. "Your impertinence is getting worse."

"I thought it was getting better."

"You see what I mean?"

Cassie rolled her eyes. "Mama, if you haven't noticed lately, I'm all grown up. When are you going to stop treating me like a child?"

"When you're sixty-five and I'm dead, and not a day sooner."

If Catherine hadn't sounded so serious, Cassie wouldn't have laughed. "All right, you win, Mama. I'll keep my impertinence to myself. But could you at least not call me baby in public?"

Catherine's lips twitched slightly. "As long as we're making allowances, I suppose I can manage —"

She didn't get to finish her sentence. Their driver suddenly hauled back on his reins, stopping the carriage and jerking them both nearly out of their seats. A large delivery wagon had come out of a side street and moved in front of them, apparently intending to turn in the opposite direction they were headed. But traffic was heavy going in the opposite direction and its driver couldn't move out into it, so he ended up stuck where he was, blocking their path.

Their driver was angry enough at the near accident he'd had that he started yelling. The other driver looked over at theirs and flipped him a rude gesture, at which point their driver retaliated with a string of curses at the top of his lungs.

Catherine's face went red-hot at some of the words coming out of his mouth that could be heard half a block away. "Close your ears, Cassie," she admonished and tossed a dollar on the driver's seat. "We'll walk."

"But this is just getting interesting," Cassie protested.

"We'll walk," Catherine repeated with more force.

She really was embarrassed. Cassie found that amusing, especially since she'd heard worse out of the cowhands on the Lazy S, and words nearly as bad out of her mama when she was upbraiding those same cowhands about something. But then that was one of Catherine's eccentricities. Unlike Cassie, who only wore her Colt on the ranch, Catherine was never without hers — except when she headed east. Then she turned into a model of fine etiquette and elegance befitting a high-society matron, with an attitude running in the same vein.

It was worth a little teasing. "You know, that wouldn't have happened if Angel were here."

"You're boasting because that man scares people just by looking at them?" Catherine said incredulously.

"I guess I am. That trait of his *would* come in handy on occasion. Imagine how easily you'd get rid of the Misses Potter if Angel walked into the room."

Catherine snorted. "Don't kid yourself. *He'd* be scared off by those two chatterboxes."

"Then there's Willy Gate who harangues you every Sunday with his Civil War stories, and you're too softhearted to ignore him."

"He was a hero — and you wouldn't happen to be hinting that Angel would be nice to have around, would you?"

Catherine's look was so stern, Cassie chose not

to answer. "We're going to be late if we don't hurry," she said as she moved ahead on the crowded sidewalk, leaving no chance for further teasing — or hinting.

A few minutes later they arrived at the dress shop, just in time to be delayed entering by another arrival, that of a well-dressed young gentleman and his overdressed lady friend. The man was so handsome, Cassie couldn't help staring at him. Catherine didn't notice that, but she couldn't help noticing that, after a brief glance at them, the man so dismissed them from his mind that he didn't even hold the door open for them, but followed his companion into the shop.

"Some people have no manners."

Catherine had said it before the door closed behind the man. He heard and turned to give her a disdainful look that had her cheeks glowing. Cassie decided she'd better not mention that that wouldn't have happened, either, if Angel were there.

But their conversation on that subject was too recent, and Catherine glowered at her, warning, "Don't say it."

"I wasn't."

"I've a good mind to complain to Madame Cecilia," Catherine continued, "and take our business elsewhere."

"It's not her fault," Cassie protested.

"Isn't it? When she schedules our fitting at the same time as that loose woman's?"

"What makes you think she isn't a lady?"

"I know a man's mistress when I see one,"

Catherine replied huffily.

Cassie rolled her eyes. "Mama, you're getting all upset over nothing."

"Am I?" Catherine countered. "When you're still thinking about that gunfighter?"

So that's what this was all about? Cassie should have figured her mama wouldn't get that heated up over a little rudeness when they'd encountered much worse before in big cities.

She gave in to avoid an argument. "So I won't mention him again."

"Good. And now I think I'll show that ill-mannered fellow some rudeness of my own — Wyoming style." And as she walked into the dressmakers shop, Cassie heard her add, "I wish to hell my Colt wasn't packed away."

Cassie wished Angel didn't have to be packed away, too.

Chapter 30

That evening, Cassie didn't wait for her mother, who stopped by to compliment the dining room staff on another excellent dinner. She wandered out to the lobby of the hotel, far enough until Catherine could no longer see her, then hurried over to the front desk to find out if any messages had been left for her.

She'd managed to get away from her mother a couple of times each day to check at the desk, even if she had to wait until Catherine retired for the night. Since they had separate, though connecting, rooms, that was easy enough to do, but she didn't like going down to the lobby that late by herself.

Tonight she wouldn't have to, or so she had hoped. But when she was only about five feet away from the desk, she was stopped.

"Don't I know you, miss?"

Cassie couldn't help staring — again. It was the young man from the dress shop, who Catherine had been disappointed to find wasn't there when they'd entered it. He'd been whisked away to a back room with his lady friend, so she couldn't repay his rudeness that afternoon. Cassie was being rude herself by staring, but he was mesmerizing in his handsomeness, with russet-tinged blond hair, dark emerald-green eyes, a smooth-shaven face without an imperfection on it, and such style in an impeccable charcoal three-piece suit.

"Miss?" he repeated.

"No," Cassie replied abruptly.

She managed to control her embarrassment at being asked twice, consoling herself that he was probably accustomed to having women of all ages stare bemusedly at him. She wondered where his lady friend was tonight, and if she really was his kept woman.

"Are you sure we haven't met?"

"Positive," Cassie assured him. "We merely frequent the same dress shop."

He smiled then. "Ah, yes, the young lady with the harridan for a companion."

She arched a brow. He was certainly consistent in his insulting manner. "That harridan was my mama. Is it arrogance that makes you so rude, mister, or maybe you just don't know any better?"

"It's an art form, actually, that the ladies of my acquaintance find quite challenging."

Cassie had a feeling he really believed that. She almost laughed, but restrained herself. Instead she warned him, "You'll be in for a challenge of the real sort if you stick around, mister, because my mama will probably unpack her gun if she finds you talking to me."

She thought that that would send him on his way, but he merely gave her a sure-she-will look and humored her by asking, "Your mama carries a gun?"

"Only when she comes to the city."

"But St. Louis isn't dangerous."

"That's why she packs her Colt away. She usually wears it, you see."

"Don't tell me you're from out West?"

Cassie wondered at the man's sudden surprise. "What if we are?"

"But I find that fascinating," he replied, and she didn't doubt for a second that he was sincere in his new interest. "Have you ever seen real Indians? Or witnessed one of those street duels we hear about?"

She wasn't going to answer that. She'd met people like him before who were avid to hear about the "wild" West, but would never try to experience it themselves. Even with the boom towns that continuously sprang up with the advance of new rail lines, the gold and silver towns that came and went with each new strike, the cow towns, all only days away now by train, folks like him wouldn't leave their safe, civilized cities to see any of them, though they thrived on hearing about the primitive frontier and all its bloody aspects.

She decided to be ornery and answer after all. "We spot small bands of renegade Indians every so often, but they only bother the isolated settler and the occasional stagecoach. They aren't nearly as troublesome as they used to be. But I was in a shootout myself just last month. It was over too quick to be all that exciting, and mine wasn't the killing bullet. That honor went to a fast gun named Angel. Actually, they call him the Angel of Death. Ever heard of him?"

"I can't say that I have," he answered. "Why

266

'the Angel of Death'?"

"Because he never misses what he aims at and he always shoots to kill." And she'd wasted enough time being ornery. "Now you'll have to excuse me, mister —"

"Bartholomew Lawrence, but my friends call me Bart. And you are?"

"Cassandra — Angel."

She'd paused too long over the "Angel." His look said he doubted she'd told him the truth. She didn't care what he believed. He was keeping her from her goal, and she'd run out of time. Catherine had suddenly appeared at the entrance to the dining room and was glancing around the lobby for her.

"But that'd be Mrs. Angel to you," Cassie added, curtly now, since she was annoyed with herself for talking to the man in the first place.

She moved off without another word to him. She had about ten seconds, before her mama joined her, to ask at the desk for any messages. She did that, and was amazed to have a note handed to her. Cassie had just managed to palm it when Catherine came up behind her. She'd walked right past Bartholomew Lawrence without recognizing him.

"Cassie, what are you doing?"

Cassie turned to find that Lawrence was still standing where she'd left him, within hearing distance. But if she did anything well, it was coming up with ridiculous excuses on the spur of the moment.

"I was just checking to see if Angel had joined us yet, Mama." And then she added meaning-

267

fully, "Right now is one of those times he'd come in handy."

Catherine followed her gaze to Lawrence and understood instantly. The man actually laughed, having heard Cassie, though he did leave then.

But Catherine was now visibly bristling. "Was he bothering you?"

"Not really. He recognized me and struck up a conversation to introduce himself."

"And to apologize?"

"I hinted that one was owed, but he calls his rudeness an art form, obviously one he strives to perfect. At any rate, I found him obnoxious enough that I tried to put the 'fear of Angel' into him. He didn't believe me."

"It takes seeing that gunfighter of yours to believe he's a cold-blooded killer."

"He's not —"

"Never mind," Catherine cut in and ushered them toward the stairs. "But I'm definitely unpacking my gun."

Chapter 31

The detective's name was Phineas Kirby. He had taken a room in the same hotel, even on the same floor. But Cassie didn't rush off to his room as soon as she read his note. As much as she deplored the necessity of having to disturb his sleep, she hated even more the thought of having to explain to her mama that she'd hired a detective and why.

So she waited until Catherine went to bed. And she wasn't taking any chances. She even prepared for bed herself and lay there for several hours in case her mama couldn't sleep tonight and wanted to come in and talk some — she'd done that before.

It was shortly after midnight when Cassie dressed again and cautiously left her room. She found Mr. Kirby's room at the far end of the hall. She knocked so quietly, it was quite a while before she finally heard grumbling on the other side of the door. A few moments later it was yanked open, and she was about to be snarled at by a very annoyed-looking man in a bulky yellow robe with socks peeking out below its long hem. He was middle-aged and on the portly side, with nondescript features and sharp blue eyes.

He must have changed his mind about snapping at her when he got a good look at her.

"Sorry, miss. I thought you were one of the hotel staff. Are you lost?"

"No, sir, I'm Cassie Stuart. I sent for you."

He was back to frowning. "Do you know what time it is, Miss Stuart?"

She winced. "Yes, I know, but I couldn't wait until morning. I'm here with my mama, and I'd rather she didn't know that I'm hiring you. She doesn't like my husband, you see, and this has to do with him."

Phineas sighed. "Then I guess you better come in and have a seat."

There were two chairs before the fireplace. He moved to drop another log in the grate before he sat in the chair that his clothes had been draped over. He pulled a jacket down from the backrest and searched through it until he found a notebook in an inside pocket.

"So what can I do for you, Miss Stuart?" He started scribbling in the notebook as he asked.

Cassie sat down in the chair across from his. "I'd like to locate my husband's parents."

"They're missing?"

"Not exactly," she said. "And he's not really my husband — well, he is, but we're soon to be divorced." At his raised brow, she assured him, "This has nothing to do with that. I'd just like to reunite him with his family as sort of a parting gift to him."

"Very commendable," he remarked. "So what are the names of these people?"

"That's going to be the difficult part. He was too young to remember their names. You see, he was taken from them, stolen by a mountain

270

man right out of this city about twenty-odd years ago, and spent the next nine years in some isolated cabin up in the Rocky Mountains. He's not sure if he was five or six years old at the time he was taken. And his folks didn't live here. He recalls coming here on a train, so they were either passing through or visiting someone here."

"He was with both parents?"

"Probably not. He doesn't remember his papa being around much."

"Well, we at least have the boy's name." Phineas said it as if it were a foregone conclusion.

Cassie gave him a small, helpless smile. "Not really. He goes by the name Angel because that's all he remembers his mama calling him."

The detective seemed surprised. "That's strange," he said, more to himself. After a moment's reflection he asked, "Are you sure you wouldn't rather find him?"

"No, I know where I can find him. I'd just like to find his parents, both of them if they're still living. I figured someone here must remember a tragedy like that happening, a small boy turning up missing and never found. I wouldn't know myself how to go about locating anyone who might know something about it. Neither did Angel, I guess, since he came back here after that mountain man who stole him died, but he didn't have any luck finding out anything." She sighed. "I know this isn't much to go on —"

"On the contrary. I should have the names for you in a day or two. It may take a bit longer to get an address where these people are living now, but my agency has excellent resources in

271

most every state, and the telegraph simplifies my job tremendously. An amazing invention, that. It's helped to capture a great many criminals." And then he was musing and mumbling to himself again. "Angel, huh? I wonder how many go by that name this side of the Mississippi."

"I beg your pardon?"

"Nothing, ma'am." Phineas stood up to escort her to the door. "I hope you don't mind if I start working on this in the morning."

She blushed. "Certainly. I *am* sorry about the hour, but it's not easy to get away from my mama during the day, and I'd never hear the end of it if she found out what I was doing. She *really* doesn't like my husband."

"Then she's urging the divorce?"

"Yes, but it was already a mutual decision, since we got married by accident in the first place."

"That's a new way to put it."

"Can you think of a better word for a shotgun wedding?" she asked.

He grinned. "I suppose not. And I can see why you would want a divorce. It can't be easy, being married to a gunfighter, even for a short time."

"How did you know he was a gunfighter?"

"With a name like Angel — it was a good guess."

Cassie was impressed. The man was obviously a genius, and her money would be well spent.

Phineas wasn't a genius, he'd just been sent here straight from his last assignment in Denver and happened to sit next to a gunfighter on the train by the name of Angel. He'd even spent a pleasant hour grilling the man with questions, his instincts telling him that anyone who looked like Angel did had to be on *someone's* Wanted list. His instincts had been wrong in that respect, and he'd come damn close to getting himself shot for his persistence, but he liked living dangerously or he wouldn't be in the line of work he was in.

And he didn't go back to bed. An hour later, after trying three hotels and getting lucky with the fourth, he was knocking on a door himself. A gun cocked in his face the second the door opened. He stared down its barrel before looking at the man holding it.

"Just met your wife," Phineas said agreeably.

"My what?"

"She's here in St. Louis."

"The hell she is. She's on her way back to Wyoming."

Phineas smiled. "Little lady with great big silver-gray eyes?"

Angel put his gun away to the accompaniment of a foul expletive. He'd gotten halfway to Wyoming before he decided he'd rather not be in Cheyenne when Cassie got home. Putting distance between them hadn't worked yet to get her off his mind, so he'd come to St. Louis to try once more to find his mother. That was one reason he was there. The other was, he figured it was about as far as he could get from his wife — and her damn divorce papers.

"I guess you were telling the truth about not

having any other name besides Angel," Phineas was saying. "At least not one that you know of. Sorry I gave you such a hard time."

"You still are," Angel said in pure disgruntlement. "So what do you want this time, Kirby?"

"Just a little information. Your wife has hired me to find your parents. It would be helpful if —"

"She did *what?*" Angel exploded. "Hell and I don't believe that woman is meddling again this soon. She couldn't even wait until she got home. And in *my* business this time!"

Phineas rocked back on his toes. He loved watching human reactions. Drop the right word or phrase, and people behaved in the most fascinating ways. He wouldn't have expected this man to lose control, though. Just went to show that everyone did have at least one weakness.

Phineas tried again. "It would be helpful if you could supply me with a description of your parents, and anything else that you can remember about them."

Black, emotionally charged eyes came back to the detective. "She hired you. Get your information from her."

"Now, how did I know you wouldn't be very cooperative?" Phineas replied. "They're your parents, but I guess the little lady you married is the only one who wants them found."

"All right, Kirby, you've made your point," Angel said disagreeably. "I don't remember my father, but my mother had black hair, curly, and dark eyes."

Phineas whipped out his notebook before he

asked, "As dark as yours?"

"No. I think they were brown."

"Any scars or distinguishing marks?"

"Not that I recall."

"What about her age or nationality?"

"She was young and pretty."

"All mothers are pretty to their five-year-olds. Did she speak with an accent maybe?"

"If she did, then I would have, too, so I wouldn't have noticed a difference, now would — ?" Angel paused, looking slightly abashed. "Now that you mention it, I recall Old Bear said I talked funny when he first took me. 'Course, he butchered the English language himself, so maybe I didn't."

"Then," Phineas added, bringing back Angel's scowl. "But, of course, you're a product of your upbringing, which I imagine was quite prim- itive."

"I don't have any problem making myself un- derstood," Angel said in clear warning.

Phineas chuckled. "I don't imagine you do. Guns always do speak louder than words." And then he got back to the subject. "Now, my first guess would have been that, with your coloring, you're part Indian, but you don't really have the bone structure for it, and that mountain man would have known enough Indian not to remark on it if you spoke one of the dialects. My second guess is you're Spanish, possibly pure. At any rate, the likelihood that she was a foreigner will help narrow down my questioning if I can't lo- cate any old newspapers."

"You really think in a city this size that the

275

disappearance of one kid would have been mentioned in a newspaper?"

"Absolutely. The problem will be finding one that keeps old issues. Most can't afford the storage space, though some of those make an effort to at least keep their front pages. Then, too, news printers come and go just like other businesses. But like you said, this is a large city and has been for a very long time, so with any luck, there will be at least one paper that's been around for the last twenty or so years."

"And with my luck, that won't be the one that keeps old issues."

"You're feeling unlucky these days?" Angel just grunted, causing Phineas to laugh. "Well, your luck's about to change. This is one of my easier assignments. It's tracking people with unlawful reasons not to be found that is time-consuming. This case won't take any time at all."

Angel wasn't going to hold his breath. "If you do find 'em, bring the bill to me. I'm not going to owe another debt to that woman I married."

"I doubt she'll appreciate that. She seemed to be looking forward to finding them for you."

"Too bad."

"But there's a matter of ethics involved. She did hire me first."

"Then I'm firing you on her behalf and hiring you on mine. Last I heard, a husband can still do that."

"Up until he's a divorced husband he can."

"Get out, Kirby."

Phineas was chuckling as he left. Angel slammed the door shut behind him. A few moments later,

276

though, it hit him, forcefully, that Cassie was actually here in the city, probably no more than a few blocks away — and his damn body reacted to that knowledge with a vengeance.

Chapter 32

"Are we divorced yet?"

Cassie woke with a start, that soft drawl echoing in her ears. "What?"

"Are we divorced yet?"

She knew instantly who he was, she just couldn't believe he was there. "Angel?"

His hand slipped into her hair as his body moved to cover hers. "Just answer the question, Cassie."

"We're not."

"Are you — ?"

"No!" she quickly assured him. "I just haven't had the time —"

His mouth came down to cut off the rest of her explanation. Obviously, he wasn't interested in her excuses just now. But what he was interested in was bundled up in warm flannel.

"How come you don't sleep naked?"

It was a question born of frustration, not one for a lady to take seriously. Cassie answered anyway. "I do in the summertime."

He groaned, knowing full well an image of her naked was going to haunt him now. And his tongue slid in deep, eliciting an answering groan out of Cassie. It was a while before they drew breath.

"You got the sweetest, softest lips I ever did

taste," he said against them.

"Your voice makes me tingle, Angel."

"What does my mouth do to you?"

"It makes me weak."

His mouth moved up to suck on her earlobe. "What else?"

"Hot," she whispered.

"Oh, God, Cassie, I'm going to burst if I can't get inside you right now."

"Then what are you waiting for?"

He laughed and kissed her again. Then he rolled to her side to shove the covers off her. She tore the top of her nightgown open, popping off three buttons in her impatience to get it off. He yanked his shirt out of his pants and sent his buttons to join hers on the bed and the floor. In seconds he was back, pressing her into the mattress. Her arms and legs wrapped around him, locking him in place. And then he was inside, deep inside, and that familiar throbbing came so quickly, bursting on her senses, pulsing around him, drawing his own climax to mesh with hers.

Cassie lowered her legs slowly. Her toes slid against leather. Angel was still wearing his boots, and his pants. She wanted to laugh, but she felt like crying.

God, how she hated the reality that surfaced after the passion was spent. She wished just once it would stay away for a while. But that was like asking winter to go away in January. Both were there to stay.

She resented that. She resented Angel, too, at the moment. And she particularly resented the fact that he hadn't taken off his boots.

She let him know it with the curt admonishment, "Next time take off your boots."

"Is Marabelle here?"

"No."

"Then I'll take them off now."

"No, you won't. You aren't staying."

"I'm not ready to leave yet, Cassie. And that was too intense. We're going to try it again, slow and easy."

Her stomach fluttered in response to those words. She suppressed the feeling.

"No, we aren't," she told him stiffly. "You're going to get out of here before my mama hears you and comes charging in with her gun blazing."

"Where is she?"

"In the next room."

"Then we'll have to be quiet, won't we?"

"Angel —"

His mouth was back, slanting across hers with tantalizing skill. She couldn't let that work this time. She couldn't.

She did. She'd missed him too much, wanted him too much, to be sensible about it. And there had been the thought, haunting her ever since he'd ridden out of her life, that she'd never know his touch again.

Now his touch was breaking the last of her resistance with a slow sweep of his hand over her breasts and belly. Gooseflesh followed in its wake; nipples tingled to hardness. She'd just had the most incredible explosion of pleasure imaginable, but her body was firing up to experience it again. And in no way did Angel hurry her toward that end. He'd said slow and easy, and that was exactly how he proceeded.

Before he was done, Cassie was sure he knew her body better than she did. No inch of her had been left untouched. He even turned her over at one point to lick his way down the center of her back. His teeth scraped over her buttocks, bringing a startled giggle from her as she was reminded of Marabelle's habit. His tongue traced circles on the back of her knees. She never knew how many sensitive spots there were on her body. He found them all, her moans and shivers of pleasure guiding him, while his hands slipped beneath her to tease the more common areas of sensitivity.

It was nearly dawn before Angel finally got his fill of her. Cassie was too sated to feel any more resentment. And he'd been right. The first time had been over with too quickly. The rest . . . Lord love him, the man was as good at loving as he was with a gun.

She wanted nothing more at the moment than to fall into blissful sleep, but she didn't dare until Angel was gone. Only he seemed in no hurry to leave, and she didn't have the strength left to urge him to go.

He lay stretched out beside her, his arms crossed under his head, his eyes closed, but she knew he wasn't sleeping. There was the barest trace of a smile on his lips. She wondered about that for only a moment. He was the very picture of a man well satisfied, after all, so why shouldn't he be smiling? He'd gotten his way — in everything. And she couldn't begrudge him that. She felt like smiling herself. Until reality intruded — again.

She was back to facing the possibility of pregnancy, and another delay in getting a divorce. She wouldn't mind that so much if she didn't have to explain the delay to her mother. *That* wasn't going to be easy. The very thought of it ruined her pleasant lethargy. And misery loved company, so she was quick to ruin Angel's, too.

"You know I'll have to wait again now, before I can get a divorce."

His shoulders moved in a slight shrug. "What's another month?"

He wanted the divorce. How dared he sound indifferent about when they got it?

But he wasn't finished. "Why didn't you start the process already?"

"I've been too busy."

He turned to look at her then. "Too busy to sever our ties? You should have found the time, honey. Leaving me with rights that I can't resist taking isn't doing either one of us any good."

Now he sounded annoyed. Cassie grew defensive. "What are you doing here, Angel?"

"Now, that was going to be my question," he replied. "Why aren't you home by now, tucked away on your ranch where I can't get to you?"

He'd managed to "get" to her tonight, which reminded her. "And that's another thing. Just how did you get in my room tonight?"

"I get my answers first, Cassie."

"Why?"

"Because last I looked, I was bigger and stronger than you — and the husband always gets his answers first."

He sounded altogether too smug for her to take that lying down. "Where'd you hear that nonsense?"

"You mean it isn't true?"

"Not in any family I know of, but particularly not in mine."

"You're talking about your mama, but you're nothing like her."

"I can be if I put my mind to it."

His answer was a doubting grin and a finger that came over to flick at her nose. "Your lying hasn't improved lately, has it?"

Cassie gritted her teeth. "You've only seen me dealing with people I've wronged. You haven't seen me deal with people who wrong me."

"Like me, Cassie?" he asked softly.

She could feel the heat climbing up her cheeks. "If I'd felt you wronged me, Angel, I would have done something about it."

"Like what?"

"You wouldn't like my spur-of-the-moment answer, so give me a minute to think about it."

He laughed. "I'll concede you *think* you can be as formidable as your mama, so we'll go by stubbornness instead. I can outwait you, honey, right up until your mama comes knocking on the door."

She opened her mouth to call his bluff, but on second thought, she decided she'd better not. She didn't want to see him and her mama squaring off again if she could help it, and he *was* just stubborn enough to let it happen.

"What was that question you wanted answered?" she asked with ill grace.

His expression changed abruptly, all playfulness gone. "Why aren't you home where you belong?"

"When my mama wants to go shopping, we go shopping," she explained with a shrug.

"In the dead of winter?"

"She figured since we were already a long way from home, a little detour wouldn't hurt."

"And St. Louis was her choice?"

"No, it was mine."

"That's what I figured. So what I want to know is, how'd I get put at the top of your meddling list?"

"What's that supposed to mean?" she asked cautiously.

"You know exactly what I mean."

She sat up, her eyes widening incredulously. He couldn't know. It simply wasn't possible . . .

"How did you find out?"

"Your detective figured I could supply him with more facts than you did, so he paid me a visit tonight."

"The man is absolutely amazing," she remarked in awe. "To locate you in a city this size, when he didn't even know you were here —"

"He knew," Angel cut in sourly. "We came in on the same train."

"Oh," she said, a bit deflated. "Well, still —"

"Forget 'still,' " Angel interrupted curtly. "What'd you hire him for, Cassie?"

"Because I didn't think you'd make the effort again to find your folks yourself."

"You don't owe me any favors."

"I figured I did."

"How's that?" he demanded. "Or are you forgetting what I took from you?"

"No," she said quietly, her cheeks hot again. "But you aren't aware what you did for my parents. They called a truce of sorts that night you locked them in the barn — at least, they're talking to each other again."

Angel snorted. Belaboring who owed whom was pointless. "Let me put it this way, Cassie. I don't want you hiring detectives on my behalf, so I took the liberty of firing Kirby on *your* behalf."

She took exception to that. "Now what'd you do that for? Don't you want to find your folks?"

"I only want to know who they were. That's why I'm here. But I'll be the one to find that out. You got that?"

"But Mr. Kirby can help."

"I'll give you that much, which is why he works for me now, not you."

Her eyes narrowed. "I don't think I like your high-handedness one little bit, Angel."

"Too bad."

"And what do you mean, you only want to know who they were? You *are* going to go and see them, aren't you, when you find out where they are?"

"No."

That answer so surprised her, her irritation with him dissolved instantly. "Why not?"

"Because we're nothing but strangers. I don't remember my father. I barely remember my mother. I doubt I'd even recognize her. And it's not as if she raised me."

"She nurtured you for five or six years."

"And then lost me."

She heard the bitterness, loud and clear. "You blame her for that? That old man took you up in the mountains where no one could find you. Your mama was probably out of her mind with grief —"

"You don't know —"

"Neither do you," she interrupted in return. "So find out. What can it hurt? At least let her know you didn't die all those years ago. More than likely that's what she ended up thinking."

"You're meddling again, Cassie," he said in sharp warning. "This isn't your concern."

"You're absolutely right," she replied stiffly, her irritation back in full force. "And this isn't your bedroom, so why don't you get out of it?"

"Finally a suggestion I can happily agree with," he shot back angrily as he threw off the covers and grabbed his pants from the floor. "And let me give you one in return. Get your butt home if you don't want me using the spare key I have to this room again."

"I'll be gone by morning," Cassie assured him.

"It is morning."

"Then by afternoon."

"Good!" he said, and leaned over to give her a hard, unexpected kiss before he swept up the rest of his things and was gone.

Cassie stared at the black bandana he'd missed in his rush to get out of there because it was half covered by the blanket. She reached down for it and raised it to her lips, still moist from his.

She'd made him angry again, though that was nothing new. For some reason, they seemed destined to part that way. So why the kiss this time, as angry as he'd been? He'd done it without thought, like a longtime habit — like he couldn't help himself. For the life of her, she couldn't figure him out.

Chapter 33

Their baggage came down first and was taken out to the coach waiting to take them to the train station. Angel only made note of it because he was watching for their departure. Five minutes later, Cassie and her mother descended the stairs and went straight to the front desk to settle their bill. The mother looked like she'd take anyone's head off who looked at her wrong. Cassie didn't look too friendly herself. But Angel wasn't planning on approaching them. He'd just wanted to make sure they were leaving today.

He'd waited nearly eight hours to find out. Cassie had obviously gone to sleep after he left her. He had spent the day sitting on a sofa in the lobby, watching the stairs, tired, and hungry, since he'd used all the money he had on him last night to bribe that spare key out of the desk clerk.

He'd gotten only a few hours of sleep last night before Kirby showed up at his door. He hadn't been back to bed since — for sleeping. He hadn't been back to his room, either, to clean up, so his cheeks were shadowed with stubble, his hair was still tangled from Cassie's fingers, and his shirt was minus the buttons to close it with.

The management had come by twice to ask

him to leave. He was frightening their guests. Two men had come by first in their fancy suits. Four had come the second time. He'd told them all the same thing. He wasn't leaving until his wife did. Apparently they'd decided not to press it, though they'd checked the registry to verify that he had a wife there. But he wouldn't have minded if they'd pressed it some. He was in that kind of mood.

Divided. He wanted Cassie gone, but he knew by tonight he'd wish she were still where he could get to her, instead of miles away. He was still irritated at her for meddling again, yet he wished they hadn't parted angry with each other this time. He could rectify that right now before she left, but he wouldn't, because it was better for her if she stayed mad at him. Then she wouldn't waste any more time in ending their marriage.

Until she did that, he couldn't go back to Cheyenne. That would be too close to her, and last night had proved he couldn't be that close without doing something about it. She'd never get her divorce that way. She'd end up having his baby instead.

The thought went through him with a jolt, and the realization that came with it was worse. He wanted her to have his baby. It was the one way he could have her for good, with no more talk of divorce, and he might as well own up to it. He wanted that meddling woman for his own more than he'd ever wanted anything else.

But that wasn't what she wanted. And it'd be a rotten thing for him to do, to wish his baby on her. So whoever said he was a nice guy?

Two men came out of the dining room just then, heading for the entrance to the hotel. Angel wouldn't have noticed them, except they suddenly stopped directly in front of him, blocking his view of the front desk. He didn't object. He'd been about to move anyway so Cassie wouldn't see him if she happened to look in his direction. Now he didn't have to . . . and to hell with that. He wasn't going to deny himself these last few moments of being able to savor the sight of her. It would be too long before he saw her again.

He got up to move to a new vantage point, behind one of the tall Grecian columns that supported the two-story ceiling in the lobby. He had to pass behind the two men to do so, and that was as far as he got when he overheard what the pretty-faced one was saying.

"She calls herself Mrs. Angel. I barely noticed her at first, but now — I don't know, there's something about her that intrigues me."

"I don't see it," his friend said in sincere bewilderment as they both stared at Cassie.

"Good, because I don't intend to share this one."

Angel reminded himself that Cassie was leaving St. Louis. He didn't need to say anything. He felt like it anyway.

"Neither do I," he said, causing both men to turn toward him. It was automatic for his hand to fold the yellow slicker back behind his gun.

"I beg your pardon?" Bartholomew Lawrence replied, then took a step back as he got a good look at the man who had interrupted him.

"The lady's married," Angel said in his slow drawl.

"Bart happens to like married women," the friend offered with a snicker, since "Bart" had lost his tongue staring at Angel.

"He tries to like that one, and he's a dead man."

Bartholomew had realized, as soon as he'd taken in the gun resting on Angel's hip, that this had to be the man Cassie had called the Angel of Death. And after that last remark, he fainted dead away.

"Aw, hell," Angel said in disgust.

The collapse of a man on the lobby floor was sure to draw both Cassie's and her mother's attention, but one glance in that direction showed they'd already left the area. He turned just in time to see them pass through the entrance and out of sight.

"Do you do that just for fun," Phineas asked at his back, "or can't you help it?"

Angel gave one more disgusted look at the man on the floor before he turned toward the detective. "What do you want, Kirby?"

Phineas laughed. "I guess you can't help it. But you really ought to cover that gun back up. You might not know it, but city folks get nervous when they see anyone other than the law wearing weapons."

"I'm used to making folks nervous," Angel replied indifferently. "So if that's all you stopped by to tell me —"

"I might mention that you look terrible."

"You could have kept that to yourself, too."

Angel turned to leave. Phineas fell into step beside him. "You're in a rotten mood, aren't you?" Angel ignored him. "Maybe this will cheer you up."

A piece of paper flashed in front of Angel's face. He stopped, but he didn't reach for the paper. Phineas drew it back when it occurred to him that Angel might not know how to read, a distinct possibility with the kind of upbringing he'd had. Phineas decided not to ask.

"You found an old newspaper?" Angel guessed.

Phineas nodded. "One that had a very conscientious reporter at the time. The story did make the front page, and damn near filled it."

"The names?"

"Cawlin and Anna O'Rourke."

"O'Rourke?"

"That was my reaction. I never would have guessed you were Irish. Every Irishman I've ever met, even second- and third-generation Americans, retains something of a Gaelic accent, but you've lost yours entirely."

"O'Rourke," Angel said, and then again, rolling it off his tongue.

He could get used to a name like that real quick. And that was all he'd wanted, he reminded himself, a name to put behind the one he had, because he was damn tired of having to tell folks, "Just Angel." But he didn't walk away from the detective when he started giving an account of that newspaper story.

"Anna O'Rourke came here with her son to visit a childhood friend. I'm sorry to have to tell you she'd just been widowed. Your father,

Cawlin O'Rourke, was a second-generation American who was a surveyor for the railroads, which is why you probably don't remember him. A job like that takes a man all over the country.

"Your mother had immigrated here from Ireland and married your father soon after she arrived in America. But apparently she was homesick, and when he died, she decided to take you back to the old country. Only she wanted to say good-bye to her friend first.

"The reporter claimed Anna had been here just over a week when her four-year-old son, Angel, disappeared from the front lawn of Dora Carmine's house. One minute you were there, the next you were gone."

"You mean she really did name me Angel?"

"Sounds like it."

"And if I was only four at the time, that would make me twenty-five now, rather than twenty-six as I'd thought."

Phineas grinned. "First time I ever heard of someone growing younger instead of older. At any rate, the story went on to mention that search parties were combing the city for you and rewards were posted. It was assumed at first that you'd just wandered off and were lost, which would explain why no one thought to search outside the city. I found one other mention in a paper dated a few weeks later, stating you were still missing and any information about your whereabouts would receive a substantial reward. You probably had half this city looking for you."

"What was the name of my mother's friend?"

"Dora Carmine."

"Does she still live here?"

Phineas nodded. "I just came from paying her a visit, to confirm the newspaper account."

"You didn't tell her about me, did you?"

"No. I told her I was from the mayor's office, compiling an official report on the increase in crime over the last twenty-five years."

Angel looked down at the floor. "Did she say if my mother's still living?"

"She's still living."

"I suppose she eventually went back to Ireland like she planned to?"

"According to Mrs. Carmine, Anna O'Rourke never left St. Louis. She refused to give up hope that you'd show up one day, alive and well. She lives about nine blocks from here in one of the older city mansions. She married a wealthy banker about eighteen years ago. He was a widower with two children. She gave him a few more, so you've got some half brothers and a sister. And to this day, she's still offering a reward for information about you."

Angel gave him a level look. "You weren't thinking about collecting it, were you?"

"I already bent my ethics once on this case. I wasn't planning to do so again."

"Good."

Phineas frowned. "That sounds like you don't intend to pay her a visit."

"I don't. She's settled in with a new family. I can't see any reason to disturb that."

Phineas stared at him for a moment before he shrugged. "You're probably right. She's just your mother, after all. What difference does it make

294

if she never finds out what happened to her first-born?"

"What happened to him isn't pretty."

"The truth is rarely as bad as what a person can imagine. She's probably imagined worse."

Angel scowled. "Worse than what I am? I doubt it."

"Aren't you being a bit hard on yourself? Compared to some of the criminals I track down, you're a saint. You got taken west through no fault of your own, but you adapted to it. I'd say you've done all right for yourself."

"So who asked you?"

Phineas gave up, handing over the sheet of paper. "The address is there if you ever change your mind. I'll drop the agency's bill off at your hotel. It's been interesting — Angel O'Rourke."

Chapter 34

"*Now* can we talk about it?"

Cassie leaned her head back on the plush seat as the train pulled out of the station. She supposed she could be grateful that her mama's private Pullman car had just arrived at the station that morning, or Catherine would have something else to complain about during the next few days. She could also be grateful that her mama had been silent this long, after coming into her room this morning and finding Cassie too tired to get up, her nightgown still on the floor, and buttons everywhere — buttons that didn't match.

All Cassie had said was, "I want to go home today, Mama, but I need a little more sleep first."

"Would you like to tell me why?"

Catherine was being sarcastic. She fully expected an explanation. She didn't expect Cassie's answer. "I don't want to talk about it."

Amazingly, she let Cassie go back to sleep, and didn't say anything when she finally got up, other than, "I've already arranged to have our new clothes shipped home when they're completed."

But Cassie had known she wouldn't get through the entire day without satisfying her mother's curiosity. She was going to avoid the truth, however, if at all possible.

"What did you want to talk about, Mama?"

"We can start with why we're on this train today instead of next week."

"We'd made our selections, finished all the fittings. Did you really want to wait around just so we could carry all those clothes home ourselves? With the weather so cold, it wasn't as if we could get out and enjoy the city. You would have been bored by tomorrow, and probably suggested yourself that we go home."

"I'm never bored in the city, warm weather or cold, and neither are you. Care to try again? Or shall we avoid taxing your store of excuses and just stick with the truth?"

"What makes you think —"

"I have eyes, baby. I saw your gunfighter in the lobby of the hotel."

Cassie had, too, but then, ever since she'd first met Angel, bright yellow had been drawing her attention no matter where she was, so there was no way she wouldn't have noticed that yellow slicker of his today. She hadn't acknowledged him, though, or even looked directly at him. She knew why he was there — to make sure she left St. Louis — and that had brought her temper back up.

"Why did he follow you to St. Louis?" Catherine wanted to know.

"He didn't. He came here for reasons that had nothing to do with me."

"Did you know he was coming?"

"No."

"I hate coincidences like that," Catherine said

with a sigh. "They're just not natural."

"Like fate?"

Catherine gave Cassie a sharp look, refusing to admit fate might have anything to do with it. "He came to your room last night, didn't he?"

"Yes."

"And?"

So much for avoiding the truth. "Angel has this problem ignoring his husbandly rights when I'm near to hand. He can't seem to do it."

"Why, that lecherous —"

"And I have a problem refusing him those rights."

"Cassie — !"

"So he suggested I go home."

That gave Catherine pause. "*He* did? You mean the man actually has *some* sense?"

"That's not funny, Mama."

"It wasn't supposed to be, baby."

"At any rate, he was entirely too high-handed about it, thinking he can order me around."

"All husbands tend to think that way. I've never understood why. Women may have gotten the right to vote in Wyoming, we can serve on juries, and we can even boast about having the first woman justice of the peace in the whole country, but husbands still think their word is law."

"Papa was never like that."

"Your papa was an exception." And then Catherine laughed. "The Summerses are another exception. We know who wears the pants in *that* family, and they fit her very well."

"That's not nice, Mama. And it's not true. I'd say they both fit into the same pants. If they have a difference of opinion, they hash it out. One spouse doesn't arbitrarily say, 'Do it,' and think that's the end of it."

"Chase Summers would never be that stupid," Catherine said with a grin. "But all right, I'll concede Jessie tiptoes around him *sometimes*. However, most times she walks all over him."

"Only because he lets her," Cassie insisted. "There's the difference."

Catherine was suddenly frowning again. "How did we get so far off the subject?"

Cassie really wished her mama hadn't noticed that. "By discussing arbitrary males. And before you embarrass us both by asking, yes, I *will* have to wait again before I can divorce mine."

Angel knocked on the front door of the massive stone house. He knew he shouldn't be there. He'd cleaned up. He was as neat as he could get without cutting his hair, which he wouldn't do until springtime. But he shouldn't be there. Only it was either come here or get roaring drunk to take his mind off his little wife. He didn't feel like getting drunk.

The door opened. A man with curly white hair and side-whiskers, in a stiff-looking formal suit, stood there. His skin was so dark it was almost black.

"Can I help you, sir?"

"I'd like to speak to the lady of the house," Angel told him.

"Who is it, Jefferson?" another voice asked, followed by the appearance of a tall, middle aged man with blond hair and green eyes.

"I don't rightly know, Mister Winston. This gentleman has asked to speak to Missus Anna."

The green eyes narrowed as they gave Angel a more careful once-over. "Might I inquire what business you have with my wife?"

"You're the banker?"

The eyes narrowed even more. "Yes."

"I just found out this morning that your wife is my mother. My name's Angel — O'Rourke."

It was the first time Angel got to say it. It felt good — and it brought a sigh from Anna's husband.

"I see," the man said in a resigned tone. "You're about the fifteenth Angel who's come to my door, trying to collect the reward." Contempt entered his voice as he added, "At least the others were Irish, or made an attempt to sound Irish. Can you prove that you're my wife's missing son?"

Doubt was the last thing Angel expected. He almost laughed.

"I don't need to prove it, mister."

"Then you won't get a penny —"

"I don't want your money," Angel cut in. "I just came to have a look at her before I head back west."

"Well, that's a new approach," Winston said, though his look remained skeptical. "Just out of curiosity, what story have you concocted to explain your disappearance all those years ago?"

"If she wants to know, I'll tell her," was all Angel said, and he was being generous in that, considering the man was starting to irritate him.

The banker hesitated a moment before he acquiesced. "For my wife's sake, I'm forced to give

300

you the benefit of the doubt. But I warn you, she'll know just by the sight of you if you've told me the truth. And if she doesn't recognize you, I'd appreciate it if you would leave without mentioning who you're claiming to be. My wife has been through enough agony over this. I don't want all those memories stirred up again for no good reason."

Angel nodded, unable to argue with that. He didn't need to talk to her. He didn't need anything from her. Just one look was all he'd like, so the image of her that he carried wouldn't be so vague. And that was probably all he'd get, because he couldn't see how a woman, even a mother, could recognize a four-year-old child in the man he'd become.

The servant opened the door wider for Angel to enter. "May I take your coat, sir?"

It was too warm in the house not to give it up. Angel didn't want to start sweating and have them think it was caused by nervousness. But as soon as he handed the slicker over, the banker's eyes went straight to his gun. He might have cleaned up, but he'd made no effort to hide what he was or where he was from. He wore his usual black, right down to a new bandana knotted loosely at his neck.

"Are you a lawman?" he was asked.

"No."

The frown was back. "I'd rather you didn't wear that thing in my house."

Angel made no move to remove it. "If you've been good to my mother, you've got nothing to worry about."

The banker's cheeks went florid, but he said stiffly to the servant, "Inform my wife that we have a guest. She may join us in the east drawing room."

The servant went away. Angel followed his host down a wide hall to a door on the right. The room beyond was large, the furniture so elegant he was leery of sitting on it. He *was* nervous — no, *scared* was more like it. He'd never been so scared in his life. He had no business here. He should have got drunk instead.

"I can't do this," he said suddenly. "I thought I could, but — tell her — no, don't tell her anything. It's better she don't know what happened to me."

"As I thought," Anna's husband remarked with enough contempt to shrivel a lesser man. "Most of them back out at this point."

"I'm not going to take offense at that, mister, because you're looking out for her interests, and I'm glad to know she's got someone to do that for her."

And Angel was being *really* generous this time, because what he'd felt like saying was, he killed men for less provocation, which wasn't true, but saying so tended to put an abrupt end to the provocation. It ended anyway, because the man nodded, either in acceptance of his remark or because he had nothing else to say.

Angel headed for the door, the tension already starting to leave him, but it came right back when his path was suddenly blocked by a young girl. She was beautiful, with her black hair floating about her waist, and big green eyes — her father's

302

eyes. She couldn't be more than thirteen years old. A sister, Kirby had said, and Angel knew in his gut he was looking at her.

A lump rose in his throat. He couldn't seem to move or take his eyes off her.

She stared at him, too, eyes bright with curiosity, and didn't look away even as she told her father, "Mother says she'll be coming right down and who might you be?"

She said it all in one breath. "Angel," he said without thinking.

"No kidding? I have a brother named Angel, though I've never met him. I've got lots of other brothers, but Mother says a girl can never have too many to look out for her."

Angel couldn't see himself looking out for a sister. He'd end up leaving dead bodies all over the place if she was even looked at wrong, and he didn't think these city folks would appreciate that.

"Katey's my name," she continued, and again in the same breath, "Are you my brother?"

The question went through Angel like lead, sharp and painful. He didn't know how to answer. The truth wouldn't get him out of there any time quick. It would likely be refuted by the banker, too. And it would commit him. One little word, and an empty part of his life would be filled.

Anna's husband didn't give him a chance to say it.

"You have delivered your message, Katey; now take yourself off to your room."

"But —"

"You know better than to make a nuisance of

yourself when we have guests."

His voice wasn't stern. If anything, it was filled with too much tenderness, telling Angel the girl was well loved. And she left with a "Yes, sir," only a slight pout drawing at her lips.

"Thank you for not answering my daughter," Angel heard at his back. "She's an impressionable child. She would have believed you."

Believed the truth? Imagine that. But Angel didn't say it, didn't say anything. He headed for the door again. If the damn room weren't so big, he'd have been gone already.

He didn't make it. They collided at the door, both rushing for it. He had to grab her to keep her from falling backward. He heard her gasp, then laugh, but she hadn't looked up yet. She was actually a small woman. The top of her head barely reached his chin. But he didn't need to see her face. The laugh told him, a sound so familiar to him, he could have heard it only yesterday.

It was her, and the memories came back with her, of gentle scoldings, and hugs and kisses, bedtime stories, and the tears when his da had died and she'd had to tell him, and love, so much love. He couldn't breathe, that knot grew so big in his throat. His hands tightened on her arms. That made her look up, and it was a good thing he hadn't let go of her, because she turned so white, she looked about ready to faint.

"Cawlin?" she said in a fearful shriek, and Angel knew she thought she was seeing a ghost.

He didn't answer. Words wouldn't get past that lump. It hadn't occurred to her yet that she was seeing the son rather than his father, and he ought to leave before it did. But he couldn't move. He couldn't even let go of her. He wanted to draw her forward and crush her in his arms, but he was afraid to, afraid of frightening her, afraid he might never let go.

The things he was feeling were choking him. He suddenly wished Cassie were there to meddle and fix things in her indomitable way, because he'd never felt so helpless and out of his depth as he did in that moment. The banker was there instead, to pull them apart and lead Anna into the room to a chair. Angel still didn't move. He ought to get the hell out of there, but his feet wouldn't obey him, and his eyes wouldn't leave his mother.

His image of her might have faded over twenty-one years, but it was back now because she'd changed so little in that time. And the things he could remember now, the little things he'd forgotten. She hadn't lost him through careless-ness. If anything, she'd been overprotective of him because he was all she'd had — then. But she had another family now, and he didn't belong in it.

Fear finally got his feet moving, fear of rejection and the hurt that went with it. It was the one thing he'd never been able to handle very well, and he wasn't going to start trying now.

He'd taken several long steps down the hall before he noticed the barricade at the front door in the form of his little sister. Katey was leaning back against it, her arms crossed, and shaking her head at him. She hadn't gone to her room as told. She'd waited to ambush him, and that was exactly how he felt, ambushed.

She grinned at him now as she reminded him, "You didn't answer me."

"Answer you what?"

"If you're my brother."

"What if I am?"

"I know you are."

"How?"

"Because I want you to be," she said simply. "So I can't let you leave. Mother would be upset if I did."

"She's already upset."

"That's nothing. She'll scream the house down if you walk out this door."

"She doesn't scream."

Katey grinned again. "According to Sean and Patrick, she does. They're my brothers — *your* brothers. They wouldn't forgive me, either, if I let you go before they got to meet you."

"You really think you can stop me, honey?"

"Maybe not, but *she* can."

She nodded behind him. He turned to see his mother at the door to the drawing room, holding onto the frame with one hand, the other pressed to her heart. She was still as pale as parchment. Her husband stood behind her, ready to catch her if she ever got around to fainting.

She looked fragile enough to break, but her voice was strong, almost accusing, when she said, "I'm believing in leprechauns as well as ghosts, but you're not Cawlin's ghost, are you?"

"No."

Tears sprang to her eyes. "Oh, God — Angel?"

He didn't so much as breathe. She didn't wait for his answer. She came toward him, so slowly, her eyes devouring every inch of him through the tears that were now falling unchecked. Then her hands were on his face, his shoulders, his arms, making sure he was real, and finally slipping around his waist and locking there as her head dropped to his chest and she began to cry in earnest.

Angel was as much at a loss as when Cassie had done this to him, except this time he had to fight back the moisture gathering in his own eyes. He hesitated for unbearable moments before his arms came up to gather her in, probably too hard, but she didn't complain.

He looked over her head at her husband. The man was pretty embarrassed at the moment, though not at his wife's display of emotion.

"I'm sorry," Winston began.

"Don't apologize," Angel said. "I don't think I would have liked it if one of those other Angels had managed to convince you he was me."

"Anna said you looked so much like your father when you were young that you were bound to be in his image when you grew up."

"I don't remember him," Angel admitted.

Anna cried harder, hearing that. Winston smiled as he came up to put his hands on her shoulders and suggested, "Anna, let him go now."

"Never!" she said fiercely and hugged Angel harder. "And I'm wanting to know what took you so long, laddie, to come home."

"It's a long story."

She looked up at him to say, "Well, you're

not going anywhere, so you've got time to tell it."

He guessed he did, though he'd never tell all of it. And he felt like laughing, now that the tension was draining out of him. Home. He finally had one. And a family. He gave in to the urge and laughed.

Chapter 35

Catherine and Cassie returned home in time to get invited to Colt Thunder's wedding at the end of the month. His sister, Jessie, had been planning it for several weeks. According to the gossip, which they got from their housekeeper, Louella, Colt had put up a fuss about having a big to-do. He just wanted it over with before the bride changed her mind. But his sister wouldn't hear of anything less than one of the biggest shindigs Wyoming had ever seen. He was marrying a real live duchess, after all, so Jessie felt they had to do it up real fancy.

Catherine was impressed. Cassie didn't mention that she'd already heard about Colt's duchess from Angel. She was looking forward to meeting the lady who had managed to change Colt's mind about white women. Angel was certainly going to be surprised when he heard about it, since, according to him, Colt hadn't liked being "stuck" with the duchess, as he'd put it.

Cassie found out more about it when she and Marabelle ran into Jessie out on the range her second day back. The older woman was looking for a stray calf. Cassie was just enjoying being able to ride out with Marabelle again. They talked as they rode along together.

"We could have used your knack for fixing

things last month," Jessie said right off. She was about the only one who'd ever been generous in describing Cassie's meddling. "You never seen two people so unhappy as Colt and Jocelyn were when they got here. They were in love with each other. I saw it immediately. But they hadn't got around to telling each other, and it didn't look like they were going to any time soon."

"Why not?"

"He didn't think she'd marry a half-breed. She didn't think he loved her. Shows how silly they both were acting, keeping their feelings to themselves."

Cassie squirmed in the saddle. Wasn't she guilty of doing the same thing? Of course, her case was a bit different. She *knew* Angel didn't return her feelings, she didn't just think it. Then why his indifference in St. Louis to the divorce? a small voice asked her. She squirmed even more. She'd have to give that some serious thought. If there was the slightest chance . . .

"You'll never guess where's he's staying," Jessie continued. "The old Callan ranch."

That took Cassie by surprise. "I wouldn't have thought he'd ever step foot on that place again after what happened there."

"I know. But the duchess bought it, you see, to live in until the mansion she's building up in the hills is completed. And once he asked her to marry him, she refused to let him out of her sight."

"I'd heard it was the other way around, that he was worried she might change her mind about marrying him."

"Actually, neither one of them is going to stop worrying about it until the deed is done. Don't ask me how I talked them into holding off for a month so I could see my brother wed proper. It wasn't easy."

They stopped for a moment to watch Marabelle rolling about in a drift of snow left over from a storm that had hit a few weeks ago. The weather was particularly frigid that morning, but both women were quite used to it.

Cassie decided to ask the older woman for some advice while she had the opportunity. "Did you ever have a decision to make that you just couldn't make up your mind what to do about, Jessie?"

"Sure, lots of times. That's where Chase comes in handy. If I can't come up with an answer, he always does."

Cassie took a moment to tease, "He must come in handy for other things, too."

"One or two." Jessie grinned. "So what's this difficult decision you're facing?"

Jessie never did have trouble getting right to the point. Cassie tried it, replying, "I happened to get married while I was in Texas."

Jessie laughed. "Well, I'll be damned, this must be the season for it. How'd you manage to keep from bursting with that kind of news? When do we get to meet him?"

"You already know him. I married Angel."

"Angel? Not — no, of course not —"

"Actually, yes, Colt's friend."

Jessie just stared for a moment before she burst out, *"You* and *Angel?"*

Cassie winced, she sounded so disbelieving. "I

311

guess it does sound pretty ludicrous, but it wasn't actually our idea. Remember how you and Chase got married?"

"How could I forget his gun sticking in my back?" Jessie replied. Then her turquoise eyes widened. "You don't mean Angel forced you?"

"Not him. It was some neighbors of my papa's who objected to my meddling."

"And Angel *let* them do it?"

Jessie's amazement was quite understandable. Anyone who knew Angel knew he wouldn't stand still for something like that, that he would prevent it from happening, with bloodshed if necessary.

"They'd already disarmed him before he knew what they were up to."

"He must have been killing mad."

"I thought he would be, and I did everything I could to try and talk them out of it, imagining he'd kill them all. But actually, he was only angry at me. My meddling had brought it upon us, after all."

"And you're still alive?"

Cassie grinned, aware that Jessie wasn't *completely* serious with that remark. "I think Angel draws the line at shooting women."

"Is that why your mother went hightailing down to Texas all of a sudden?"

"No, she thought I might need help with those neighbors of Papa's," Cassie explained, "but Angel had already defused that situation."

"What was he doing down there, anyway?"

"I ended up being a favor he owed someone."

"That's Angel for you. He takes debts he owes

312

real seriously. He's been trying for years to pay my brother back for saving his life. In fact, Colt mentioned that Angel had helped him out with the duchess down in New Mexico, so their debt's finally squared."

"Yes, Angel told me about that."

Jessie gave her a concerned look then. "Your mother must not have been too pleased to hear about you wedding Angel, even if it wasn't intentional."

"That's putting it mildly. As it happens, she's taken a real dislike to him ever since."

"Well, don't worry about that. She'll get over it just as soon as you get it annulled. I'm surprised she hasn't already taken care of that for you."

Cassie couldn't hold back the blush her answer generated. "She can't. Getting an annulment was no longer an option after Angel insisted on having a wedding night."

Jessie's eyes flared. "Well, hell, when did he get to be so ornery?"

"Possibly after he met me. We don't exactly get along too well — all the time."

"Who does? But didn't he know he'd be forcing you to get a divorce?"

"He knew."

"Then I don't get it. What could he have been thinking of?"

Cassie's blush got a great deal brighter. Jessie noticed and said, "Oh," and did some blushing of her own. "Did you mind — no, don't answer that." Jessie's blush got worse now. "That's too personal —"

"It's all right, Jessie," Cassie interrupted. "That's part of the problem. I didn't mind at all."

"Are you saying you have special feelings for Angel?" Jessie asked carefully.

"I guess I am."

"Then you aren't going to get a divorce?"

"That's the rest of the problem. He expects me to. My mama expects me to."

"Well, who the hell said you have to do what's expected?" Jessie asked.

"But Angel doesn't want to be married."

Jessie snorted. "He should have thought of that before he had himself a wedding night."

Cassie sat back, bemused. Now why couldn't she take that attitude? But she knew. Jessie wasn't the type to let anyone walk on her without stepping right back on them, but Cassie had to be good and mad before she even thought about stepping on anyone.

In fact, she'd already tried to get mad at Angel again, to remember all the things about him that irritated her, to remember their last encounter — at least how it had ended. Mad, she could be arbitrary and make him wait some more for that divorce. She *hadn't* thought about flat out not giving it to him.

She looked at Jessie helplessly. "I don't think I could do that to him."

Jessie shook her head. "He didn't have any qualms about making your marriage legal. I wouldn't have any about keeping it that way — if that's what I really wanted. If that's *not* what you want, Cassie, go ahead and divorce him."

314

But it was what Cassie wanted. She had no doubt of that anymore. She just had every doubt about the wisdom of trying to get what she wanted from a man like Angel.

Chapter 36

Jocelyn Fleming, Dowager Duchess Of Eaton, wasn't paying the least bit of attention to the flame-red hair she was brushing. She was watching her lover in the mirror of her vanity as he sat on the bed they'd just spent a pleasurable hour in, toying with a piece of paper in his hand. He was dressed already, in his usual casual attire of tight black pants, blue shirt, red bandana — and knee-high moccasins. His fringed buckskin jacket hung on her bedpost. He wouldn't need it again tonight, for his sister and her husband were coming over for dinner, would in fact be arriving shortly.

She wondered, not for the first time, if she would be able to get him into a suit for their wedding. She seriously doubted it. She wondered, too, if he was ever going to cut his past-the-shoulder-length black hair again. The last time he'd worn it short, he'd nearly been whipped to death — on the front porch of this very ranch.

She still ached for him each time she saw his scars, and he no longer hid them from her. She'd already decided she would never ask him to cut his hair, since he wore it long deliberately so no one would ever again doubt that he was a half-breed. The decision would have to be his alone — when and if he could ever put all of that old bitterness to rest.

She liked to think she was working on helping him toward that end. At least now he was more like the happy, contented man his sister had described to her, rather than the surly, near savage man she'd tricked into escorting her to Wyoming. Until the day she died, she'd never forget his expression when she'd called his bluff and agreed to pay him fifty thousand dollars to be her guide. Dear Edward's money had never given her as much pleasure as it had that day.

"All right, I give up, Colt," Jocelyn said, drawing his light blue eyes to the mirror. "My curiosity simply can't bear it anymore, so tell me, what *are* you sitting there frowning about?"

"This damn letter from Angel."

"When did it arrive?"

"It was there when I went to town this morning. And I shouldn't even call it a letter. Two damn sentences is all he wrote, though I can't really complain about that, since he probably had to have someone write it for him, and he's never been long-winded."

Her brow rose slightly. "Are you trying to make me feel sorry for that despicable friend of yours by telling me he can't write?"

"I never asked if he could, but I seriously doubt it, with the way he was raised — and you can't still be mad at him for that stunt he pulled in New Mexico."

"Can't I? I truly thought I was going to die that day. He could have told me he was on my side, instead of letting me think the worst."

"If you'd thought any differently, Longnose

317

might have suspected something, and who's to say you and Angel would have got out of there alive? Now I'm not condoning what he did, but he did have the best intentions. You'd been running from that man for three years without knowing what he even looked like. It was time you knew."

"I give you only that," she allowed.

"Well, give me one better," he said. "If you'd had to waste time guessing who Longnose was when he showed up here in your bedroom that day, you wouldn't have acted as swiftly as you did, and you might have been dead by the time I got up here to kill the bastard."

She hadn't thought of that, but still, she really detested the idea of being grateful to Angel. Pointedly, she said, "You were telling me about his letter. What has you so upset about it?"

Colt grunted. "I'm not upset, I'm baffled."

"And you're handling it very well, too."

He gave her a sharp look. "He says he'll be home within the week."

"Wonderful." She sighed. "In time for the wedding. *Just* what I wanted to hear. Does *he* at least own a suit?"

"You're going to pay for that one, Duchess."

She smiled sweetly at him. "Do you promise?"

He came up to stand behind her. "My brother-in-law has the right idea. A woman's neck needs to be wrung every once in a while."

"If you put your hands on me, Colt Thunder, I can't promise we'll be available when your sister arrives."

He bent down to lick the bare skin on the

318

inner side of her camisole strap. "Jessie would understand."

"Philippe wouldn't."

"That's all right," he assured her. "I feel like shooting that temperamental French chef of yours once a day anyway. So today I give in —"

"Stop!" She chuckled. "What else did your wretched Angel have to say?"

The frown was back as Colt glanced again at the letter in his hand. "He asks me to keep an eye on his meddling wife until he gets here."

"I didn't know he was married," Jocelyn said. "Have I met her?"

"How the hell should I know?" he replied. "I haven't met her yet myself."

Her frown appeared to match his. "Then how does he expect you to keep an eye on her?"

"I'm damned if I know," Colt said in exasperation. "It's not like Angel to be cryptic — well, it is, but not *that* cryptic. He must think that I'd know who he's talking about, but I'm damned if I do."

"Did he describe her?"

"Honey, I told you word for word all he said. Two damn sentences."

"Well, actually, he does describe her — as meddling. Do you know anyone like that?"

"There's only one woman in these parts that anyone refers to as meddling, but it couldn't be her. She was visiting her father in — Texas."

"Isn't that where Angel went when he left us in New Mexico?"

He shook his head, not in answer, but in bafflement again. "I refuse to believe Angel married Cassie Stuart."

"There, you see, you *did* know who he was talking about after all."

"Jocelyn, Cassie Stuart is a very proper, very well-brought-up young lady. She and Angel would be so mismatched it'd be laughable. Her kind scares the pants off him."

"That would certainly be interesting." She grinned at him through the mirror. "I rather hope it is her, though, of course, that means I'll have to start feeling sorry for the girl immediately."

He placed his hands slowly around her neck.

"What do you mean, you know?" Jessie scowled. She hated having a good surprise spoiled. "Cassie just told me today. When did she tell you?"

"She didn't," Colt replied, his bafflement back. "I got a letter from Angel. But I still refuse to believe it. *Angel* and *Cassie?*"

"That's what I said," Jessie told him. "But it's true enough, though how long it remains so is another matter. They didn't get married because they wanted to. They were helped to it by some angry Texans."

"All right, now *that's* a little more believable," Colt allowed. "Though I still can't imagine why Angel would let it happen."

"Maybe because he wanted it to happen."

Colt, Jessie, and Chase all looked at Jocelyn in surprise. It was Colt who asked her, "Where did you get that crazy notion?"

The duchess shrugged. "If he didn't want to be married, would he be in the habit of calling her his wife when referring to her, instead of by name? Would a man who hates to be indebted, as you've assured me he does, ask you to keep an eye on this lady when he's going to be here shortly himself? And by the way, why would he be so concerned about her? Is she in some kind of trouble?"

It was Chase who answered, since Jessie and Colt were still mulling over Jocelyn's astounding logic. "If you knew the lady, you wouldn't have to ask. Cassie Stuart is in the habit of always being in trouble of one kind or another because of her meddling."

"I don't like that word, Chase," Jessie complained in defense of her friend. "Cassie just has a big heart and likes to help people —"

"Whether they want help or not."

Jessie gave her husband a dark look for that interruption. Typically, he merely smiled back at her.

And to dispute some of Jocelyn's logic, Colt added, "Cassie's mother is perfectly capable of keeping her out of trouble. She's been doing it for years."

To which the duchess simply tossed out another bit of logic for them to chew over. "So maybe Angel feels that's his responsibility now."

"She may have a point there, Colt," Jessie conceded. "After all, Angel insisted on having a wedding night, when if he'd kept his hands off the girl, she could have had that shotgun wedding annulled."

"Well, *that* must have been an interesting conversation you two had this morning," Chase remarked with a chuckle.

"Cassie actually told you that?" Colt asked his sister, a bit embarrassed himself.

Jocelyn, seeing his flush, laughed. "Men do seem to have that problem every once in a while."

"I'm more than likely to have it tonight," Chase said.

His wife threw her napkin at him from across the table — but she didn't push his foot away. It had slipped beneath her skirt and was presently rubbing up and down the back of her calf. She concealed a secret smile that only he recognized.

"Well, I don't care what you say," Colt said to the table at large. "I happen to know Angel better than the rest of you, and I'm not accepting any of this until I hear it from his own mouth. But in the meantime, I guess I better go over to the Lazy S tomorrow and make sure Angel's so-called wife is behaving herself."

"I'll go with you," Jocelyn volunteered. "I'd like to meet this poor, unfortunate girl for myself."

"Duchess —" Colt began, only to be cut off.

"It doesn't matter what you say, Colt Thunder. I am never going to like that particular friend of yours."

"You weren't planning on telling his wife that, were you?" Colt wanted to know.

"Certainly not. I hope I have better manners than that — though *someone* ought to encourage her to get a divorce while she still can."

"But you won't, Duchess," Colt said without expression. "We only allow one meddler in each county, after all. We shoot the rest."

"More Western customs?" she asked in a tone quite as dry as her friend Vanessa's had ever been. "How quaint."

Chapter 37

Angel hadn't expected to be back in Cheyenne before the end of the month. But the plain fact was, he couldn't stay away. The short time he'd spent with his family had actually given him a new sense of self-worth. They'd accepted him as he was, without looking down on him for the profession he'd drifted into. It had made him rethink his situation with Cassie, and once he had, there was no way he was going to delay doing something about it.

That was what he'd thought when he left St. Louis. But when he was only a few hours' ride away from her, the doubts had started to re-surface — not enough to change his mind about the decision he'd made, but enough to put brakes on the urgency that had been hounding him.

He was going to tell Cassie that he wouldn't give her a divorce. No, maybe he ought to ask her first if she wouldn't mind staying married to him. If she said she did mind, *then* he'd tell her, "Too bad." And he'd keep her in bed in-definitely if he had to, until she changed her mind. In bed they were compatible in every way. It was only out of it that she could find a hundred reasons why they would never suit. He aimed to convince her otherwise.

Now it was just a matter of getting up the

nerve to do it. Seeing Catherine Stuart right after he'd arrived hadn't helped. She'd been on her way to the bank and had seen him, too, but hadn't acknowledged him other than to fondly caress the gun on her hip.

That lady was definitely going to be a problem. Trying to get on her good side would be pointless. She didn't have one. So his best bet would probably be not to deal with her at all. He didn't exactly need her approval to win Cassie, he just needed Cassie's.

That decision put one of his worries to rest, but it was a short rest. The knock on his door came before he'd even had a chance to unpack. He thought it was Agnes, the owner of the boardinghouse where he lived whenever he was in town, but when he opened the door, Cassie's mother was standing there looking her most formidable.

She didn't waste any time getting to the point of her unexpected visit. "There's twenty-five thousand dollars in this bag. Find yourself another town to live in."

He glanced down at the black bag in her hand, took in her stiff posture, the determination in her expression. He didn't close the door in her face, though he sure felt like it. He didn't invite her in, either.

"I like this one," was all he said to her.

"So find yourself another one to like."

Angel kept his tone polite — just barely — and only for Cassie's sake. "Keep your money, Mrs. Stuart. I've got no use for it."

"It's not enough? You want more?"

"Ma'am, I earn five thousand a job, sometimes

ten, for just a few days' work. I don't want your money."

She wasn't expecting to hear that. It turned her expression even more sour than it was. "If you're so damn rich, why don't you retire?"

"I'm thinking about it."

Catherine scoffed. "You won't. You're not suited to anything else."

"That's what I always figured — but there does happen to be something else I can do now," he said in his slow drawl. "I can be a husband to your daughter. Keeping her out of trouble would be a full-time job."

He said it to rile her. She'd made him angry, thinking she could buy him off. And it worked.

She damn near screeched, "You stay the hell away from my daughter, or I'll — !"

She didn't finish her warning. Angel grinned, guessing her problem. "Can't think of anyone who's fast enough to kill me, can you?"

She about-faced to march off, without giving him the satisfaction of a reply. "Mrs. Stuart?" he called after her. She didn't stop. "You can tell Cassie I'll be out to see her soon."

"Step one foot on my —"

"Yeah, I know, you'll shoot me yourself. Folks just love to tell me that." He said the last to himself, though, since she was already gone.

Her mama was late. Cassie had taken care of the few purchases they'd needed while Catherine had gone to the bank and to the depot to see if Madame Cecilia's gowns had arrived yet. They'd had lunch first in one of the several restaurants Cheyenne boasted, then gone in different directions to complete their errands.

She didn't mind waiting in the carriage on a day when the sun was out, but this afternoon the sky was looking kind of gloomy. She hoped the snow would hold off for another two days, until after Colt's wedding.

Imagine him coming by the ranch just to introduce his duchess to her and her mama the other day. That had been an unexpected surprise, but one that Cassie had appreciated. It gave her the opportunity to mention to him that Angel was in St. Louis. She'd hoped he might know how to reach him there to invite him to the wedding, but Colt hadn't taken the hint, at least not that she'd noticed, and she wasn't bold enough to come right out and make the suggestion.

She'd tried talking to him about Angel when her mama wasn't there, but he kept changing the subject. In fact, now that she thought of it, about all he'd been interested in was knowing if she'd found anyone who needed her special "fixing" skills since she'd been back.

"I think we should go to Mr. Thornley's office right now if it's still open, and if not, we'll hunt him down," Catherine said as she hopped into the carriage so suddenly she scared the breath out of Cassie. "He's been my lawyer for years. He can probably work miracles and get those divorce papers delivered to Angel today."

"I can't yet, Mama," Cassie said, adding a pointed reminder. "The baby?"

"Damn, I forgot about that. Well, the very minute we know for sure —"

"What did you mean 'today'? Is Angel back? Have you seen him?"

Catherine sighed and picked up the reins to get them started down the street. "I saw him," she mumbled through gritted teeth.

Cassie's heart picked up its beat with the knowledge that he was back — and near at hand again. "Did you have words with him?"

"None worth mentioning," Catherine said evasively, keeping her eyes straight ahead, a clear sign she wasn't going to be any more enlightening than that.

Cassie frowned thoughtfully. It might not be worth mentioning, but *something* had obviously upset her mama enough for her to start insisting on the divorce again. Cassie wondered if she ought to tell her right now that she wasn't getting a divorce, possible baby or not. No, that kind of unpleasantness could wait.

She ought to tell Angel first anyway, and that wasn't going to be pleasant, either. Of course, she could hold off telling him until she knew one way or the other about a baby. That gave her another week or so to figure out how she was going to tell him she wasn't going to set him free.

They were nearly out of town when Cassie noticed the man standing in front of one of Cheyenne's more disreputable saloons with two other men. She stared, rubbed her eyes and stared again, and still didn't believe it.

"I'm seeing a ghost, Mama."

Catherine turned to look in the same direction, but didn't see anything out of the ordinary.

"There's no such thing," she said firmly.

"But that man over there, the tall one," Cassie said in a shaky voice. "He's dead. Angel killed him in Texas. I put my own bullet in him, too."

"Then maybe he didn't die."

"They buried him."

"Then it's just someone who looks like him," Catherine said reasonably.

"The spitting image?"

"You're not seeing him close up, baby," Catherine pointed out. "If you did, you'd see you're mistaken. Dead men don't walk again."

Cassie's heart dropped to the seat when one of the men suddenly pointed at her. She recognized him as someone she'd frequently seen around town though didn't know by name. And he walked off after pointing her out. The other two were returning her stare now.

She might be mistaken in what she'd just seen, but not about the man. She almost couldn't find her voice to answer, "I know dead men don't walk, but — but it *is* him, Mama. He's not someone I could forget. He broke into my room one night in Caully and would have raped me if Marabelle hadn't fetched Angel. That's why Angel called him out and shot him."

Catherine nearly pulled up on the reins. "How come your papa never told me about *that?*"

"Because I didn't mention it to him."

"What else didn't you mention to him?"

Her mama was definitely annoyed now, so Cassie did some evading herself. "Nothing that I can recall."

Catherine snorted. "Well, don't worry about

329

that fellow. He's certainly not dead. If anything, maybe he's a twin brother of the other one."

"Another Slater?" Cassie said with a groan. "One was one too many."

Chapter 38

It was nearly dark by the time they got home, but that didn't stop Cassie from saddling up and riding out. She did it without her mama knowing, of course. Only old Mac, who had the care of the Stuart horses, saw her. She asked him to tell her mama that she'd felt the need for a brisk ride before dinner — if her mama asked. If she rode full out, she just might make it back in time before Catherine got around to asking.

She was going back to Cheyenne.

Seeing that man who was the image of Rafferty Slater hadn't merely shocked her, it had set her to fretting all the way home. Her mama undoubtedly had the right of it. He was probably Slater's brother, more than likely his twin brother. And his showing up in Cheyenne, where both she and Angel hailed from, was just too coincidental for her peace of mind.

Even if he wasn't here seeking revenge for his brother's death, she had to warn Angel about him. Rafferty had tried to shoot Angel in the back, and dirty tactics like that tended to run in the family. At any rate, she wasn't taking any chances, not where Angel was concerned. She wasn't about to lose him to a no-account, cowardly back stabber just when she'd decided to keep him.

She reached Cheyenne faster than she ever had before, but it was still dark when she rode in, and the clouds that had been hovering all day were going to hold back the moon, so she wouldn't be able to ride as fast on the return trip. She might not make it home before dinner after all, but she'd worry about explaining to her mother when the time came.

She knew where to find Angel. It was standard knowledge that he resided at Agnes's boarding-house because the old lady was so fond of him, and never rented out his room to anyone else, even when he was gone for months at a time. Whether he was actually in at this time of the evening was another matter. She hoped she wouldn't have to wait around or go hunting for him in town, but if she had to, she would.

She tied up her mare in front of the board-inghouse. Only a dim light from a parlor window was lighting the porch, but it was enough to keep her from tripping on the steps leading to the door. Cassie didn't quite get that far.

"Don't move lessen I tell you to, little lady, and don't make a sound."

A gun jabbing against her back reinforced that order. Cassie had no difficulty recognizing it even through the thickness of her jacket. And she wasn't wearing her own. She never did to Cheyenne, and she hadn't wasted time to fetch it at home before she'd returned to town.

Obviously she should have. But she hadn't been thinking of danger, just of getting to Angel to warn him. It was too late to berate herself for not examining Agnes's porch more closely, too.

She knew better. Such carelessness could easily cost a life. It was possible she was going to find that out firsthand.

A hand on her shoulder turned her, so that the gun was now jabbed into her belly. She'd had a feeling she would recognize her accoster, and she did.

"Nice of you to come back to town to make this easy for me."

She didn't acknowledge that remark. She knew him, but she had to ask, "Who are you?"

"They call me Gaylen," he said. "But you know my last name, don't you? Folks don't usually forget someone they help to kill."

Cassie went quite pale, though common sense made her insist, "You're not Rafferty."

" 'Course I'm not, but no one ever could tell us apart, so it's the same, ain't it? Lookin' at me is lookin' at the man you killed."

It wouldn't do to point out that Rafferty had deserved it. "What do you want?"

"I was gonna take care of that Angel fellow first, then you after, but now that I have you, I'll have to rethink on it. Come along. My horse is tied up out back."

Cassie wasn't given much choice with his hand clamping on the back of her neck and his gun moving to her side. She thought about screaming, but didn't care to get shot for the effort. And he wouldn't hesitate to shoot. It was dark, with no moon and nothing but flat plain behind the boardinghouse. He'd be gone before the smoke cleared, while she wouldn't be alive to say who'd done it.

He put her on his horse in front of him. He didn't holster his gun, so she didn't consider trying to jump off yet. They rode out onto the plain so he could circle around the town without being seen; then he headed toward the foothills in the east.

It was nearly five hours later before he found the small, one-room cabin. Cassie had a feeling he'd been lost for the past two hours. Smoke curled out the chimney. Another horse stood in the lean-to nearby. Seeing it, she finally remembered that he'd had a friend with him in town earlier.

The friend was sleeping, curled into his bedroll before the fire, when Gaylen pushed her into the cabin. He didn't bother to wake him yet. The only furniture in the room was a table with one chair. Neither looked very sturdy.

He gave her a brief glance as he set his saddlebags on the table and started to rummage through them. "Your folks got money, don't they? Lots of it?"

"Yes, why?"

"Some of it might compensate me for my loss."

"Then you won't try to kill Angel?"

"Didn't say that."

He pulled out a bandana and a strip of rawhide and motioned Cassie into the far corner. The bandana ended up around her wrists, the rawhide around her ankles — after he'd yanked her boots off and tossed them across the room.

"I've decided to send Harry down with my demands," he told her when he had finished.

"This has worked out better'n I first figured on."

"How's that?"

"It'll be easier killin' that fast gun up here. Won't have to rush off after or worry about no posse. Your ranch ain't far from here, is it?"

"How should I know?" she said unhelpfully. "I couldn't tell where we were going."

"I reckon it's not far."

Never once had he raised his voice or sounded like a man enraged over his brother's death. His attitude wasn't natural, but she took some small hope from it. Maybe he wasn't as bad as Rafferty had been. Maybe he wasn't all that happy about the killing he felt he had to do. And maybe he didn't even know what kind of man his brother had become. She decided to enlighten him, just in case.

"You know, your brother was no good. He stampeded cattle. He tried to —"

"Don't be talkin' against my brother," was all he said, and even that was said mildly.

He ignored her then to go over and kick Harry awake. They conferred quietly by the fire for a while, with Harry glancing her way more than once. He wasn't as tall as Gaylen. His eyes were a dull gray, his brown hair long and stringy, his clothes ill-fitting and stained. He was, in fact, an ugly little man, the kind easily led by others.

Cassie strained to hear them, but couldn't catch more than a word or two. After they did some scribbling on an old newspaper, using soot right out of the fireplace, Harry shrugged into his jacket and left. Gaylen settled down in the vacated bedroll by the fire.

Cassie waited a few minutes, but it really did look like the man was going to go to sleep, and never mind that she hadn't been fed, or offered a blanket or even a position closer to the fire. Warmth wasn't her immediate concern, however.

"Just how did you plan to get Angel up here?"

"He's gonna bring me your ma's money."

"What makes you think he'll do that? It's more likely my mama will send —"

"She'll send Angel, or it's no deal."

"She might *ask* him, but that doesn't mean he'll agree to come," Cassie pointed out.

"He's a gun for hire, ain't he? So your mama can hire him if he don't want to do it for nothing. And he don't know who's got you or that I aim to kill him, so why wouldn't he come? 'Sides, I heard you got hitched to him 'fore you two left Texas. It would look pretty bad if the man didn't come to get his wife, now wouldn't it?"

Cassie didn't hear much beyond the mention that Angel would be coming up here unaware of what was waiting for him. That hadn't occurred to her. She wished it hadn't been pointed out now because with it came a sick feeling of dread. Would her mama remember that she'd seen Rafferty's brother in town and draw the right conclusion? Would she even mention it to Angel if she did?

Cassie had to do something, get away, or think of some way to warn Angel. If Gaylen hadn't tied her hands behind her back, she could have scooted over to him and hit him with one of the logs stacked next to the fire. If he hadn't removed her boots, she would have tried kicking him senseless. There was nothing but two logs in the fireplace, so she couldn't even fish out a burning stick to maneuver against the cotton bandana. And sticking her hands in the fire completely to burn off the cloth just didn't appeal to her, nor did it guarantee she'd be alive afterward to do anything.

Her only option at the moment seemed to be to help Gaylen into rethinking the matter. But as she stared at him lying there, his arms tucked behind his head, looking so peaceful, as if he weren't contemplating murder, she wasn't the least bit confident.

She still had to try. "Would you kill a man who'd tried to shoot you in the back, Slater?"

"Sure I would."

"Well, that's why Angel shot your brother."

"Lady, I heard what went on down there. That man of yours was lookin' for my brother to kill him, and he's known to be faster'n lightnin'. Either way Rafe woulda died, so what he tried was the only chance he had, as I see it. You gonna tell me that there Angel of Death wasn't out to kill him?"

She couldn't very well do that. "Your brother tried to rape me. That's why."

He glanced over at her then, showing her the first bit of emotion. It was surprise. "Well, shoot, what'd he want to do that for? You ain't nothin' much to look at."

Heat stole up Cassie's cheeks. "That doesn't change the fact —"

"Even if he did rape you," he broke in, "that'd

be no reason to die."

With *that* attitude, he'd never admit his brother
might have deserved what he'd got, so she
changed tactics. "You won't get away with this.
If you succeed in killing Angel, I'll hunt you down
myself. There won't be anywhere —"

He cut her off again with a snort. "Lady, what
makes you think you'll be leavin' here alive? The
only reason you ain't dead yet is in case that
fast gun wants to see you 'fore he comes in close
enough for me to shoot him. You're the reason
he killed Rafe, so you gotta die, same as him."

He probably thought that would shut her up.
It nearly did. "You — you still won't get away
with it. I saw you in town today. I told my mama.
She's smart enough to figure it's you, so the name
Slater will be on Wanted posters in every state
and the Western territory. You'll never have another moment's peace if you murder us."

"So I'll leave the country," he replied with a
shrug. "That won't bother me none. But you're
botherin' me, so shut it up, girlie, 'fore I stuff
something in your mouth. They won't be able
to get the money until the bank opens in the
mornin', so that gunfighter won't be gettin' here
until near noon. I need some sleep 'fore then."

Cassie decided against telling him that her mama
would have him hunted down, no matter where
he went. His answer would probably be that he'd
kill her, too.

She gave up for the time being. She'd have
time in the morning to work on him some
more, and his friend Harry, too. The smaller
man would be easier to scare, and maybe *he*

could talk some sense into Slater.

But she refused to let him have the last word. "I'm hungry," she complained.

"I ain't wastin' food on a dead woman."

She let him have the last word after all.

Chapter 39

Catherine pounded on Angel's door at two o'clock that morning. It sounded like she was breaking it down. The other boarders were out in the hall having a look at what woke them by the time Angel had opened the door.

She had two of her tougher-looking cowhands with her. Angel stood there in just his pants — and his gun. His first thought was, she'd intended to escort him out of town, especially since she was carrying that damn black bag again. But if so, she should have tried it more quietly. The gun he leveled at his visitors said he was staying right there. And having been awakened from a *very* pleasant dream about her daughter, he was in no mood for any more of her insults.

"You try to give me that money again and I'll burn it," he told her.

"It's not for you. I'm here to hire you."

"To leave the country?" he sneered.

"No, to get Cassie back. Was she here? Her horse is still out front."

"I haven't seen her — and what do you mean, to get her back? Where is she?"

"She's being held in a cabin up in the foothills. From the crude map they drew, I'd say it's an old trappers cabin not far from my ranch. I don't know how many men there are, but they want twenty thousand dollars or they say they'll — they'll kill her."

Angel's gun slowly lowered. It was only then he noticed how pale Catherine was. He probably looked the same.

He hoped she was lying, that this was no more than a setup to get rid of him. Could she be that underhanded? Probably, but the fear he saw in her eyes told him this wasn't one of those times.

"How did this happen?"

"She was with me in town today. When we got home, she took off by herself. She left the message that she was just going for a ride, but with her horse here, I have to assume she was coming to see you. But since you haven't seen her, she must have been taken almost immediately after she got here."

"And all they want is twenty thousand?"

His surprise was understandable. Everyone who knew the Stuarts knew they came from old money.

"Apparently they don't know how much I'm worth," Catherine said. "Which is fortunate in one respect only. I just happen to have that much on hand, so I don't have to wait until the morning to visit the bank."

Only because she'd tried to bribe him out of town. Her slight blush said she was remembering that, too. It got worse when she added, "The other five thousand is still in the bag. That was what you said your price is, wasn't it?"

"Take it out."

"I beg your pardon?"

"Take the five out. I won't work for you, Mrs. Stuart, not for any reason."

He turned away after saying it. Catherine took a step forward, which put her inside his room. "You have to," she said in a beseeching tone. "I don't know why, but they say they'll only take the money from you. If anyone else tries to deliver it —"

He was putting his shirt on when he interrupted her. "I didn't say I wouldn't deliver it."

"Then let me pay you."

"To collect my wife?" He paused to give her a dark look. "She is still my wife, isn't she?"

Catherine went red in the face again because she suspected he wasn't going to move another inch unless she answered him. "Yes," she bit out.

He didn't rub it in, but he did continue dressing. "Where is that cabin?"

"Jim here can show you where it is, but he can't back you up. They say specifically, you're to go in alone."

"Didn't figure it otherwise. Do you have any idea who these men are? Enemies of yours, maybe?"

"Mine, no — but possibly yours."

"What makes you think so?"

She shrugged, her look uncertain. "It could be just a wild guess, but Cassie saw someone in town today that shook her up pretty bad. She claimed he was the man you killed while down in Texas."

"I killed more'n one down there."

"That Cassie knew about?"

"No. That would be Rafferty Slater," he said.

"But dead men don't walk."

"That's what I said," Catherine replied. "But she insisted this man looked exactly like the one you killed. The only reasonable explanation is that they're brothers, maybe even twins."

"And a brother might be after a little revenge," Angel concluded as he shrugged on his slicker. "Thanks for the warning."

Cassie's teeth were chattering. The cabin hadn't been made very well. The cold had been seeping in along the floorboards all night. An icy wind was coming in through one larger crack in the wall near her back. The fire was still going, but Gaylen had tied her up in a corner on the opposite side of the room, so its warmth wasn't reaching her.

She could have managed to scoot across the floor to get nearer to the fire if she'd tried to. But Gaylen was hogging it, and she couldn't bear to get close to a man who was going to shoot her while she was bound tight and helpless to prevent it, so she stayed where she was. She supposed he wouldn't have minded waking up to find her frozen stiff. It would save him a bullet.

Then Harry had returned and had done a lot of staring at her before he settled back down — again in front of the fire. He even added another log to it, but the heat still didn't reach Cassie. And after the way the little man had looked at her, like he wouldn't mind warming her himself, she definitely wasn't getting near either one of those two, no matter if she did freeze.

She must have fallen asleep at some point,

though that hadn't been her intention. What woke her, she wasn't sure. Possibly her chattering teeth. But it was still night. The cabin didn't boast a single window, but the cracks in the walls would have shown up sunlight if it was out there.

Her hands were completely numb now. She'd spent a good hour earlier trying to stretch the cloth to slip at least one hand out, but Gaylen had tied her so tight, she'd have to be cut loose. She doubted he'd bother to do that before he shot her.

She'd stared at the door for a long time, debating whether to try to leave. No more than a loop of rope hooked to the wall was locking it from intruders. She might have been able to work that loose with her teeth, and her chin could have taken care of the latch. But the door was a lot closer to the fire and the two men than to her, and she was afraid the cold that would blast in when she opened it would wake them both, if not immediately, then soon, because she doubted she'd be able to close the door behind her with the wind pushing at it. Besides, she wouldn't get very far, rolling and scooting down the foothills. And Gaylen might just go ahead and kill her now if she put him to the trouble of having to go after her. That wouldn't help Angel when he arrived. And it certainly wouldn't help her.

She tried moving her legs, and found out that she had aches all over from her cramped position. Her head fell back against the wall, causing her to groan. She couldn't remember ever having been so cold, and miserable — and afraid. She didn't want to die. She wondered, if she told Gaylen that, whether he might reconsider. She almost laughed. He was as conscienceless as she'd once thought Angel was. But Angel had a deeply ingrained sense of justice. Gaylen's justice was cold-blooded murder.

"Cassie?"

It was the wind, making her hear things she wanted to hear. That couldn't have been . . .

"Cassie, wake up, damn it."

She leaned forward to turn and stare wide-eyed at the wall. "I am awake," she whispered excitedly. "Angel?"

"Can you open the door?"

"I'll try, but it may take me a while. They've got me tied up."

"Never mind. I'll break the door in."

"No," she hissed. "If that doesn't work, you'll just wake them. Let me try first."

"All right, but hurry."

Hurry, when she ached so much she could barely move? Actually, with rescue imminent, her cramped muscles didn't seem to hurt nearly as bad as they had earlier.

Since there was no furniture to block her way, lying down and rolling got her across the room quicker than scooting would have. Getting up on her knees when she reached the door wasn't as easy, though, but she managed it after several tries.

Her real difficulty came from the rope lock. It hadn't looked all that secure from across the room, but it was stretched tighter than she'd figured, and hooked over a curved nail. She was able to grasp one side of the loop with her teeth, but no matter how hard she bit down and pulled, the end wouldn't slip over the hook. And trying to stand up to turn and use her hands would be a waste of time. Her fingers were too numb.

She finally had to put her mouth to one of the cracks in the door. "Angel?"

He was right there waiting. "What?"

"I'm having trouble with this rope lock. Maybe if you open the door and push against it some, it will stretch the rope enough for me to work it loose."

His answer was to do just that. Cassie watched the rope carefully, ready to tell him to stop if she saw it stretch even a little. She should have watched the opposite edge of the doorframe instead. The pressure Angel was applying popped the rusted hinges loose and the door suddenly swung in on her from that side.

Her cry of surprise came too quickly to silence it. "What the — ?" was heard almost immediately behind her, and right after it, "Please do," was heard from in front of her.

Cassie wiggled her way out from under the door, which was now hanging from that damn loop of rope, to see Angel holding his gun on Gaylen and Harry, and itching for any excuse to pull the trigger.

"You must be Angel," Gaylen said.

"The Angel of Death," Angel replied for the first time in his life.

"So you came without the money?" Even now, faced with an abrupt end to his scheme, Gaylen wore an expression that seemed almost indifferent. Beside him, Harry looked about to faint. "I hadn't figured on that."

"The money is outside. Her mama happened to have it on hand. You want it, draw for it."

"That'd be real sportin' of you, 'cept I heard you never lose."

Angel just smiled. Cassie got mad, listening to them. She was cold, hungry, sore, and the door had hit her on the head when it fell sideways.

"If you aren't going to shoot them, would you mind doing something else with them so we can leave?"

Her voice was about as frosty as it could get. It didn't draw his gaze, just a nod, before he walked forward and motioned Gaylen to turn around. As soon as he did, Angel's gun butt cracked against his skull.

Harry stared bug-eyed as his friend went down and Angel turned to him. "Couldn' you just tie me up instead?"

"I could shoot you instead."

Harry turned quickly to receive his blow. Cassie made a sound of disgust. Harry had had a good point.

"Why *couldn't* you have tied them up?" she wanted to know.

Angel glanced at her for the first time. "Because that's easier to do if they're like this. I'll do it now."

"Do you have a knife to cut me loose with first?"

He pulled one out of his boot. Her mama would hate to know that they shared that habit in common.

"You all right?" he finally got around to asking as he sliced through her bonds.

"Couldn't be better," she snapped.

She wasn't sure why she was so angry with him. Possibly because she'd seen how much he'd wanted to kill Gaylen — or maybe because she'd like the comfort of a hug and knew she wouldn't be getting one.

"Actually, I'm amazed you let him live," she said. "He'll probably only get a few years in prison for what he tried to do here. You aren't worried he'll come after you again when he gets out?"

"I never heard of Rafferty, but Gaylen Slater is another matter. That was him, wasn't it?"

"So he said."

"Well, he's wanted in Colorado and New Mexico for murder. One of those juries ought to end up hanging him."

"I thought it didn't bother you to kill someone who you knew was headed for the hangman."

"With you watching, it bothers me," he said, then asked, "How did they get to you, anyway?"

"I came to town last night to see you."

"Alone? And without your gun?" he said in a tone that implied she couldn't have done anything more stupid. "What did you want to see me about?"

"I don't think I'll tell you now," she said stiffly.

"You wanted to warn me about Slater?"

"What if I did?"

"I didn't think you cared."

"I care."

"How much?"

"Too damn much," she replied sharply, in contrast to his soft tone, only to spoil that confession by adding, "But then, we aren't enemies, so I'd like to think that makes us friends. And I care about *all* my friends."

He gave her a dark look that said he wasn't going to take much more of her sass. Then he left her to attend to the binding of the two unconscious men. She stayed where she was, rubbing the circulation back into her hands before she sought out her boots.

She moved stiffly, her muscles still sore. And she started getting annoyed at herself. She should have been nothing but relieved. She was safe. Angel was safe. She should have been thanking him instead of snapping at him — but she still hadn't had that hug.

"This was too easy," he said, coming up behind her.

She turned to face him. "They weren't expecting you until noon, so they didn't bother with a watch."

His eyes narrowed suddenly. "Did either of them touch you, Cassie? And tell me the truth."

"So you can still kill them yourself?"

"Yes."

He was nothing if not honest, her Angel.

"No, they weren't attracted to me."

"They must be blind."

Her cheeks started glowing pleasurably. "Are *you* attracted to me, Angel?"

"What the hell do you think?" he said before he yanked her into his arms.

Chapter 40

Cassie got a few hours' sleep on the way home, sitting in front of Angel on the saddle and using his chest for a pillow. He made the ride nice and slow so she could, but not before he offered a confession in a low-voiced grumble. "I'm damned if I want to take you home." They were both remembering that kiss and crushing hug he'd given her in that relic of a cabin. "If your mother weren't waiting . . ."

He didn't finish, and Cassie didn't answer. But she was smiling as she went to sleep — and more determined than ever to keep her Angel.

The sun was just up when they rode into the yard of the Lazy S. Catherine was on the porch to greet them. She hadn't gotten any sleep last night herself.

After a backbreaking hug, Cassie forestalled any interrogations with a quick "I'll talk to you later, Mama. I have to settle something with Angel first." And she turned to him to add, "I'll be right back, so don't go away."

They both stared after her as she ran into the house. Catherine finally looked at Angel, who hadn't come more than halfway up the porch steps — to keep his distance from her.

"Did you kill them?" she asked.

"Not with her there."

"I would have."

He didn't doubt it. "Cassie tends to get upset at the thought of me killing folks. She does crazy things to prevent it. Even wanted to challenge Rafferty Slater herself, so I wouldn't."

Catherine digested that slowly and with a good deal of dread, though her expression didn't change. She wasn't about to mention to him that it sounded like her daughter didn't want him hurt, at any cost.

She raised a brow. "What'd she do with the Slater who's still alive?"

"Started bitching at me instead of thanking me for getting her out of there."

"Then let me thank you —"

"None's needed."

She hadn't thought so. "Do you know what she means to settle with you?"

"No."

Catherine was afraid she did, but she wasn't going to warn him. A gunfighter for a son-in-law. She supposed worse things could happen.

With a resigned sigh, she said, "I'll send someone to the sheriff to take care of those men. Tell Cassie you did the explaining for her. I'm going to bed."

Angel frowned before the door had closed behind her. She was leaving him alone with her daughter? The same woman who'd wanted him as far as he could possibly get from Cassie?

When Cassie stepped back out onto the porch, it was to find Angel with one arm around Marabelle's neck and the other hand scratching at her ears. "When did *that* happen?" she asked incredulously.

"What?"

"You and Marabelle getting along."

"Why shouldn't we?" he said in all innocence. "She's just a big ol' pussycat."

Cassie snorted to tell him how much she was accepting that. He just grinned up at her — until he noticed that she was now wearing her gun. His frown came quick and furious.

"Just where do you think you're going with that?" he demanded.

"Nowhere."

"Then what'd you put it on for?"

"Because I'm challenging you to the draw, Angel."

"That's what you think."

"You want that divorce, don't you?"

His frown got darker. "What the hell's the one got to do with the other?"

"If you win, I'll go straight to the lawyer's office and get the divorce started.

"And if you win?"

"There won't be any divorce."

Angel went very still, his eyes riveted to hers. "Why would you take that chance?"

"It seems to be the only chance I've got — to keep you."

"You *want* to stay married?"

His amazement made her hold back a decisive answer. She said instead, "I've kind of gotten used to it."

"All right, we'll draw," he said, stepping slowly up onto the porch to pace off with her. "But there's no way you can beat me, honey."

She grinned at that point. "I might just surprise you, Angel."

A few seconds later he was surprised. She was damn near as fast as he was. But she was more surprised because today he'd been slow, so slow a child could have drawn faster. He'd let her win. When it occurred to her why, she ran to him and threw her arms around his neck.

"You lost!" she cried happily.

"That's what you think," he replied before his mouth found hers and rendered her breathless.

It was a long time later when she said, "I don't understand. Didn't you want the divorce?"

"Honey, why do you think I didn't stop the MacKauleys from marrying us?"

"But you couldn't stop them."

"Couldn't I?"

Her eyes widened. She'd seen him turn and draw within the blink of an eye. He *could* have prevented Richard from taking his gun that day. And he'd been close enough to Frazer on the way to the house that he could easily have disarmed him and put an end to it there.

"Then why were you so mad at me that day?" she wanted to know.

"Because you all but begged them not to do it," he replied.

"But that was because I was scared to death you were going to kill them all if they did."

"Was that your only reason?"

"Actually — yes," she said with a slight blush. "I didn't half mind marrying you myself. Of course, I was worried about what my mama would say about it."

"Are you still?"

"Not really. You wouldn't believe it, but she's really been a lot more mellow since she and my papa started talking again."

"No, I wouldn't believe it."

Cassie laughed. "Did I tell you he's coming for a visit, my papa? I wouldn't be at all surprised if they actually get back together soon."

"Are we back together, Cassie?"

"I expect you to collect your things and move in here today."

"I don't know if that's such a good idea."

"Why? You already know the house intimately. It really is an exact copy of my papa's."

She was deliberately missing his point — her mother's guaranteed objection. He let her for the moment. "Did you ever find out why he did that?"

"Not exactly. I would imagine it was to keep the memories fresh."

"That, and because he still loves me," Catherine said from the other side of the window they were standing near.

Cassie and Angel turned toward her, only to see her abandon her eavesdropping post and walk away. They both burst out laughing.

"She *said* she was going to bed," Angel told her.

"Before she found out just what was going on? Not my mama."

"Then she's gone to get her gun?"

Cassie grinned up at him. "That's not something you'll have to worry about anymore. If you didn't notice, she just gave us her blessing

354

by not saying anything."

"I didn't notice."

"You'll figure her out eventually. You'll have lots of time to try."

He pulled her closer. "You can't imagine how nice that sounds to me."

"So tell me."

She was putting him on the spot. Words like he wanted to say to her didn't come easily.

"I don't know how you came to mean so much to me, Cassie, but you do. Hell and I couldn't get through a day without thinking about you, and wishing you were mine."

"Angel, are you telling me you love me?"

"I guess I am. But you aren't going to turn me into a cattleman."

She was laughing and kissing his face. "I wouldn't try." But her meddling instincts made her add, "The next sheriff of Cheyenne, maybe . . ."

Chapter 41

"I think that's the first time I've ever seen Colt Thunder in a suit," Cassie told Angel as they watched the newly wedded pair circulate among their guests. "And do you know how long it's been since he cut his hair?"

"I know," Angel replied. "I hardly recognized him at the church. I would have waited until spring myself, but I doubt cold ears even entered his decision. I'd say he's finally put the past behind him, thanks to the duchess."

"It always takes a woman —"

"Not always."

"Most of the time, to set things right."

He snorted. "With an opinion like that, it's no wonder you meddle." And then his black eyes took on a warning cast. "But we're breaking you of that habit, aren't we?"

"*We're* going to try," was all she allowed, but she hadn't quite met his gaze to say it.

"Cassie —"

"I'll be right back."

He frowned at her departing back — and the end to *that* subject. But after a moment he grinned to himself. He'd already decided to go easy on her. Cassie wouldn't be Cassie if she weren't meddling in *someone's* business. But she didn't have to know that yet. He'd like at least a few weeks of peace before he had to shoot anyone on her behalf.

Cassie headed straight for her mother, sure that Angel wouldn't follow her there to continue their conversation. He'd been ill at ease this morning, being in Catherine's dining room when she entered it, a clear indication that he'd moved in. But all she'd said was, "Are there any eggs left?" That hadn't made him relax, as it had been intended to, but he would with time.

"You know, I'm going to have to throw one of these myself," Catherine said as Cassie reached her side.

"One of these?"

"Weddings. I missed yours, and since you're obviously not going to get rid of that gunfighter, I suppose I ought to see you married to him properly."

Cassie smiled brilliantly. "Do you mean that, Mama?"

Catherine sighed. "Unfortunately, yes." But she had to ask, "Are you sure, baby?"

Cassie didn't need that clarified. "I love him, Mama. I can't get more sure than that."

"All right," Catherine said, then warned, "But you'll never make a cattleman out of him."

"I wasn't going to try."

"Why not?"

"It would be a waste of his peacemaking abilities."

"Angel? A peacemaker? Have you been hitting that punch Chase spiked?"

Cassie laughed. "I never would have thought so, either, Mama, but Angel really does have the ability. Look what he accomplished down in Texas. I only set it in motion, but Angel was the one who made it possible for that feud to end. And look at you and Papa, on speaking terms again — and maybe more. That was Angel's doing, too."

Catherine didn't correct that "maybe more." She said instead, "It is a total contradiction to associate peace with a man who leads such a violent life."

Cassie merely shrugged. "So his ways are a little different from Lewis Pickens's."

"A little?"

"All right, a lot. And Mr. Pickens might work at it, whereas Angel doesn't — intentionally. Yet they basically do the same thing. Just look at Angel's profession. He solves people's problems, Mama. He leaves peace behind, where there was contention. He *is* a peacemaker. He just doesn't know it."

"I'd advise you not to spread that around. He might object to having his reputation whitewashed."

Cassie grinned. "I'll wait a few years before I point it out to him."

"Smart girl."

"Nice suit."

Colt barely managed to keep from glowering at Angel. He'd already been told that one too many times today. It didn't stop him from satisfying his curiosity, though.

"I know you showed up today with her on your arm, but are you and Cassie Stuart really going to stay married, or are you just lending her your protection for some reason?"

"I'm not all that sure anymore that she can't protect herself," Angel said. "Did you know she's about as fast as I am at the draw?"

"Who do you think taught her?" Colt shot back.

"You?" Angel said in surprise.

"I showed her the rudiments. She was only a kid at the time. I guess she's been practicing."

"Apparently."

"But her mother never let her do much more than keep the accounts on their ranch. It's no wonder she meddles in so many people's lives, with so much free time on her hands."

"She won't have all that much free time anymore," Angel promised.

"So you are staying married?"

"I'd like to see someone try to separate us."

He said it so forcefully, Colt laughed. "Well, don't look at me. I wasn't thinking of trying."

Angel grinned sheepishly. "What she makes me feel — I haven't gotten used to it yet."

"It's changed you, all right."

"How's that?"

"I never thought to see the day *you'd* ask for a favor," Colt said.

"Neither did I, but don't worry about it. You didn't come through, so we're still square."

"What are you talking about?" Colt demanded. "I was keeping an eye on her."

"Not enough to keep her from nearly getting killed yesterday."

"From *meddling?*"

"Indirectly. It was the tail end of what she started down in Texas."

Colt shook his head. "Hell, you've got your work cut out for you, being married to that one."

Angel grinned. "I know it. But what happened to you? I thought you and the duchess didn't get along."

Colt's eyes sought his wife's across the room, and he smiled. "She grew on me."

"Must be contagious," Angel said, his own eyes searching out Cassie. "I ended up with the same problem."

"So Mr. Kirby came in handy after all?" Cassie said.

She'd finally got around to asking Angel if he'd found out who his parents were. She hadn't expected him to reply in the affirmative, not this soon anyway.

"I suppose you're going to take the credit for that?" he asked.

"Certainly." She waited, but when he said no more, she poked a finger in his chest. "Well? What is your name?"

"Angel."

She laughed. "You mean it wasn't just an endearment?"

He shook his head. " 'O'Rourke' goes with it."

"Irish? Well, that's unexpected. But I do like the sound of it. Cassandra O'Rourke. It has a much nicer ring to it than Cassandra Angel. And did you find out where they are now?"

"My father died before my mother and I went to St. Louis. She's still living there."

"I'm sorry about your papa, but I hope you know I won't let up on you until you agree to go see your mama."

His arm went around her waist to squeeze her close to him. "This is one time you can't meddle anymore, honey. I already did."

"I knew you would," Cassie said smugly. "So what's she like?"

"She's wonderful. Her whole family is wonderful — with only one exception, but I'm not even displeased with him."

"What do you mean, family?"

"She remarried. I have two half brothers and a sister, and even two stepbrothers. My sister, Katey, is a delight. You'll love her, Cassie. You won't be able to help it. She wants to be a cowgirl. She was after me the whole time I was there to teach her how to shoot my gun."

"Did you?"

"No. She'll have no use for it there."

"She will when you bring her here for a visit."

He grinned at her. "So you teach her."

"Don't think I won't," she assured him. "So which one is the 'exception' you mentioned?"

"The oldest stepbrother, Bartholomew."

She frowned thoughtfully. "That name sounds awfully familiar for some reason."

"Possibly because you met him in St. Louis."

Her eyes widened. "Bartholomew Lawrence! *He's* your stepbrother?"

"He and I were equally surprised when he finally walked in on the reunion. But then, I'd already had words with him at your hotel when I heard him talking about you. I'm happy to say he nearly fainted — again."

"Just what did you say to him to make him faint the first time?"

"Not much," he replied innocently.

"I'll bet," she snorted. "Well, whatever you do, don't mention him to my mama. She had a run-in with his rudeness and came close to shooting him."

"I'm starting to like your mama better already." That got him a sour look, so he added, "Actually, I'm grateful to ol' Bart."

"Why?"

"It's damn nice knowing I'm not the only rotten apple in the family."

Cassie took exception to that. "You aren't rotten. I happen to know you're just as sweet as you can be."

He grinned at her. "Don't spread that around. You'll ruin my reputation."

"I was talking about the taste of you, honey."

His eyes fired up immediately. "Why don't we go out to Jessie and Chase's barn? Last I looked, they had a damn fine hayloft."

"It's going to be cold out there."

"You won't be," he promised.

Chase and Jessie did indeed have a damn fine hayloft. Cassie couldn't recall ever appreciating a soft bed of hay before, but she did now. She lay with her husband's arms around her, in no hurry to return to the wedding party.

"You know, if you hadn't agreed to stay married to me, Cassie, I was going to come to you once every month until you got pregnant."

She sat up so she could turn to look at him. "Even after you said giving me a child wasn't your intention?"

"It wasn't, then. But I'd like nothing better now, and I'd reached the point where I was willing to do anything I had to do to keep you."

She cupped his face to bring his mouth closer to hers. "All you had to do was ask, Angel," she said against his lips. "That's really all you ever had to do."